Picture Me Now

Clare Cogbill

Picture Me Now

DEDICATION

To all who believe there's something that links us, not
only in the life we have, but in the connections between
generations and across intercontinental populations …
Perhaps there are occasions when we catch a glimpse of
someone and know, know for sure deep in our heart, that
our worlds have been connected before.
This book is for those of you who believe this to be
possible. It is also for those who consider the links
between us are fragile enough that across time they may
be broken.

And it is for those who question such things.

CONTENTS

ACKNOWLEDGMENTS

Writing a book is both an utter joy and one of the most arduous accomplishments. This is not my first book, but it is my first piece of fiction (because dogs really can talk, right?). It is hopefully the first of many such novels, as I itch to get this one published now so I can move onto one of the others I have in the pipeline.

Through the process my husband Alun has been happy to have garage time, while I pursue writing the products of my dreams. You have read every word and let me know when something hasn't been quite right, and that is so important to me.

To my son Connor, thank you again for an amazing cover and painting such a perfect image – while I lacked inspiration at what the cover should be like, you knew. The book is also all the better because of your critical editing and proof reading.

Our rescue dogs Ralph and Nell, you are our perfect companions – I hope you feel the same way about us.

I know I am lucky to have you all in my world.

PART ONE

NOW

CHAPTER 1

'Dad.'

'Dad!' Jenna repeated. 'Are you listening to me?'

A distant drone of people chatting drifted closer to me, lifting me from my daydream. Jenna's indignant voice had penetrated the background noise, jolting me back to where I was. I wasn't sure for how long she'd been tugging at my sleeve.

Where was I? Who *were* all those people around me?

Realization filled my pores as I became aware of what was going on. The zoo! I was at the zoo! We were sitting in the over-priced cafeteria which overlooked the bird house. I was with my wife Ellie, and Jenna, our six-year-old daughter.

On the table in front of us was a tray full of the remnants of our café lunch – one we'd supplemented with a hastily-made indoor picnic of nutty bars and fruit. Paper cups and packets were strewn across the tray. Our three apple cores bore tooth marks from half an hour before; their flesh by then tinged with pale shades of beige and brown.

Alongside the apple core on Jenna's plate lay a couple of discarded crusts of bread. Cries from her grandparents that unless she ate her crusts she wouldn't keep her curls, had clearly fallen on stubborn ears. She hated her curls and wanted straight hair just like her school friend Emma-Louise. I had to smile to myself each time she left those crusts parked neatly at the edge of her plate. She'd inherited much of Ellie's determined character.

'DAD!' Her voice was by then incredibly loud and insistent, demanding my attention and that of everyone else within earshot. But while I looked in her direction, my mind was elsewhere. Something had just happened, some weird déjà vu, and through the haze I was desperately trying to process it.

While I sat smiling at Jenna, from the other side of me I felt Ellie nudge my arm, 'Nate, are we going now?' I jolted with the ferocity of her nudge. With her head cocked to one side, she picked up my brown paper cup from the rickety, pale green plastic table. She turned it upside down a few inches above the plate on which a toasted teacake and some strawberry jam had recently resided. 'Look, Nate! It's empty!'

I watched silently as three tiny drips of coffee emerged from the cup and fought back the urge to tell her that it clearly *hadn't* been empty. Like tar, the drops of coffee eagerly formed the smallest black puddle on the plate. I nodded in defeat, 'Okay, come on, let's go.'

Their insistence was distracting me from figuring out what was going on inside my head. What *was* it that had just happened? And then, from across the room I sensed someone watching me. My heart missed a beat as I recalled what had just happened.

Her. There was a woman across from us who I'd previously noticed. With my heart pounding, I looked away, and then immediately fought the urge to look back at her.

I made moves as though I was complying with Ellie and Jenna's eager demands to get going for our afternoon itinerary. Essential to their (Jenna's really) list were the red pandas, flamingoes, the penguin feed, the chimpanzees, and the reindeer. They were not necessarily in that order, but we apparently had to see them all, and then drop by the gift shop on our way out. Ah, yes, of course, the gift shop with prices that were even more inflated than the coffee shop.

As I shifted my body so I could shuffle my denim jacket and coat from the back of my chair, I boldly stole one more glance over to where the woman was sitting. I'd noticed her as soon as she walked through the door about five minutes after we arrived. Straight away there was a presence about her; something incredibly familiar. I'd also been instantly distracted by her smile. I was sure that I'd seen her before somewhere, but if I had, there seemed to be no mutual recognition.

I continued to sneak surreptitious glances at her, quickly trying to absorb as much about her as I could. I'd already guessed she must have been in her fifties. She had tell-tale wrinkles around her eyes and neck, but she had a youthful glow and looked much younger. Her hair was curly and dark, and pulled back into a ponytail. I imagined when loose it was probably down to her shoulders. Her cheeks were slightly pink from the biting wind outside, and her eyes were blue, or perhaps green?

Like the sea.

On her neck was a scar which was only partially covered by her jacket. I found myself wondering how she'd done that – it was such a strange place to have such an obvious injury.

She wore a name badge on her dark grey fleece and had a lanyard around her neck. I strained to see her name, but she was too far away. I sensed Ellie peering at me and immediately felt guilty that I was paying this stranger so much attention. But there was something about her – something I couldn't fathom.

Earlier, as she walked over to the table that was diagonally opposite ours, she laughed at something her companion said. She had a loud, infectious laugh, and tossed her head back, reinforcing the depth of her joy at being in that moment. I tried to catch what they were talking about, but they were clearly discussing something only they knew of. Some in-joke, I guessed.

Her companion was probably in her late twenties and had short, strawberry-blonde hair, with a long fringe pulled back behind her ears, which sometimes fell forward in soft bangs. She had fine, elfin-like features and her complexion was quite fresh and beautiful. Normally my attention would have lingered on her and taken in her beauty, wondering how I could recreate such an exquisitely perfect face in my studio back home. But not then. The older woman – there was something incredibly mesmerizing about her.

Ellie glanced at me and sighed. She wore that familiar expression which told me she reluctantly understood what I was up to, but that she was not altogether happy – especially on a family day out. We'd been together for ten years, and she'd got used to how my absorbing the detail of strangers' faces had become integral to how I worked as an artist. I imagine that as the years passed, I'd developed the role of an intrepid people watcher, someone who used the people around me as inspiration for my pictures.

Since I was a young child, I'd had a knack for remembering people: their expressions; what they wore; how they looked; fine details such as scars or beauty spots. There were times growing up when, several months after family gatherings, I could describe and draw details like scarves, hair accessories, and the clothes worn by aunts, uncles, or cousins. Eventually, my parents noticed the same detail was matched in how I drew their faces, and the rest, I suppose, is history.

It felt different with that woman, though, because as soon as I saw her, I felt a shudder weaving its way down my spine. It was something beyond the thrill of the impending creativeness that I felt each time I was inspired by someone. That creative notion was spontaneous, and enough for me to later apply each stroke of the brush to the blank world on the canvas in front of me; to carefully paint each of my subjects from memory.

Was what I'd felt with her the feeling that people got when they became instantly attracted to someone? It was like something I'd never felt in my life before. They talk of love at first sight – was that what that rush of feelings had been?

Nothing like that had ever happened with Ellie and

me. We met at university and were in the same social circle for about a year and a half before we got together. One evening at a party we found ourselves sitting next to one another, and we ended up talking all night about the things we loved. She said she adored romantic comedies and foreign language films, while I loved horror and science fiction.

We talked about the things that made us angry about the world and how we were going to change it for the better. Under the influence of just a bit too much alcohol, we pinky-promised one another that we'd do everything in our power to make the world a better place for future generations. There would be no war; no fossil fuels; we'd create a world in which people would appreciate art, and everyone would value the beauty of nature because it would be integral to everyone's early education. We found we shared a love of cats, but she also told me she'd always wanted a dog.

By the end of the evening, we'd arranged to go on a date to the cinema; just the two of us – a proper date without any of our friends. That date forged the beginning of the bond we developed over the years to come. Ellie was perfect in every way, but there had never been any thunderbolt, there'd been no strike of lightning to tell me that she really was the one. I'd always been happy with that and felt lucky to have her by my side. I felt a great sense of contentment with her and that together we were sharing our life adventure. There were times, though, when I wondered whether that was only because I'd never experienced anything else? There'd not until that point, that moment in that zoo cafe, been a cavernous, gaping hole of doubt develop deep inside my heart. For the first time, I realized I'd felt something which could challenge my love for Ellie, and the whole thing, the whole concept, seemed preposterous – I knew that with every bone of my body. I'd only just seen this woman, but there was something there; something I had never felt before; something entrancing.

Ellie knew that in the weeks which followed me having spotted someone I'd like to paint, I would disappear into the studio to recreate my impression of them. We decided to name them muses in a deliberate effort to make them relate to what I did for a living, rather than them being related to some weird voyeuristic appetite I had for staring at strangers, which is how we both knew it could be seen. Once the picture was finished (and only then) I would reveal the finished article to Ellie in my studio, nervously asking her to cast her critical eye over my work. Sometimes the painting took months; sometimes only days; other times I lost the inspiration, and nothing happened.

Jenna sometimes came into the studio and watched me paint. Secretly I hoped she would feel inspired one day to do something creative with her life. There were times when her young critical eye was welcome. Her honesty wasn't tainted by the politeness we gather as we get older, when we avoid risking offending someone. I'd set a small easel up beside mine, but so far, she was showing more interest in spending time with the cats.

Some friends had suggested they found my subconscious search for muses a little voyeuristic – some even said they found it creepy. They often said it jokingly, but I felt there was some underlying truth in their jest. Nevertheless, I would sometimes sense them scanning my paintings as though they might be trying to find a hint of themselves in the image. When each piece was complete, I hoped my reticent critics saw the image was generally so different to the actual person that they realized the subject was simply a source of inspiration – a fleeting, nameless, mysterious source of stimulation for my creativity.

Straight away I felt excited about painting this woman. Her image had instantly become embedded in my mind. There was a complexity about her which had caught my eye. What was it? Her face? Her character? For the very first time since I met Ellie, my remote, detailed examination of a stranger felt as though I was betraying her. Something bothered me about the woman. I'd seen her before somewhere; I was sure of it, but I didn't feel I could approach her. Not then, not in that situation.

While still fumbling with my jacket, I explored the recesses of my mind; trying to remember. I was sure I couldn't have felt that familiarity without there being some justification for it. I had some hasty recognition process going on – like some matching card game we would play with Jenna.

But there was nothing. There were no matches to give me that penny-dropping moment; nothing to help place where she had been that I'd also happened to be. Perhaps it was something as simple as I'd subconsciously noticed her browsing one of the galleries or museums in town – the places I went for extra inspiration when my mind was blocked. Or perhaps I had passed her in the supermarket; our trolleys nearly brushing one another as we'd idled over the oranges and apples in the fruit and vegetable aisles – contemplating food miles, or how much more you had to pay for organic food? Or perhaps I'd stood behind her at the checkout, said thank you to her after she'd placed the conveyer belt divider between my shopping and hers, and then patiently watched her food items being bleeped through the till – maybe it really was something as simple as that. I knew deep down, though, that there had to be something more, for if I'd previously seen her face, I wouldn't have forgotten where or when.

As I wrapped my scarf around my neck, the woman turned and looked at me; her face still bearing the remnants of a smile she'd shared with her companion. The blonde turned around too, but then turned back towards the table, when she clearly hadn't recognized me.

People often noticed me watching them. It was as though they sensed I was looking – they would feel someone's gaze on them and be compelled to look over. I would usually smile at them, inviting them to return my modest offerings of friendliness. But with her, it was me who quickly looked away.

I stupidly glanced back at her, the residual smile on her face had disappeared, but she was still looking right back at me; confidently holding my gaze. Usually someone would by now have looked away in embarrassment, but not her. Her smile gone, small lines furrowed her brow and the corners of her eyes, making her look older, however in my captivated state those lines simply added to her beauty. I turned my head away from her gaze and closed my eyes to fix the image of her – the one I would be painting. I willed myself not to look back again.

But there was something more there, not just an

image forming in my mind – more like déjà vu. I often had feelings like that. There were times when the feeling simply washed over me, but later, once I was alone in my studio, I would think again about that moment, going over it in my head, trying to make that all-important match. I would wonder for days afterwards what the significance of that feeling had been, but I rarely managed to work out who the person was, or when and where I may have met or seen them before. If ever it happened when I was observing someone, then later when I was painting them, I would try to recreate that feeling of déjà vu, and desperately search for how everything fitted together. There were times when my paintings felt to me to be inadequate, and I would tear them from the easel and rip them into pieces.

And start again.

Often later, Ellie would drift into the studio after a hard day at the courts, and she'd despair at what she saw as the nonsensical waste of what she thought was a beautiful piece of art. Holding up a torn painting, she would try to piece together the broken image. The time she became most cross about it was when I was painting a picture of Jenna sitting beside an oak tree in a bluebell wood. Whether it was my state of mind at the time, I don't know, but for some reason I couldn't get a bough of the tree to cast a shadow across Jenna's face just right, and so, down the picture came. Ellie came home to find me sitting on the step in the doorway of the studio; my paintbrush broken in two on my lap; the picture screwed up behind me on the floor. Months later, I gave her a finished version of the painting. Jenna helped me carry it from the studio to the office where Ellie was writing a report for work. The look in her eyes was enough for me to know that she loved it. I had finally made my peace with that picture and, more importantly, Ellie had forgiven me for giving in to what she half-jokingly called my 'artistic ways.'

I could sense the woman was still watching me as I placed some coins on the table, but I vehemently willed myself to stay focused; to concentrate on Ellie and Jenna. I told myself to keep my mind fixed on Jenna's small hand now in mine, and the chattering and rambling of the two people I loved most in the world.

We were on our way. We walked away from the table, leaving empty cups tidily stacked on the brown canteen tray. I felt Ellie's hand on my arm, and concentrated on that tiny, six-year-old hand perfectly fitting my other hand. I fought the urge to turn around to catch the woman looking at me; to see her inviting my gaze.

Just a few steps from us being safely through the

door, Ellie became temporarily distracted with buttoning up a top button which had come undone on Jenna's coat.

My heart sank as I fought my opportunity to look again! I justified it to myself by declaring I would, just to see whether she was still watching me. I suddenly felt as though I was some hormonal kid in a school dining hall trying to catch the eye of a girl I liked.

I turned my head, and out of the corner of my eye, I could tell she was still transfixed on me. She had felt something too. I was sure she had. The woman opposite her was animated; she had her hands on top of her head and was perhaps mimicking some behaviour she had observed in one of the zoo's animals. She hadn't seemed to notice what was going on. I thought I heard her say something about feeding the chimpanzees their afternoon selection of fruit.

I couldn't meet her gaze. She had, I guess, outstared me; like a staring game a child would play with a friend. If I looked back at her, I was worried that the seed of betrayal which had been planted inside of me in those few moments would grow. It would begin to flourish and develop into something more than an image in a painting.

Instead, I looked out of the window and pretended I

was looking at what the weather was doing. It had been freezing cold earlier and it didn't look as though it was improving. I muttered to Ellie that it looked cold outside but fought back the urge to suggest we cut our losses and went home. Who ever thought of going to the zoo in the middle of winter? Apparently, *we* did. Ellie nodded, pulled her hat on, and smiled at me.

Outside, the blustery, wintry breeze attacked our faces. The wind was littered with fine flakes of snow. I buttoned my warm coat over my thin denim jacket and tucked in my striped black and yellow scarf. We had forgotten to bring along Jenna's gloves, so I gave her mine, and Ellie and I walked along one either side of her, each holding onto a tiny hand which was sliding about inside an oversized glove. I pushed my other hand inside the deep pocket of my overcoat, but it was so very cold outside. It was probably about two degrees Celsius with a little winter sun, but there was an extreme wind chill factor going on, which made it feel like we were several hundred miles further north.

The animals secreted themselves away in their dens, sheltered from the elements under trees, or huddled beside whatever buildings they had available to them. We stood shivering in the cold outside each enclosure, and I could understand why there were so few people there.

The winter day was short, and before long, night-time began to descend. We didn't get to see all Jenna wanted to, but she was satisfied. She'd clearly had enough and was longing for the comfort of our living room, and to sit and watch a film fit for a six-year-old. She was happy leaving the zoo animals behind to go home and cuddle up with our much more liberated creatures: Tommy and Jeremy, our imaginatively named sibling black tomcats. I sighed and imagined we were home in front of the fire with the two of them nestled beside us, softly purring as we obediently stroked them along their backs.

I often wondered at the ethics behind having animals on show simply for human interest and entertainment. Even at the age of six, Jenna had picked up on that, asking as we made our way back to the car along the main path through the zoo, why the animals had to live in cages, and why they couldn't be free to wander where they wanted. She told us she thought the animals were sad. I vowed to myself that I would paint something which reflected that and give it to her; something which showed the ways in which wild animals had become such a commodity. She was saying things way beyond her years and both Ellie and I were encouraging her – both of us frequently astounded at her prematurely adult vision of the world.

Returning from my thoughts, we were nearing the

zoo's exit when Jenna, seeming to have spontaneously forgotten her proclamations of the plight of captive animals, requested that as we were heading towards the birdhouse, we could perhaps go in for another look.

Earlier, there'd been a large toucan in the trees in the middle of the enclosure, and Jenna wanted to see him again before we finally left for home. Perhaps although he, too, was captive, because he was more tangible and not behind physical bars, she saw him as being free, and not confined like the other creatures. But he was clearly anything but free. From a practical point of view at least we could warm ourselves in there before we headed back to the car. And so, we headed through the floppy rubber doors, which closed behind us sealing the heat into the stiflingly hot aviary; at the same time preventing the birds from making a bid for freedom.

The bird house was adjacent to the café where I'd seen the woman. I looked at my watch and saw that almost an hour had passed since lunchtime. Surely she wouldn't still be there? I felt a lurch inside my gut at the possibility of seeing her again, and immediately chastised myself for even imagining such a thing; reprimanded myself for even having wanted to see her.

The toucan was high up in the branches. As though he had been trained to do so, he fluttered his undersized velvet black wings, and came down to perch himself on the lower branches. He landed not far from our heads. Jenna laughed her innocent, six-year-old laugh, as the handsome bird cocked his orange-beaked head from side to side. I lifted her up so she could see him more clearly and take a photograph of him to show to her friends at school.

I stole a glance through a small square window toward the coffee shop, and the woman was nowhere to be seen. I felt ashamed that my enjoyment of this time with Jenna was tainted by what had happened earlier. I was with her and Ellie, but my mind was clearly elsewhere.

What *was* I doing?

I concentrated hard and tried to be in the moment, to enjoy the time with my wife and daughter. But still, while my body and face entertained the distractions of the day, the memory of the woman's face, her soft features, her smile, her easy laugh, were all imprinted in my mind. What was it? What had that thing been which had happened between us? I was positive it had been something, but I didn't know what. Had she felt it too? Her lingering gaze certainly meant she had noticed me, but perhaps she thought I was some lecherous weirdo, attempting to hit on her while on a day trip with my wife and child. I imagined I could see why she might have thought that!

But if there *had* been something between us, I had no idea how I could possibly find out. Not without trying to see her again. And somehow, despite all the guilt and misgivings on embarking on such a thing, the concept of seeing her again excited me.

Chapter 2

I tried to forget her, really I did. I attempted to focus on the New Year and getting my paintings ready for the major exhibition I had coming up in late spring.

For the rest of the Christmas holidays, we were busy visiting family in the south of England, but all the time there was something niggling me, silently nibbling away at my core. There was something I knew I needed to do, but there was no way I could share it with Ellie. I couldn't tell her that all the time I was with her and Jenna, I was thinking of someone else. I hadn't been able to get the woman from the zoo out of my head.

Her face; her laugh; those eyes.

How is it that you can wake up on an ordinary day, utterly captivated by your partner, but later that very same day, and in just a single moment, your wife and all she means to you is stored in the recesses of your mind? How is it that a person can become so utterly infatuated with a complete stranger? I wasn't even sure if it *was* infatuation, but *something* had happened that day.

Keeping secrets from Ellie was such a huge betrayal of her trust. We'd never kept secrets from one another, but that thing, how I was feeling, I knew that it would hurt her. I was sure it was something she wouldn't understand. How could she? Why would she ever understand that in the blink of an eye, that woman had become someone I saw in every image in my studio. I also saw her in every TV show – lingering in the background as though she was a poorly-paid extra. Several times I thought I saw her walking past the house, and each time I got up from my seat to check just in case it was her. In the throes of falling asleep each night, I heard her laughing. She had become an earworm – an annoying song that had stuck in my head, penetrating my every brain cell – constantly repeating itself in my mind, over and over and over again.

The more I tried to understand how I was feeling, constantly questioning my bizarre thoughts, the more I tried to acknowledge I was experiencing something akin to a teenage crush. I was having those intense emotions which arise from the first flush of feelings you have as a hyper-hormonal fourteen-year-old, when you idolize someone you may have met only once.

In the weeks following our day out at the zoo, on evenings when various friends were over for festive dinner dates, ethical debates about the existence of zoos invariably drifted into debates about other problems going on in the world. Meanwhile, I would sit with my attention only half-focused on what the others were talking about, my mind constantly drifting in and out of the conversation. Hoping no one would notice, I tried to smile at the relevant points, using everyone else's grins and laughter as cues to reciprocate.

It was at one of those dinners that my friend Marc noticed something was up. He's the owner of a local art gallery which is frequented by tourists – a place where I sometimes sold my work. While Ellie took Jenna, and Marc and Christina's son Jacob, a bowl of sweet and salty popcorn to have while they watched Bambi in the other room, and Christina had nipped away to the bathroom, Marc seized his opportunity to talk.

Looking around him before he spoke, he leaned into me from across the table. 'You okay, Nate? What's up? You're really subdued tonight.' His dark curls flopped against the side of his face as he checked behind him again to make sure neither Ellie nor Christina were within earshot. A deep frown created crevices in his brow.

My heart sank, as I realized my distraction had been more obvious than I'd thought. 'Yeah, sure, of course,' I replied. I tried to stall for time while I thought what to say next. A few heavy moments passed. Marc tilted his head to one side as he waited for me to say more. Finally, I replied, 'I guess I'm just worried about the exhibition. It's a big one for me, you know. It's going to be a big step. Into the big league, I suppose, and I can no longer be the pretty much anonymous painter! With publicity comes exposure. You know – a lot of pressure!'

Marc's rescued brindle (and thankfully cat-friendly) lurcher Bruce, who always came with them to visit, came over to the table and nudged Marc's elbow for some attention. Marc looked away from me, his face softening into a smile as he dutifully stroked his canine companion's silky smooth, striped head.

Marc nodded thoughtfully, despite the distraction, clearly still pondering over what I'd said. He looked up and smiled across at Christina as she returned from the bathroom. She smoothed her faded jeans as she walked across the room. 'I love the burgundy paint in the bathroom – it's a great contrast to your plants,' she called through to Ellie. Ellie was settling a rising dispute between Jenna and Jacob about who loved Bambi the most.

'Thank you!' Ellie shouted back. 'It was our pre-Christmas holiday project. It'd been annoying me for so long. I'd totally gone off the turquoise – it was far too bathroomy, if you know what I mean!' Christina laughed and said she'd also liked it when it had been turquoise.

The evening passed without any more mention of

my apparent inattentiveness, but I felt it was more through a lack of opportunity to finish our conversation, rather than Marc being happy that things were resolved.

Much later in the evening, we watched them buckle a sleepy Jacob into his car seat. Christina then opened the back of the Jeep for Bruce to leap into his cozy travel bed. For the first time ever, I was relieved they were going. I figured Marc was onto me. I felt as though he knew I was up to something, that he could see right through me. I wasn't that transparent, was I?

Although she was quiet, Ellie didn't mention anything when we were tidying the kitchen before bed. Once I'd checked the cats were in, I locked the cat flap and went to bed, feeling determined that no one would ever know there was something … someone … on my mind. It was simply a phase I was going through. It would pass.

After Christmas had been packed away into its boxes in the loft for another year, and once Jenna was back at school, we settled back into our usual school and work routines. Each day once Ellie had left home to go to her job at the courts, I would take Jenna to school and then go home to work in the studio. When it was time to collect Jenna, I would go back again and bring her home. The timing could sometimes be inconvenient if I'd been focused on a particular painting, but my time was more flexible than Ellie's, and it had become the way we managed.

My exhibition was only four and a half months away and I was due to go for a pre-exhibition meeting at the gallery. Niggling away at me was the fact that it was taking place only about a twenty-minute drive from the zoo. The closer the meeting got, the greater the urge to spend a couple of hours at the zoo became. I thought that somehow fate was driving me towards engineering an accidental meeting with her, this person who had entered my every waking hour, and all my dreams. But what would I say?

The conniving, scheming thoughts I was having were really worrying me. I wasn't *that* person, yet this seemed too important an opportunity to miss. I was sure this stranger had experienced that same immediate connection between us. That old story about eyes meeting across a crowded room and you'd know, just know that whatever it was would last forever, well I'd just never got that before – not in that way anyway. For me it really had felt like one of those occasions people talk about – the times when someone meets a stranger at a party, or in a bar, and gets chatting to them, and they know instantly that they will become a big part of their

28

life.

I suppose that kind of thing happens sometimes with friends, too, but in a different way. Like when you meet someone and find them funny or kind, or you have something in common with them. Very quickly you know you'll be there for one another through thick and thin, probably for the rest of your life. It had been like that when we first met Marc and Christina.

We'd just moved to the area to be close to Ellie's job as a lawyer, and we were still carrying the then tiny baby Jenna around in a papoose. Ellie and I were in town getting to know the place, taking it in turns to carry our baby girl. We drifted into Marc's gallery for a look around, and to ask whether he might be happy to display some of my paintings. We got chatting to him and both immediately liked him, and from the photographs I showed him of my work, he was keen to see more.

We chatted as though we had known him for years. I removed Jenna from the papoose and rocked her from side to side because she was a little grizzly. While admiring some pastel landscapes by another local artist, the reason for Jenna's distress manifested in an extremely stinky nappy moment, so Marc offered the use of the back room to clean her up. As I changed Jenna's nappy Ellie made a big fuss of the (much younger then) newly rescued lurcher Bruce. Marc had discovered him at a local rescue shelter's adopt-a-dog day where Bruce was stood on the high street with a volunteer who was shaking a collection can. Bruce had been wearing a vest emblazoned with the words 'I need a home' … and the rest, as they say, is history.

With Jenna's nappy changed, we ended up staying for coffee. As it was later in the day, while we were finishing our drinks, Christina arrived with baby Jacob to collect Marc and Bruce to take them home. Instead, we all got a takeaway and stayed for the rest of the evening. And so, the bonds between our two small families were forged.

Indeed, in the years that had passed since that day, we had become like family – we were all living far away from our hometowns, and as the years had passed we'd become quite dependent on one another. Perhaps Marc really did know something was up with me. Perhaps he sensed it – he and I had got to know one another as though we were brothers, so it's possible he was more perceptive to my mood than even Ellie was. Could he really see right through me?

I was so conflicted – I was being disloyal and obsessive. And yet, the more I thought about it, the more I knew that I had to try to see the woman from the zoo again. A huge part of me wanted to stop this obsession, and yet the only way to put an end to it seemed to be to take it further. I had to satisfy my curiosity.

For meetings about my exhibition, I had to drive about a hundred and fifty miles, so Ellie and I booked Hannah, our occasional after-school childminder, for a few hours one Tuesday. That way I was able to leave for the gallery as soon as I dropped Jenna at school. I was keen to get working on the arrangements for the exhibition as soon as possible. After the meeting I had decided I would go for a fleeting visit to the zoo. No one back home would ever need to know – surely if no one knew, then no one would get hurt? And at least my curiosity would be satisfied. For that's all it was – just curiosity.

That Tuesday morning, I watched Jenna run across the playground to join Jacob, Emma-Louise with the straight hair much-coveted by Jenna, and their other friends. Once she reached them, she turned to wave me goodbye. My heart fluttered at the sight of her. She was all that I had ever hoped for in a child. And yet, there I was about to embark on a mission which could change the course of everything we had all known together.

I felt as though I was a silly schoolboy with a crush

on a teacher – but deep inside I felt a burst of mixed feelings. Were they feelings of fearful dread, or flutters of excitement? I really didn't know what was going on with me, or why I was behaving so irresponsibly. Or, at least, at that point I didn't know.

Chapter 3

The zoo was quiet. I guessed not many people went there in the sleety, rainy months. This was particularly so on one of those unpredictable weather days; days when the rain falls hard across your face and it can't decide whether it should be wintry cold, or whether to fall as soft, warm droplets. That afternoon the rain had decided to keep itself at bay, as the sun feebly attempted to break its way through the remnants of the morning's storm clouds.

I idly wandered past pens full of bored creatures, with enrichment activities they'd seemingly lost interest in and cast aside. All the time I was distracted and keeping a look out for her. I was ruminating about the eventful visit I'd had to the gallery that morning.

The gallery owner was Joanna Dewhouse – a brightly-dressed, tall, slender, thin-faced, and extremely flamboyant woman. She had round, green-framed spectacles perched on the end of her nose. Her hair was harshly cut into the nape of her neck, and an auburn fringe flopped around her face, her grey roots just visible close to her head. Her age was deceiving – she could have been anything from thirty-five to sixty.

When Joanna saw me waiting for her at reception, she came marching over. Straight away she was overwhelmingly enthusiastic about my forthcoming exhibition. 'I just love your work, Nate!' Her emphasis was on the word love, making it sound more like 'lurve'. 'You have a capacity to bring portraits alive; for making them ooze reality. They are positively and sincerely charming.' As she spoke, her arms were animated, elaborately emphasizing everything she said. She paused, seemingly waiting for me to say something. I don't take praise easily, though, always seeing inaccuracy in what I've created, so I merely smiled and thanked her.

'Yes … hmm …' she gazed at me for a little while longer, with her hand clasped thoughtfully to her mouth and chin. She seemed to be considering my facial features. It went on for perhaps twenty or thirty seconds, which didn't really help my already high-alert anxiety levels. She then eagerly, and quite scarily, grasped hold of my arm. 'Come!' she declared, 'we have work to do!'

As we advanced along the network of short corridors that were akin to a rabbit warren, I noticed little dens of activity at each corridor's termination. Some of Joanna's extensive team scurried around from room to room, while some of them followed us and fussed around us. Each of them held a diary or clipboard clutched in front of their chest. Others remained focused on their computer screen or their work. They all seemed a little wary of Joanna. I could sense why – she was really domineering. Quite frightening, in fact.

The exhibition really was going to be a big thing for me, and being frog-marched around the gallery by this eccentric woman as she showed me the extensive wall space, I wondered whether this was in fact too big for me, too big a deal. Was I really that good? Was I actually good enough to have a major exhibition in a big city? Could I really pull this off?

Joanna's voice called me back from my thoughts, 'Nathaniel, young man, I was serious when I told you I love your work. There's a depth to your portraits that makes them almost, I don't know ... authentic, heartfelt ... genuine? I can't even find the words to describe them, which is unusual for me.' She paused and then let out a chortle, which I found alarmingly terrifying. She held onto her absolutely flat belly as she cackled. She tossed her head, and her fringe collected the light which streamed through the window. The waves in her hair became embellished in copper tones. 'Honestly, Nathaniel, that's what your pictures do to me – they are overwhelmingly, viscerally, I don't know, sincere?' She shook her head and began to cackle once more.

'But no, Nathaniel, not even that word can describe them.' I smiled at her, willing the day to be over, so I could go home.

But I wasn't going home, was I?

The meeting with Joanna concluded with her introducing me to Davey Jones, who insisted he'd never been a member of the 1960's group The Monkees. I later discovered that this was something he told everyone he met. He was average height with a little paunch. He wore deep purple trousers and a matching lilac-trimmed waistcoat. His shirt sparkled with silver glitter, as though he'd shaken a pot of the stuff over himself. His spectacles were black with a sprinkling of silver glitter at the turned-up corners. Looking as though he'd just stepped out of a fashion magazine circa 1970, at his neck a lilac dickie bow complemented his attire.

Joanna enthused that Davey was going to oversee my exhibition. I felt a great sense of relief wash over me that Joanna was taking more of a back seat in the organization of my event, but just a little nervous that the glitzy Davey was deputizing for her. Weighing up the pros and cons of the two of them, however, Davey Jones, not of The Monkees, was my guy. I was sure I could work with him much more easily than I could the overpowering Joanna.

'I'll be here for you, though, Nate!' Joanna offered her reassurance. 'Oh yes, I'll be here if you need me! And on the opening night we shall have one whale of a time – you mark my words, young Nathaniel! It will be marvelous.'

I couldn't wait.

All too soon, once we were left alone to get on with things without Joanna's interference, Davey and I got things sorted quickly. By the end of the meeting, we both had a good idea of how we were going to proceed. I declined more coffee, which made me feel a little antisocial. Perhaps I just liked being at home in my studio. Maybe the idea of the apparent fame I was being forced into to get my paintings and my name out there in the big wide world – well, maybe that just wasn't me?

Relieved the morning was over, I made my way back to the car. Sitting at the steering wheel, I had a choice to make. I could just go home and forget my seemingly stupid plans, or I could go to the zoo and see whether I could find the woman. If I did find her, though, what would I say? What *was* there to say? I didn't know her – I was going there on some whim, a whim which even *I* didn't understand, so how on earth could I expect *her* to?

In the end, the drive to the zoo was like an automatic reflex. After just a couple of streets from the gallery, I arrived at a T-junction. It was the T-junction which would decide my fate. At that point, I could have gone home, but I didn't. Instead, hardly without a second thought, I drove the car in the direction of the zoo. Very quickly I found myself heading through the large metal gates which bore a carving of an elephant. In the car park I almost did a loop and drove straight back out again, but I'd gone so far that I felt compelled to keep on going. With the car neatly parked between the allocated lines, I willed myself to not switch off the engine, the inner turmoil almost too much to bear. But with a swift movement, my hand reached down to the key, and the engine became quiet.

Requesting just one ticket at the reception, I felt a little odd, as though I'd left a child in the car park. 'Just one adult?' The guy behind the desk asked, looking around me to see whether there was anyone else I intended paying for. I also looked around me, and immediately felt stupid for doing so, I was clearly on my own.

'Um, yes please, just one.' The shame of what I was undertaking was humiliating enough, but what I was doing was apparently even amiss to those who were around me. It seemed I wasn't going to be able to accomplish my task completely unnoticed. I paid cash so it wouldn't show up on our joint account statements, and then immediately felt guilt wash over me in doing so. I took my ticket and secreted it away, deep in my overcoat pocket. I was behaving like some unfaithful husband, arranging a secret rendezvous. I should have taken my sketch book or a camera, but I'd never really been a sketcher or a photographer. Just paint. Paint was my thing, the medium I loved; I loved its versatility, how it could portray accuracy, or a sense of vague suggestion.

I walked out of the lobby past the stuffed toys and toy dinosaurs. I wondered at the educational value of there being toy dinosaurs there. While I could see it would be fueling the imagination of youngsters, it might also raise small children's expectations that they would see dinosaurs during their visit. I pondered over that thought for a while and reflected on reports I'd heard about mammoth DNA being combined with elephant DNA to bring the mammoth back from extinction. Crazy, especially when there are so many endangered animals which could use the help of scientists!

I walked past the flamingoes and the African wild dogs, occasionally feigning interest at the viewing points to avoid looking too conspicuous. It didn't sit comfortably with me that the wild cousins of these creatures would travel widely, yet here these animals would spend their whole lives in captivity. Was it that we had already arrived at a point where this was the only way some of these animals would avoid the fate of said woolly mammoths? That thought made me incredibly sad.

I continued reflecting on my morning, but all the while I was aimlessly searching for her. *Perhaps it was her day off?* I thought, and immediately a wave of disappointment swept through me. What if this risky venture of mine was a complete waste of time?

Brushing such thoughts away, I headed over to the bird house and optimistically went inside to look for her. As soon as I passed through the rubber flap doors, I became surrounded by exotic pigeons, doves, thrushes, and that toucan. They rustled in the leaves above my head and sang their individual song. I had a near-miss when a bird with ornamental crests on his head relieved himself just centimeters from my shoulder. The bird was beautiful! I reached in my pocket and got out my phone to take a picture, but then remembered that what I was doing was a secret. I felt a deep pang of guilt and turned toward the door.

Sliding the phone back into my pocket, I noticed a woman with dark hair who was dressed in the same kind of fleece the woman had been wearing. She had her back to me and was crouched down low, offering some crumbs to a small, ground-dwelling bird. I felt as though my heart had fallen into the pit of my abdomen. What should I do next?

But then, she turned, and it wasn't her – this woman was much younger. Surprisingly, I felt a sense of relief wash over me. She looked over and smiled. 'They each have their own personality, you know?'

'Really?'

'Yes, this one here is the leader of his little group. He's always the one who comes over first for food.' She pointed over to a slightly smaller bird and added, 'that's his brother hiding over there, he's a shy little thing.'

I considered asking her about the woman, but the moment passed. Our conversation over, she smiled and turned back to talking to the fat little birds.

Suddenly feeling stupid and alone, I decided to leave. I was a fool. I tried not to look over at the stuffed toys as I made my way past the gift shop. I knew it would've been difficult to have explained the toy once I got back home. Any lies I told would become embellished with more lies – something like 'Oh, I just happened to have to take a diversion on my way back from the gallery, and I ended up in the zoo shop and bought you this fluffy penguin. Jenna … what will you name him?' I suppose it might just have sounded feasible, but I wasn't going to risk it.

That evening at dinner the three of us ate home-made pizza with vegetables piled so high that olives and artichokes were scattered across our plates. We were sharing the tales of what we'd all been up to that day. It was incredibly hard for me not to mention the zoo. Instead, I focused on telling stories of Joanna and her gallery, offering an exaggerated impression of her, 'I luuurve your work, Nathaniel …'

Ellie and Jenna laughed and for the first time (I think the first time anyway), I noticed they had the same smile, the same curve at the corner of their mouth, the same impression of a dimple in their left cheek. I couldn't recall whether they'd always been like that, or whether as Jenna was getting older, she was becoming more like Ellie. People had said from the moment that Jenna entered this world that she was like me, that she had my eyes and the same shaped jaw line, but I was glad she was starting to look more like Ellie.

It wasn't just how she looked, though, because Jenna was also showing the same level of determination and drive that I'd always seen in Ellie. At university Ellie always worked hard and got everything completed well before her deadlines. She said that way she could enjoy herself knowing it was all done. *Just get it done and draw a line under it*, that had always been her motto.

Jenna was the same and would often become a little impatient with me when I was vague about what she needed to do if she was struggling with her homework. 'Where's Mummy?' she would ask quite indignantly, and I would dutifully phone Ellie and see how long it would be before she was home. If it was going to be longer than an hour, Jenna would sigh at me and go and phone one of her friends for help – usually Jacob. Jenna would then inform me quite matter-of-factly that Marc and Christina were much better at helping Jacob with his homework than I was at helping her. 'It's because your head's all over the place, Dad. You really need to focus more.'

That was her mimicking Ellie, who frequently said that to me. Whenever Ellie said it, she would sometimes add that she was aware that marrying someone like me would mean that not every day was the same, but that it would be nice every now and then to have a bit more of a regimented structure to our lives.

I smiled at how different I was to the two of them and felt myself absorbing the bliss of our disjointed domesticity. To conceal what I'd been up to that day, I pushed any thoughts of the woman and my clandestine zoo visit to the back of my mind. But, still, there was something not quite right, and every spare moment I had in the days that followed, I thought of the woman. I was finding it hard to, as Ellie would say, *draw a line under it.*

The fact that I was painting a picture of the woman was probably not helping. The emerging image of her was getting clearer each time I was in the studio. The picture was almost complete, but I was struggling with painting her eyes. They had been a specific shade of blue-green, and I needed to get them right.

Each time I stood in front of the easel I grappled with my memory. Closing my eyes before mixing the paint, I desperately tried to bring forward the image from the depths of my mind. I could see her so clearly when I closed my eyes but recreating it once I opened them again and stared at the swirls of blue, green and yellow on my palette, had become a problem. At one point I'd been on the verge of ripping the painting up, but she was getting to look so much like how I wanted her to be, that I didn't want to waste time. It would get there, each day I felt more positive that it would.

I just had to be patient.

Although time was short, I wanted to get the picture finished in time for my exhibition. All the time, though, still bothering me, was why she'd become such a part of my waking hours. I got that I would inevitably think about her at night because I had less control over that, but during the day I should have been able to have pushed my thoughts of her away. But the more I thought of her, the more I became frustrated with the situation.

Little did I know that very soon something would happen which would only deepen my obsession.

Chapter 4

A few days after my clandestine zoo visit, Jenna and I were in the kitchen together cutting some slices of fruit to have as an after-school snack. In the background, an antiques show was playing on the kitchen television. An old guy from Halifax was having a painting valued by one of the antiques specialists. The presenter held the painting up in front of him and, commenting on its scratches, he told him it would need some work to bring it to its true value, and hence valued it at about half what the old man had been expecting. 'That's okay,' the old man said, tangible disappointment etched on his face, 'I'll sell it anyway.'

'Shame,' I muttered to myself. Jenna rolled her eyes at me talking to the television.

The camera returned to a lingering shot of the painting. It was of a red fox. A sudden sense of realization shot through my body. *What was it? What was it with the picture?* I dropped the vegetable knife on the chopping board and raced to get the TV controller. 'Dad!' Jenna screeched as she got covered in sticky orange juice.

She tutted and shook her head at me.

Standing just a couple of feet from the television screen, I pressed the rewind button and then paused the image on the painting.

What was it? There was something about the painting on the screen. *What was it? Think, Nate. Think! Red fox, red fox! What was it about the fox? What did all this mean?* The thoughts shot through my head like a machine gun firing rounds.

And then, I gasped, as realization washed over me.

A deep, visceral understanding suddenly flooded my pores, my flesh, my bones, my nerves. 'Why didn't I think of that before?' I exclaimed out loud. I clasped my hand around my mouth. 'Oh my God! That's it!'

'Don't use the Lord's name in vain, Daddy.' Jenna exclaimed, sounding just like her very religious grandmother.

I irresponsibly left her to her own devices amid the knives and partially chopped fruit and rushed out of the room. I called back to her, 'Jenna, we're not even religious!' I raced upstairs to the first-floor landing. I precariously balanced myself on the banister and reached up and pulled down the ladder to the attic. '… and Jenna, don't touch anything, I'm just going up into the attic. In fact, just come up here onto the landing and wait for me.'

As keen an art collector as I was a painter, in the

attic I'd accumulated an extensive collection of paintings – a couple of hundred or more. It was mainly stuff I'd taken a shine to in house clearance or antique shops, and I was keeping hold of them to display whenever we managed to buy a much bigger home. The collection had clearly become so large that I really should have been selling some of them, but it would've taken weeks to have sorted them out. And so, they remained there, ten or twelve deep, stacked against the walls, or leaning against the rafters of the roof. Luckily the attic was floored and dry, but I did sometimes worry that if ever we had a leak in the roof the whole collection could be ruined.

Amid the assortment of metal or mousy-smelling, wooden framed pictures I was sure there was an oil painting of a woodland scene, with a flock of birds silhouetted across the sky. In the foreground of the image was a young girl sitting on a wooden bench. She wore a blue and white, floral, sleeveless dress, and white sandals. Beside her, a bright red fox cub stood on his hind legs and was raising a front paw to 'bat' at a red admiral butterfly. The girl was looking at the fox and smiling. The dark red of the fox was a sharp contrast to the girl's pastel blue clothes; the butterfly was as large as the fox cub and out of proportion to the rest of the picture. It had one wing dripping in shades of red, black, and white. It was such a strange combination, but it somehow worked.

Once the memory of the painting's existence had come to me, I was suddenly able to recall the whole image, and the picture was definitely somewhere in the attic. But where?

'But Nana always says we mustn't say what you just said.' I heard Jenna call up to me from where she had shifted herself from downstairs and plonked herself on the low rungs of the ladder. She clearly hadn't given up on my recent, apparently blasphemous, misdemeanour – her grandmother would have been horrified at my poisoning of the poor child's mind! If I'm honest, both grandmothers would have been.

'I know, but Nana is really a bit of a nutcase.' I replied under my breath. I'd never really got on with Ellie's parents – I always felt they thought she could have done better than me. Adding to that, their more recent determination to try to indoctrinate Jenna into their way of religious thinking, well, it was just the final straw.

'What did you say, Daddy?'

'Nothing, Jenna. Yes, you're right, Daddy won't say that again.'

'What are you doing, Daddy?'

'Nothing.'

'Whenever I say that to you, you always want more information,' she protested.

'I'm looking for something.'

'What?'

'A picture … you just wait down there by the bottom of the ladder for me, Jenna, I'll just be a few minutes.'

I heard her singing 'Crazy Nights' to herself. I smiled and got on with trying to find the picture.

'Crazy, crazy, crazy, crazy nights …' came echoing up the ladder into the attic. She very quickly ran out of lyrics and decided to hum the tune instead, interspersing it with more renditions of the words she could remember.

And then, I found it!

It was as though the picture melted into my hand; my heart pounded against the wall of my chest. The copper frame needed some tender loving care, and I could see why it had been chosen to complement the redness of the fox, but the picture itself was as though it had been painted yesterday. As I had remembered, it was of a girl in a blue and white dress and a fox cub was vividly painted, the careful brush strokes of his fur even visible in the gloom of the attic. The dark ginger was a stark contrast to the pale greens of the leaves on the trees and the shades of blue in her dress. The girl was just off-centre in the picture. She was sitting on a wooden bench – her head was turned so she was looking at the fox chasing the butterfly. But there was something more to her – it was as though she wasn't actually looking at the creatures around her, but was gazing out of the picture, to whoever was looking in. For such an innocent image, it was quite haunting.

The picture reminded me of old paintings from the echelons of societies past which you see hanging in castles. The ones where a museum attendant will tell you to look at the image from anywhere in the room and you will see the person's eyes following your every move.

The picture was about two feet wide by eighteen inches high, and as soon as I examined the face of the woman, everything became so clear – this painting was what had been bothering me all those weeks. It was her – the woman from the zoo, I had no doubt that the image in the painting was her. She was younger, but I was sure there was no mistake about this. I strained my eyes in the dim light and could see the picture was painted in 1985. Above the date there was a signature, but it was an illegible scrawl.

I heard the distant sound of Ellie calling upstairs.' Hi guys, I'm home. Where *are* the two of you?'

'Daddy is in the attic and I'm on the ladder.' Jenna called back to her.

Ellie shouted up, 'It's an absolute tip down here.' And then she realized what Jenna had said. 'You're what? On the ladder? And what's Daddy doing in the attic? What *are* you two up to?' She came rushing up to the landing to rescue her daughter and waited for an explanation. Jenna willingly gave her version of events, allowing me a little time to think about what I was going to say to them.

'We were cutting fruit and then Dad paused the TV on a picture of a fox. Then he went rushing away, leaving me alone with those sharp knives. I came up here so I wouldn't hurt myself,' Jenna offered. I could imagine the look of horror on Ellie's face as Jenna threw me to the wolves.

Allowing my desire to defend myself against Jenna's accusations pass, I focused on the painting. I considered putting it back and going down empty-handed, telling them I hadn't found what I was looking for, but I didn't want to lie to them. I never had, so why would I start? I told myself I hadn't properly lied about the zoo visit – I just hadn't told them anything about it. Was omission of information a form of lying? I wasn't sure.

'Nate, what are you looking for? And why is the television paused?'

Taking a deep breath, I passed the picture down to Ellie. 'Here, take this please, Ellie.' I climbed down the ladder and jumped off the last four rungs, feeling proud that I still had a piece of that daredevil schoolboy inside me.

'What is it?' Ellie asked. Then she nodded in recognition, 'Oh, of course, the fox cub – just like the one on the TV downstairs!'

'Wow, Daddy, the fox in that picture is just like the one on that TV programme. It's so cute.'

'What is it, Nate, do you think it's by the same artist? Is it someone famous?' This was my get-out, my escape route, my getaway car! I could sense her imagining our early retirement.

Deciding not to lie, I took a deep breath and took the wind out of her planning-our-retirement sails, 'No, not at all. Ellie, not the fox, look at the woman.' Ellie looked away from the fox cub and concentrated on the woman's face.

'Who is it, Daddy?' Jenna chirped.

'Do you see it? Do you see who it is?' I quizzed Ellie, frustrated that she hadn't had an immediate sense of recollection. While Ellie looked doubtful and was clearly racking her brains to offer an answer, I stole the opportunity to let Jenna get a closer look. 'Jenna, have you seen this lady before?'

Jenna pondered for a few seconds and then slowly nodded, her small face breaking into a grin as she recognized who was in the picture. Looking up at me, and obviously feeling extremely pleased with herself, she said, 'Yes, Daddy, in your studio.'

For a minute Ellie looked horrified, as though I'd been welcoming young ladies into my studio when she wasn't home. It was my turn to tut. 'Exactly, Jenna.' I smiled at her and offered her a high five, which she eagerly accepted. 'Look, both of you – come with me.'

On our way to my studio at the bottom of the garden, I began to have regrets, but then told myself it was better to get this over with. At least then there would be no more doubt – I could move on with my life and stop wondering. I had at last discovered what that weird attraction had been. It wasn't an attraction at all, it was purely recognition, which I'd wrapped up as something much more meaningful. I *had* seen her somewhere before – in a painting which had found its way into my collection. The thing that had been playing on my subconscious since I saw her had finally become clear.

A dark red sheet enclosed the painting on which I had been working. As I revealed the picture, Ellie looked a little puzzled, her brow furrowing in that way it did when she was worried about some case she was working on in the courts. 'The woman at the zoo? But she was much older than this girl in the painting.'

'I know, Ellie, but can't you see? It's her. It's definitely her. The eyes, the heart-shaped face, high cheek bones, the dark, curly hair, the complexion, even the thin nose. And look,' I held the painting close to my eyes and strained to see the girl's neck, 'there's a birthmark – right here. Just like in my picture.' I held the painting in front of Ellie and pointed to the blemish on the right side of the girl's neck, and then at my own painting on the easel, where the mark was so much more obvious. It was small on the picture of her in the painting I had recovered from the attic, but you could clearly see it.

'Possibly, but you know yourself how much people change through the years. We couldn't possibly be sure.'

'No, but the mark on her neck, surely that on its own would be significant enough?' I began to feel my heart sinking.

Ellie didn't answer, but just stood looking at the image in front of her. And then she spoke. 'So, are you sure she had a birth mark or some kind of scar there? Did you really observe her *that* closely? How on Earth did you manage to see her in such detail?'

My heart sank as that familiar feeling of being some weird, voyeuristic monster washed over me. I nodded, 'I did, sorry, I saw it when she took off her scarf.' Feeling sheepish, I meekly pointed toward the image on the easel and shrugged, not really knowing what to say next.

Ellie looked pained, hurt. It was as though we'd gone all the way back to square one, back to that point ten years earlier when I'd had to explain how I found my inspiration for my paintings. I carried on – I was in trouble, so I figured I might as well get it all over in one fell swoop. 'If it is her, don't you think she should have this painting back? Don't you think that she would want it?'

Ellie looked doubtful. 'I don't know, Nate. What if it isn't her? We'd feel a little stupid, wouldn't we?'

'It's worth a try, though, isn't it? I'm sure if it *is* her, she would be delighted to have it back. It really is a beautiful painting.'

I had found the *Girl with Fox Cub and Butterfly* painting, as I'd named it six years earlier, in an antiques shop named Auntie Abigail Annie's Antiques (I'd remembered the shop's name because of the catchy alliteration), just north of Leeds. The dealer (disappointingly, not named Abigail or Annie) told me she'd picked it up at an auction, thinking it would sell on quite quickly. She'd had it for more than two years when I saw it, so she let me have it half price. She said she thought that many couldn't see how it might fit into their colour schemes at home.

We agreed it was such a shame that more people hadn't liked it. I told her I loved it. I tucked it into the back of the car, alongside a brightly-coloured teapot I thought Ellie would like and headed for home. When I got the painting home there was never really anywhere we thought it would go with any of our other pictures. And so, it had ended up in the attic, along with the multitude of other *can't quite place* pictures in my *I'll hang them somewhere when we get a bigger house* or *sell them on one day* collection.

And that's where it had remained until that day when it emerged from the loft.

Putting the painting to one side once again, I told Ellie I'd do a bit of research on Monday and try to find the woman at the zoo – perhaps even go in there the next time I had a meeting. I felt relieved that by my mentioning it to them I would at last be doing everything above board.

Jenna said she would want to go along too, but I quickly told her she would be at school. Perhaps that response was too quick. I glanced at Ellie; I didn't think she'd noticed. 'Can't we go over the weekend?' Jenna asked. She was getting to an age where she questioned everything, and it was becoming much more difficult to fob her off with excuses.

Ellie saved me. 'Not this coming weekend, Sweetheart, we have a few busy weekends looming just now, especially with Dad's exhibition being soon. Dad can go sometime during the week. We'll all go together again in the holidays. I promise. We could even see if Jacob or Emma-Louise could come along too?'

A least Ellie was on board, and she always got away with parental bribery much easier than I did. It was that quick thinking way she had, and I was sure she put it to good use in the courts.

'Okay then,' a suitably satisfied Jenna answered, as we walked back into the kitchen to continue chopping fruit. The picture incident forgotten, the three of us talked about our day. Once the bowls were full, Jenna topped her fruit with dark chocolate chips. I thought better of challenging her about the logic of sprinkling chocolate all over fresh fruit and decided I'd do the same, adding some pumpkin and sunflower seeds to make myself feel more self-righteous.

That evening, the three of us hugged the cats Thomas and Jeremy close to us, while we cried over what felt like our zillionth viewing of Dumbo. Before Jenna headed off to bed, to cheer ourselves up we played twenty minutes of Sonic the Hedgehog on my old cherished Megadrive.

Later that night, once Jenna was tucked up nice and soundly sleeping in her room, Ellie and I collapsed into bed. Ellie told me about a case that was going on in the courts. I'd heard about it on the news but had been so caught up in my own world, I hadn't even realized Ellie was involved in the prosecution team. It was a child abuse case concerning three children about the same age as Jenna. Ellie told me as much as she could about what had been going on, and how she couldn't possibly imagine how anyone could be so cruel. 'What is it that makes someone end up doing such horrific things to the children they've created ... to *any* child?'

She was emotionally drained, and by the dim light of the bedside lamp, I noticed dark circles under her eyes. I shook my head in disbelief as her tears finally washed away the sadness of her day. My mind was with her, but not entirely, and while I comforted her, I simultaneously chastised myself for what I had done a few days earlier. How could I have gone off like that with barely a thought to the wonderful family I had back home. But that problem was solved, and once I found the woman from the zoo and gave her the picture, there would be no more need to contact her. The job would be done. Finished!

How strange it was that I should have in my possession a painting that was so clearly of her. As I drifted off to sleep that night, lying on my back with Ellie hugged close beside me, I wondered about how (and why) the painting had come into my possession. It had been a chance finding in an antique store, but what a coincidence that we should have come across that very same person on that cold, wintry day back in January. Perhaps Ellie was right, though, perhaps it wasn't her? But then I recalled that Jenna had recognized her from the picture too – and Ellie had as well – once she'd been prompted anyway.

It had to be her.

Chapter 5

I didn't go back to the zoo that week. I was busy with painting, preparations for the exhibition, and making sure each piece of work was properly framed and presented in the most complementary way. I hoped the exhibition would bring a massive boost to our household income for the year. It was comforting knowing that, for once, things might be a little less of a financial struggle.

There was something else holding me back from going to the zoo. I wasn't sure what, but I wondered whether I was using the exhibition as an excuse to not go and confront her. In the end, I realized I had to get the whole thing over with – have the meeting with her, pass on the painting, and then dust myself down and get on with my life.

I also wondered whether my delay in going had been deliberate because there was a part of me that hadn't wanted Ellie to go with me – perhaps I was biding my time to keep the meeting just for me. Maybe I was just waiting for it not to be such a hot topic in the house? Or perhaps I hadn't wanted it to seem as though I was rushing off to see some woman I had been inspired to paint. This was particularly a concern after Ellie's renewed insecurity, when she'd quizzed me about having noticed the mark on the woman's neck.

When I got around to visiting the zoo, I suppose all those conflicting thoughts resulted in my not telling Ellie I was going. I don't understand why I didn't tell her, but with her being so busy with the case at the courts, the subject hadn't come up in a week or two. So, one Wednesday I decided I would just go. Ellie knew I was going to the gallery, so perhaps she would assume I would also go to the zoo. Or at least that's what I told myself so I would feel absolved of any guilt.

It was a bright, spring-like day that I ventured back there, with the intention of going straight to the zoo after my next pre-exhibition meeting. Learning from my previous visit, in an attempt to look like something resembling a professional photographer, I had my SLR camera around my neck.

I walked along the increasingly familiar pathways, following a route past all the different species, which had by then also started to become quite familiar to me. I very quickly made my way to the area by the bird house and café and wondered why I was convinced I would see her in that area. Just because I'd seen her around there the first time, didn't mean she'd be in the same place again – she could work in any part of the zoo. She could even have been on holiday! She might not even work there! I felt that familiar sinking feeling I'd had on my first solo visit. But then, she'd had a lanyard and fleece, so I was pretty sure I'd find her – my spirit lifted.

I'd left the painting in the car, and for the previous week to ten days had been imagining speeches in my head, about how I had a painting I'd like her to see, I'd left it in the car, and would she like to go and look at it with me? However I tried to wrap it up, it always came out sounding unnervingly sleazy, something like, 'Do you want to come up to my apartment and see my etchings?' I felt my whole covert visit was doomed for failure for one reason or another. I admitted to myself that what I was up to was definitely odd. I was behaving quite irrationally.

I focused most of my time around the bird house and shifted away from there each time I saw someone who wasn't her. I began to think people might be thinking I was up to no good. Eventually, after an hour of searching, I decided to inject a little *carpe diem* into my mission and headed back to the reception area to find someone who could help me.

Joe, which was apparently what the tall, gangly guy at the desk was called, looked as though he had spent four hours gelling short spikes into his hair. Perched on his chin he had a neatly manicured, apparently trendy-of-late, sculpted black beard. He wasn't at all helpful when I tried to quiz him about the zookeeper who worked there. Describing her in as much detail as I could, I asked him whether she was around, so I could have a word with her.

'About this tall,' I added, holding my hand level with my shoulder, 'with brown, curly hair and blue eyes.' I paused, while he looked at me with a blank expression. I frustratingly pointed to his lanyard and fleece, both of which had the words *Joe Davies Reception Staff – Loves Boa Constrictors* on them, and added meekly, 'and she was wearing one of those lanyards, and a fleece just like yours.'

'I really don't know who you're talking about Mr. … er?'

'Campbell. Nate … Campbell. Please … just Nate.' I had a sudden thought that I was in the casting line-up for a 007 movie. I smiled to myself.

Joe Davies looked at me as though I had three heads.

'Okay … Mr. Campbell,' he replied. 'You just wait here, and I'll go and try to contact one of the keepers.'

Joe walked over to another desk where he would be out of earshot, picked up the phone and embarked on deep conversation with someone. He smirked and shook his head. I strained to try to hear what he was saying, but he was too far away. He eventually made his way back over to the desk, 'Okay, Mr. Campbell, if you just take a seat over there by the window, the Head Keeper will be here for you in about ten minutes.'

I thanked him and walked over to the red, very uncomfortable-looking, plastic seats. I nervously wondered whether the Head Keeper would be the woman in question.

It was the spring holiday in that area – Jenna's school wouldn't be off until the following week. Kids of all ages were excitedly tugging at their parents and one another, all desperate to be allowed through to see the animals. I felt again that sense of sadness for the animals that were all limited by their enclosures. I imagined them being laughed at and screeched at by passing families and school groups.

I watched one woman who looked about forty. She had three excited noisy children and a baby with her. The baby was wailing as she maneuvered him around her handbag and purse. As the volume of his shrieks increased, she rocked him from side to side. She caught me watching her. 'Nappy!' she confirmed. She looked skywards and then back at me and smiled. I nodded and smiled back in understanding, recalling the first time we met Marc and Christina. Once her tickets were bought, she kept one ticket back and handed over the rest to another woman with her, who looked as though she was in her early twenties. She rushed off toward the door marked *Parent and Baby,* with the baby expertly balanced on her hip.

With them gone, I switched my attention to some other people. They were a group of young adults who were reaching into their pockets to find identification to prove to Joe Davies that one of them was old enough to be responsible for the whole group. 'I AM an adult,' one girl declared. She triumphantly thrust her driving license under his nose. 'Look, I'm twenty-two years old.' She looked as though she was ready to stamp her foot in defiant indignation at the unjustness of being asked for her identification.

Joe took the license from her and squinted as he held it close to his eyes to read the tiny print. To add insult to injury, he held the card up in front of her so he could compare her to the image. I had to admit she looked as though she might only have been fifteen, I was definitely with Joe on that one … but he was also being a bit of a pain. His face a little flushed, Joe handed her back her driver's license and took their money. Triumphantly, the five young people grasped their tickets and headed through the huge, glass doors.

Distracted by them as they walked away, I focused on one of them. He was an interesting-looking guy of about seventeen, who had blond dreadlocks. I realized I'd never painted anyone who had them. I tried to imagine the paint strokes I would use to create such an effect. Caught deep in thought about the possible technicalities of painting dreadlocks, I hadn't noticed the keeper approaching me.

The pretty young keeper, who was not the woman I'd seen before, smiled down at me. 'Mr. Campbell?' A huge part of me was disappointed that it wasn't the other woman stood in front of me holding her hand out to greet me. I stood up and shook the red-haired keeper's hand.

'Um, yes, er, Nate.' I suddenly felt quite flustered. She was about eight inches shorter than me, but still taller than average for a woman. I quickly noticed her pale green eyes, which complemented her straight, red hair. She had a dusting of freckles across her pale skin, and the loveliest smile, which made me think how awful it must be to ever see such a beautiful face sad. If ever I painted her, I would seize that moment and capture that smile of hers. It could be a strange feeling to have the ability to recreate and immortalize a moment in that way – but it could be both a gift and a curse.

'Elise.' She smiled again.

I paused, wondering how I was going to explain what I needed from her. She nodded as though she were prompting me, biting her bottom lip as she did so. 'What can I do for you?'

'Okay, Elise. I'm afraid this is a bit of a strange request, but I'm looking for someone – a woman.' While I searched for what to say next, she appeared to look a little uncomfortable. She looked around her – perhaps for an exit?

'Okaaaay?' She replied.

Realizing the possible connotations of what I'd said, I quickly continued. 'Oh no! Gosh, not anyone, a specific person. And not in *that* way. I'm happily married with a daughter.' I was embarrassed and I felt my face flush as I tried to justify what I was saying. I could be such a bumbling idiot at times.

Realizing what I had to say was never going to be easy, I decided to get it over and done with. 'In late December I was here with my wife and daughter. When we were having coffee, one of the keepers came in and sat down close to us. She caught my attention.' I felt I needed to quickly explain, as a confused and slightly alarmed look washed across Elise's face. 'I'm an artist and mostly paint portraits. Anyway, I couldn't get her out of my head.'

Elise looked puzzled and even more concerned than she'd seemed before.

'No. Gosh. No. Again, not in that way. She had such striking features, and I knew I had to paint her. That's sort of what I do, I remember people's faces and then paint them. Sometimes they look like the person, sometimes it's a surreal version of them, but I try to capture the essence of how I imagine they might be. You know, their personality, and so on?'

I felt I was providing more information than I needed to, and I wasn't really making the situation any better by meandering. I wasn't making sense, and I considered that perhaps in hindsight I should have asked Ellie to take the picture to the zoo.

'Anyway, to cut a very long story short, I'm also an art collector, and just a few weeks ago I came across a painting I bought years ago. I'm positive the image is of her – the keeper I saw! Not as she is now, but when she was younger. Anyway, that's why I'm here now – I want to give her the painting.'

Elise's alarm had turned into curiosity. 'Oh? How interesting! Are you sure it's her?'

'As sure as I can be – even my six-year-old daughter, Jenna, thinks it's her.'

Elise seemed doubtful but was now much more on

board with this. I began to relax. 'Okay,' she said, 'I can't guarantee I can help you, but can you give me some idea of what she looked like?'

As I described her, I saw a look of recognition appear on Elise's face. 'Wow! You know who she is? Can I see her? Is she here today?'

Elise's expression shifted to one of concern. *Crikey*, I thought, *don't say she's dead.* I wasn't exactly sure where that thought came from, but what she said next was quite unexpected.

'Um, yes, I think I know who you mean, but she doesn't work here.'

'But she was wearing ...' I pointed to her fleece.

'Yes, I know. She was here temporarily for a few months doing some conservation work with us.'

'Ah, I see.' I considered the situation for a few moments and then asked her how it might be possible for me to contact her.

'Look, maybe given the unusual circumstances, if you leave me your contact details, I can get in touch with her for you, and then it's up to her to get in touch with you. I've probably already said too much about her.'

I realized that was perhaps as good as I was going

to get. 'Okay. Thank you!' I dug deep in my coat pocket and found a small metal case Ellie, in an effort to organize me, had given me to keep my business cards safe. I handed her one of the cards and then added, 'Listen do you have ten minutes, only I have the painting in the car – do you want to see it?' That concept of going up to someone's room to see their etchings sprang back into my mind. I hoped she wouldn't go back to thinking I was strange. But luckily, she nodded.

'Yes, sure, I'm intrigued. I can't be long, though.' Elise told a girl at the desk she was going to the car park and would be back in about ten minutes. Was she telling them so they'd know where to get her, or was there still an element of doubt about my authenticity? Was it possible she still thought I was some lecherous weirdo?

At the car, I removed the picture from the boot and walked around to the front and balanced it on the bonnet. I peeled back the brown paper I'd carefully wrapped it in the previous afternoon.

Elise took a sharp intake of breath as the picture was revealed. She clasped her hand around her mouth. 'Wow! My goodness, you're right. How strange is that? It looks so much like her. Even the mark on her neck. It's obviously someone much younger, and if it's not her then it's certainly an excellent doppelganger!' She smiled and shook her head slowly, seemingly in awe at the likeness. 'Wow!' she repeated, 'and what a lovely picture!'

Finally feeling vindicated in all my efforts, I simply nodded and said, 'I … we … felt that if it really is her, then she should have it. It's such a good likeness. She has such striking features!' I held the painting up in front of the two of us. We both stood and admired it for a moment or two.

As I wrapped the picture back in its brown paper, Elise said, 'Look, I can't guarantee she'll get in touch with you, but I'll do my best.' She held my card up to confirm she was keeping it safe. 'I'll let her know I've seen the painting.' I thanked her and headed on my way.

Later at dinner I told Ellie and Jenna all that had happened. I decided it was better to be open about it and explain that as I'd been down there anyway, I thought I'd drop by the zoo. After all, there was nothing to hide.

'I really think it's her, Daddy. I think she will be very excited when she sees it.' Jenna was clearly becoming as intrigued as I was about the concept of searching for this nameless woman.

'As long as she gets in touch, I suppose,' Ellie pulled a funny face and wrinkled her nose up at

Jenna and added, 'she might just think Daddy's a weird stalker!'

'What's a stalker, Mummy?'

The phone rang and I left Ellie absorbed in an in-depth conversation with Jenna about how stalkers were bad people, that Daddy wasn't really a stalker, and Mummy was only joking.

The call was from Elise the zookeeper. 'I hope you don't mind me phoning in the evening, I just thought I should let you know I've emailed her and given her your contact details. I tried to phone her, but she could be away working. I just didn't want you to be hanging on waiting for her to get in touch, when it could be weeks before that happens. *If* it happens, of course …'.

'Of course. Okay, Elise, thank you so much for letting me know.' I felt our conversation was drawing to a close and asked her, 'Elise, just before you go, I meant to ask you her name.'

There was a pause at the end of the line. 'I'm probably better leaving her to introduce herself, should she decide to do so … I'm sorry!' She sounded genuinely apologetic.

'Gosh, yes, of course, confidentiality and all that.' I felt a little stupid. She must have thought I was going to go straight to my computer and try to find her, which, if I'm honest, was something I probably would have done. I suddenly felt as though I actually was that stalker!

'Indeed. Good luck with your search! But Nate, I also wanted to say that I couldn't believe the likeness in the picture. It really is quite something …'.

I imagined her smiling at the other end of the phone, and once again promised myself that when I got the chance, I would paint her. She really was quite stunning. I thanked her and went back through to Ellie and Jenna, who were still discussing the concept of stalking someone. By the end of their extended discussion, I didn't feel any better about my predicament. I got some reassurance, however, from telling myself I simply had a painting which needed to be returned to its rightful owner.

That was all.

Chapter 6

A week or so later when an email arrived from her, it was short.

Dear Mr. Campbell

I believe you've been trying to contact me about a painting you have. I admit I am just a little intrigued. I wonder whether you would mind sending a photograph of it to me.

Yours

Dayna Marshall

I immediately sat down in front of my computer and composed a reply. I spent the first ten minutes wondering whether I should be formal or informal – what would she think if I were too casual? Do I call her Miss, Mrs., Ms., Dr. or Professor? I was sure she was a doctor or professor – she had to be, but her email signature was giving nothing away. I searched the Internet and found her: she was a professor of zoology. Of course she would be, given what she did for a living. Perhaps she'd deleted her professional details before sending her email – in some effort to hide her true identity, in case I was someone she needed to be careful about. Or perhaps she didn't feel she had to tell everyone her status. Maybe I was overthinking it.

I deleted my response four times before eventually phrasing the message how I wanted it to be. I decided in the end that relatively informal was best.

Dear Dayna

Thank you for getting back to me.

The picture is quite something. I have attached a photograph of it. I really don't think the photograph does it justice. Do you recognize it?

My kind regards

Nate

A few days passed before I heard from her again. During those days I imagined her amid the jungles of somewhere like Borneo, surrounded by rescued orangutans, a baby one clinging to her side. I obsessively checked my emails several times an hour. It was interrupting my work and I began to feel ashamed that, while I was focusing so much of my time on the painting and its potential owner, Ellie and Jenna were functioning as two-thirds of our family normally functioned.

The second email was slightly longer and a little more informative:

Dear Nate

I apologize for how long it's taken to get back to you – work has been very busy, and it's been extremely difficult to find a location where I can get access to the Internet. Most of my work this last month or so has been in dense forest.

The picture you attached to your message is certainly fascinating. It without a doubt shows a likeness to me when I was (much!) younger. How very strange!

I certainly don't recognize it, but I am interested to see it. I fly back to the UK a week on Saturday, so could possibly meet you one day the following week at Raven's Nest Coffee Shop on Station Avenue near to the zoo. Do you know it?

I'll be out of range for the next few days but will pick up your reply once I get back to relative civilization.

Cheerio for now

Dayna

I had been right when I'd imagined her walking around clutching a baby orangutan to her hip, and it made me wonder what exciting conservation projects she was involved in. When Ellie and I were at university, so many of us talked about how once we graduated, we'd go off and make a difference to the world. How many of us think that about our lives? And yet so few of us do anything about it.

I wondered whether she was married. I went online to search for images of her, and beside her at various charity events there was a tall, bespectacled man. Beneath one of the images, it said his name was Jackson Marshall. One photo I found was of the two of them in what looked like a lighter moment, either side of an African elephant, all three of them looking as though they were posing for the camera – the elephant reaching his trunk toward Jackson's face. I wondered whether Dayna and Jackson were still together, and then mentally chastised myself for even wondering. After all, it really didn't matter to me whether she was married. A niggling worry kept on coming back to me – what did I *actually* hope to gain from our meeting?

I arranged to meet her the Tuesday after she got back. I didn't tell Ellie. Once again, I wasn't sure why I didn't. I had nothing to hide, after all, Ellie knew about the painting and that at some point I'd planned to meet with the woman who I hoped would claim it as her own. But I suppose time had passed since it was something we were talking about, and, well, she'd been busy at work with that horrendous case, which by then had been unexpectedly suspended while new evidence was examined. Our spring holidays had passed, and we were on the countdown to the summer, and before that my exhibition.

Excuses … it seemed I was constantly finding excuses for my absurd behaviour.

That Tuesday, the cafe was busy with customers grabbing pre-booked sandwiches, salads, and cakes to take back to their desks for their lunch. I thought of the packed lunches Ellie and I made after dinner each night for the next school or work day. We even prepared one for me so I wouldn't have to stop if I was suddenly mentally consumed by a piece of work. Just like all those commuters and office workers I could see paying at the till, I was also prone to eating while working, usually grabbing a fork and food container, and making a mess on the floor as I stood in front of my work; all the time contemplating my next strokes of paint.

At the table next to where I was sitting waiting for Dayna to arrive, there was an old gent. He had deep tracks of wrinkles across his face and neck; lines and craters exposing the story of his life. He held tight to a walking stick, which even though he was sat down, was clearly helping him to balance. His companion, a man in his twenties who had medium-length, Marc Bolan style brown curls, placed a pot of tea and a cup and saucer in front of him, along with a piece of almond cake, which had a generous layer of pure-white icing on top. The old man thanked him and smiled, deepening those facial fissures as he did so.

'You want it poured just now, Grandad, or shall we leave it to brew for a little while?'

The old man reached for his slice of cake and broke a piece off the edge. Crumbs of sponge cake dropped to the floor and over his lap as he manoeuvered the cake into his mouth. 'We'll give it a few minutes, Jamie-son.' His ill-fitting false teeth shifted as he chewed.

The young man named Jamie saw me looking over at them. I smiled, hoping he didn't think I was being nosy. He acknowledged my curious gaze with a smile and a nod. Feeling a little uncomfortable for once, I looked away from them and gazed out of the window. Recalling what I was doing there, I felt a flutter of butterflies pass across my abdomen.

And then, there she was. I spotted Dayna weaving her way between the traffic as she crossed the busy road. She saw me as she opened the glass door and smiled and waved. I wondered how she knew what I looked like and then remembered the power of the Internet. Or perhaps she actually remembered me from the day at the zoo? I hoped that was the case, but it was probably more likely she really had done an Internet search and found pictures of me with my work. I had a website that was advertised on the bottom of every email I sent, so it was pretty easy to find me.

Nothing was secret anymore. There was no need for anyone to say, 'I'll be wearing a red rose,' or 'I'll be carrying a rare copy of Time magazine which has Marilyn Monroe on the front of it.' Nope, with just a few casual taps of the fingers, you could find out practically anything you needed to know about anyone.

She walked straight over to me. 'Nate! Hello.' She smiled and assertively reached out to shake hands. 'I looked at your web page – your paintings are wonderful!' Her confidence and immediate honesty were a little overwhelming.

Dumbstruck, I reached my hand out to her.

When our hands touched, I felt an immediate spark of electricity. The sensation permeated the cells of my fingers, sending a current shooting through my body. As I felt the jolt pass through me, she looked at me and smiled. I held on tight to her hand. I felt sick. Dayna seemed to realize that something was wrong, and the smile disappeared from her face. She tilted her head to one side. I continued to hold onto her hand and locked eyes with her – they were blue-green and as pale as the sea on a bright, sunny afternoon. I sank into those pools of green and felt as though my legs would collapse beneath me. As I continued to hold onto her hand, now with both of my hands, the electric bolt continued to flow right through me. Her look was replaced by one of concern. Was it concern? Or had *she* felt something too?

'Nate, are you okay?' She'd clearly noticed something, but had she felt the same extreme bolt of, well, whatever that had been? While I nodded my head with every ounce of energy I could muster, I tried to brush away the million thoughts that were raging through my mind. We let go of one another's hands and she smiled again. 'Shall we sit down and order a coffee?' She looked concerned, flushed, and just a little confused.

'Gosh, yes, of course. I'm so sorry, I don't know what's wrong. I suddenly felt as though I was going to faint.' I shook my head and glanced over to where Jamie and his grandfather were sitting at the next table. Had either of them noticed what had just happened? The guy named Jamie looked as though he was ready to get up and come over to us, but as I sat down, he settled back into his seat. Some people were like that – observant, perceptive, and just, well, sensitive to such things, I guess.

'It's okay – I was worried about you for a minute or

two there. Do you feel all right now?'

I nodded to her and lied, 'Yes, I'm fine, I don't know what came over me.'

She smiled and removed her waterproof jacket and her fleece, revealing an array of layers underneath – cardigan, sweater, blue and green checked shirt, and there was evidence of a khaki green T-shirt peeking out from beneath all those layers. Noticing me watching her, she said, 'Layers, Nate, I always dress in layers – at least you can take them off one by one, and you're prepared for any weather!'

Within seconds, the waiter appeared beside the table and offered us the lunch menu, which we declined and just ordered two black coffees.

The bitter scent of coffee permeated the air as I waited for my beverage to cool in front of me. Clearly much less sensitive to the heat of the steaming liquid than I was, Dayna began to sip hers straight away. As though we'd been friends for years we talked about our work and our families. She talked about Jackson, who she'd met at university. He was a recently retired computer scientist. She said they couldn't be more different to one another, but that somehow it worked. She flashed a photograph in front of me. It was of her family surrounded by an array of animals.

She and Jackson had two daughters who were both at university, the eldest studying environmental science, the younger one physics. She said it was as though they had created younger versions of themselves in terms of their daughters' personalities and interests.

Their home in Yorkshire was also home to several rescued dogs and cats, and they had some rescued pigs and sheep running about the place. She laughed about how they had to pay extortionate amounts to get good pet sitters to go and stay in the house whenever she was away working. She said the girls were too busy with their own lives now to spend weeks on end at home looking after the menagerie. Since his retirement, Jackson had accompanied her on some of her trips away and having spent his whole working life in front of computer screens, he was apparently becoming quite good at handling young primates and a variety of other wild animals and birds – even the odd reptile or amphibian.

Primates were, indeed, Dayna's life's passion. She had been working with them for almost twenty-five years and had more recently spent most of her time trying to secure sanctuary places for orphaned or displaced primates of all types; the displacement due to the animals' ever-shrinking habitats. In the last few years, the mainstay of her work had been with orangutans because of the growth in monoculture palm plantations that were making the natural habitat of the orangutan uninhabitable. *Wow, that had been some intuitive guess*, I thought to myself as I recalled my mental image of her with a baby orangutan clinging to her side.

She began to tell me things I was already aware of about the crisis in Borneo, but hearing her tell it with such passion seemed more urgent than any appeal for action I'd ever heard from anyone.

'Palm oil is in so many foods and other products such as shampoos – it is so difficult for people to avoid. And yet their habitat is being replaced with hundreds of miles of palm trees.' Her raised voice expressed such deep concern for these beautiful, dark orange primates. 'It makes me so angry – I just wonder when it will all stop … will it have to be too late, and then one day we, the human race, will collectively look back in anger, regret everything resulting from our carelessness, and ask ourselves 'What *have* we done?' Do we have to completely break the Earth before we have any chance of fixing it? But then what? Perhaps it will be irreparable! Maybe it's already too late?'

We'd never properly met before, and yet I felt utterly inspired by her, mesmerized even. We were nothing to one another, but for those few captivating moments, I felt that she was mine and I was hers, both compelled to find an answer to the way the world was turning a blind eye to the issue of ever-shrinking natural spaces in the world.

She went on to tell me that her work at the zoo had been to help them establish a new enclosure specifically for a group of seven previously orphaned orangutans. She and her team had managed to get them living quite happily as a disjointed family group. That was why she'd been there on that freezing cold winter's day when I first saw her.

She explained that moving the orangutans over to the UK would free up space in the sanctuary back in Borneo, enabling more to be rescued. These babies had become so tame that rehabilitating them to the wild would not ever have been an option. Their mothers had been killed when their forests were destroyed for palm trees to be planted. What's more, for the most part, their habitat no longer existed. The jungle they had called home was gone, to give way for these gigantic land-hogging industrial scale monocultures, which extended for miles and miles.

The rescuers tried not to let the baby orangutans become too dependent on people, but when the apes stayed in their care for too long, they became too attached. Some of the youngest ones also became imprinted and thought themselves to be human. The safest option for the group unfortunately became a life in captivity. She said it was a seemingly never-ending conveyor belt of displaced animals, and that some of the circumstances under which they arrived at the sanctuary still broke her heart. She told me each case was different and every new creature who came along needed someone to take care of them. She said you would think that with all she had seen she would have become hardened to it, but even after all the years she'd been working with great apes, it still got to her.

Her eyes began to well up with tears. I felt an urge to reach across the table and wipe away her sadness but held back. She must have been around twenty-five years older than I was, but the age gap between us seemed insignificant. The conversation was easy, and within those couple of hours together I felt as though I had known her my whole life. It's like that with some people, I suppose there are those you immediately bond with.

I could have listened to her talking about her work all day, but she blinked away her tears. Tears that would remain hidden until another time. Instead, she changed the subject, asking me more about Ellie and Jenna. It felt strange suddenly talking about them – I guess to me they weren't a part of this – whatever *this* was. She listened and smiled when I talked about Jenna and how she could be quite forthright – bossy even. In return she shared stories about her own two girls when they'd been a similar age.

When the waiter came over to see whether we wanted any more coffee, Dayna glanced up at the clock that was on the wall behind me. 'Um, no thank you.' She looked from the waiter to me and added 'Sorry, Nate, I shall have to go soon.'

I reluctantly asked the waiter for the bill. Meanwhile, Dayna's gaze shifted towards the painting, which throughout our conversation had remained on the bench beside me, still protected by its brown paper.

'Is that it?' She nodded towards the package and smiled inquisitively. 'May I?'

'Oh yes, of course.' I helped to lift the painting over the table to her. I was glad we still had the picture to discuss, because the more I spoke to her, the less I wanted my time with her to end. A couple of hours had passed, and I felt as though I could have sat there forever: talking with her; listening to her; watching her; laughing with her; consoling her.

She carefully peeled the brown paper from around the painting. 'What a lovely frame,' she said, admiring the intricacies of the decorated copper surround. I willed her to look at the image, but her line of sight lingered on the frame.

Go on, look at it ... I mentally willed her to look and look properly.

She eventually shifted her gaze to the girl in the picture. I watched her, waiting for a reaction, but she didn't move; didn't speak. I thought I saw her eyes begin to fill up with tears again. 'Is it you?' I asked her, 'Is it really you?'

I looked at the image and back at her face and the likeness was striking. She had unusual features – those beautiful eyes, of course, but her face was unusually heart-shaped, and she had high cheekbones. Her perfectly formed lips were fairly plump and coated in a thin film of clear gloss, accentuating their natural pinkness. And then, of course, there was the mark on her neck, which I could see quite clearly was a scar, perhaps over the top of a birthmark.

My heart was beating fast. I could hear the echo of it deep inside me: thump, thump, thump. I was spellbound, waiting for her to speak; for her to acknowledge it was her.

It had to be her!

The lines around her eyes and mouth were those

created by smiling and laughter. In the centre of her brow, I could see fine lines of concentration, worry, and of sorrow. While the lines entrenched on the face of Jamie's grandfather beside us at the next table indicated he'd had something of a tough life, when Dayna reached his age, despite the intensity of her work, she would still have only a light scattering of fine lines marking the history of her life.

I waited for her to say something.

Still, there was no response from her. She sat absolutely still, looking deep into the image.

When she eventually spoke, her voice sounded saddened. She looked at me apologetically. 'No, Nate, I'm sure it's not me. Unless someone painted my portrait all those years ago without my knowledge – a little like you do with your own paintings, and your quite unsuspecting subjects?' She laughed, a little at my expense, I thought. And that by then familiar concept of being a stalker wheedled its way back into my mind.

'But it looks so much like you – even Jenna recognized it as you,' I pleaded.

'I'm sorry, Nate, I would have loved for it to have been me. You know, it would have been flattering to have had some secret admirer when I was younger. It really is such a wonderful picture – but unfortunately it's not me, even though I can see a likeness.' She quickly shuffled the brown paper around the picture and hurriedly passed it back across the table to me.

Looking back up at the clock she said, 'Nate, I'm so sorry, I really must go. I've been quite opportunistic, and when I knew I was going to see you this morning, I arranged a meeting for 12.30 at the zoo. I didn't think we'd be so long … but it's been nice – I've enjoyed our chat!' Her eyes were the colour of shiny blue-green pebbles in a gently flowing, crystal-clear stream. I was sure she was on the verge of tears, yet she seemed so determined it wasn't her. She was desperate to get up and leave. Our time was up.

'Sure, yes.' I was disappointed. 'I'll get these' I said and picked up the picture and the bill and went over to the till to pay.

She waited by the door to say farewell. We didn't shake hands, but instead she took hold of my arm and smiled. 'Thank you, anyway, Nate, it's been an interesting morning. Good luck with your exhibition. And thank you for the coffee.' She looked as though she was going to say something more, but she simply added, 'It's been really nice meeting you.' I thought I could see tears beginning to well in her eyes – but perhaps that emotion was what I hoped to see.

With a heavy heart, I stood and watched her walk along the street. A few yards from the corner, she looked back and waved. I waved back and kept on watching until she was out of sight. The picture felt heavy in my hand. I had achieved nothing.

On the way home in the car, I tried to remember every word she'd said, every glance, every animated gesture of her hands. It was as though it had been a first date, except of course it hadn't, and yet that feeling I had experienced when I first saw her back in the winter, that was still there – and yet much more. I had a cascade of emotions running through me, infiltrating every part of my body.

I'd been convinced when she was looking at the picture that she *had* recognized it. But why would she recognize it and then not admit it was her? It was so bizarre. Me, Ellie, Jenna, even Elise the zookeeper, we were all convinced it was her. Dayna admitted that she'd seen a likeness, but perhaps she was overwhelmed by everything. Perhaps, too, as Dayna suggested, it had been painted by someone without her knowledge. Why would someone do that, though? Ah, yes, apparently *some* people even did that for a living, something which she'd taken the opportunity to remind me of ...

It was going to take me a good hour and a half to get home – I wasn't sure what I'd say to Ellie about how my day had been. I regretted not having told her I was going to meet Dayna. There was certainly nothing to be secretive about, or there hadn't been before I'd met up with her in such a covert manner. I was still not sure what it was I felt for Dayna. She was quite beautiful – and despite her clearly stressful and eventful hard-working life, the years had certainly been kind to her.

I felt confused about her. I had something of an attraction to her, but I didn't know whether she felt the same. We hadn't arranged to meet again, so our meeting was certainly not the beginning of some torrid affair! And yet, all the way home, I was desperately trying to think of how I could engineer another meeting with her.

In the end, because I got back before Jenna finished school, I didn't even mention to Ellie I'd been out of town. She asked whether I'd managed to get much painting done during the day. I made excuses about having to go out and buy some materials, and that before I could gather my thoughts, the day had been over, and it was time to go and collect Jenna. Telling her I'd been out to buy supplies, I suppose, was big, whopping lie number one.

Later on, as we were getting ready for bed, she

asked me what I'd bought in town. 'Oh, you know, I was short of paint, and while I was there, I thought I'd replace a few brushes,' I replied.

Lies number two and three.

'Ah, right …' there was a pause, and out of the corner of my eye I saw her pulling on her pyjama bottoms. I could tell she was contemplating this. My heart sank as I realized the conversation had clearly not yet ended. She asked me how Edgar, the old guy who owned the art and craft shop, was getting along with his arthritis.

'Edgar? Ah, yes, he's doing well. He says the painkillers are suiting him, and he hopes that soon enough he'll get a new knee. He's still got a bit of weight to lose before the surgeons will operate on him. And well, you know, waiting lists.'

Lies numbers four, five, six, and seven. Those lies were coming through thick and fast. Was that how easy it was for people who cheated on their partner to lie to them? Just tell one bare faced lie and the rest would come trickling through like droplets of water from a dripping tap? Does each lie embellish the last, until all the imaginary moments heaped on top of one another seem real to the person who is lying?

She gave me a look. Was that doubt? But then she

smiled. 'Good, I'm glad he's coping.'

I was out of the woods.

Chapter 7

In the darkest hours the night after I met Dayna, at about 2 am I woke with a start. My brow was covered in fine beads of sweat. I couldn't move – my back was transfixed to the bed. Something wasn't right – something had startled me. I must have been dreaming. I've always tended to remember my dreams, but that dream wasn't there. There was nothing – simply a void wrapped in confusion … and my heart was pounding.

Perhaps I'd heard a noise outside? Perhaps one of the cats had knocked something over downstairs?

I thought of Jenna fast asleep in the room next to ours; adrenaline rushed through me, forcing me from my prostrate position on the bed. In that moment of realization, whatever had been keeping me transfixed was overpowered by my urgent need to check on Jenna, I had to make sure she was okay.

Once on the landing, I could see the gentle light from her pink, pig-shaped night light giving its usual rosy glow to her room. I tiptoed across to her doorway and quietly peered over to her bed, where I could see she was soundly sleeping. A feeling of relief washed over me. She was lying on her back with her face slightly turned to the side, her dark auburn curls snaked around her head, mimicking a child-like Medusa. Soft breaths were just about audible and I could see her thumb lingering near her mouth.

She'd stopped sucking her thumb a few months before she started school. Her teacher had mentioned that sometimes she still sucked it in class, but that she had been doing it less often of late. We used to think she must have emotional problems; that we were to blame as her parents, so we took her to the doctor. She had reassured us, saying she was just fine and not to worry – she would simply grow out of it. And, for the most part, she had. Even before she was born, and as birthing day had drawn closer, we could sometimes see Ellie's belly rocking from side to side, as the not-yet-born Jenna inside her seemed to be searching the dark, fluid-filled cocoon for her thumb. Seeing her lying there deep in slumber, I could sense there remained an innate desire for the comforter that had consoled her during those months before she was born.

Satisfied that she was okay, and still puzzled about what had disturbed me, I left her room and went downstairs to investigate whether the two pesky felines were to blame. Whenever they were indoors when we went to bed, we always closed the cat flap to prevent any wayward strays from dropping by for a feline party. Some of them had even become territorial in our kitchen in the middle of the night. This was something a ginger tom named Marmalade, who'd moved to the area just after us, was prone to doing. He was a people-friendly cat, but he'd made it obvious he didn't tolerate other cats in what he felt was his new territory.

The cats hadn't been in when we'd gone to bed, but there they were, the two of them curled around one another among a basket full of dirty washing. Their jet-black fur blended into one giant cat with two heads, four ears, eight legs, and two tails. They looked as though they hadn't moved a muscle for hours. On hearing me, only Jeremy acknowledged my presence by half opening one eye – just one. He squinted over at me and seeming to realize I hadn't come down to feed them, he immediately closed it again, joining Thomas in their mutual, comforting sleep. Smiling to myself and not wanting to disturb the two of them, I crept to the back door and dropped the cover on the cat flap, lest Marmalade was on the prowl.

Whatever had woken me clearly hadn't been Jenna or the cats, so I figured I must have simply had a bad dream which had startled me. I made my way back up to the bedroom. It was just after 2.20 am – just over four hours until the alarm would wake us for the day. I sighed and wondered how people coped who regularly worked nights. I hated it when my sleep was broken.

At 4.37 am I woke again, and as consciousness crept through me, I had an increasing awareness of something. Something which made my heart pound furiously against my chest wall. With a sinking heart, I realized the world as I had known it had just crumbled around me. I felt sick to the pit of my stomach.

I had, that time, remembered my dream.

I lay there on my back until the alarm went off. Just like before, I felt as though something had riveted me to the bed. It was like those times when you are an angst-ridden teenager and you feel as though the end of the world is coming, so you lie there transfixed and try to figure out all the worries of the world. But then it dawns on you that for some things there really are no solutions. I hadn't felt that way since I was fourteen years old, and my grandmother had suddenly passed away. In the end, you understand that worrying about existentialism is futile because we're all in this together, and we'll all eventually pass away, leaving nothing except footprints on the hearts of those we've loved; or memories of a song, a painting, a place, or the words we've uttered or written.

As I lay there wondering what I was going to do with the information which had penetrated my mind in those borderline asleep-awake moments, Ellie lay on her side facing away from me, soft sounds emanating from her mouth and nose. She was right next to me, but she could have been a million miles away.

Continuing to feel I couldn't move, I lay there trying to interpret what had been going through my mind, and what had jolted me from sleep. I'd been dreaming – a vivid dream which had felt so real it had been tangible. In the dream, I saw Dayna. She wasn't how she was when I saw her in the cafe, but how she appeared in the painting – the young version of her.

In my dream I couldn't see me, just her. We were in a room, and I was painting her. She was sitting by a desk in front of a window and her eyes were sparkling in the light. I reached out to touch her, to stroke her face. I could see my hands and arms in the dream, but the rest of my image was hidden – just like when you have dreams about yourself, you often only see the people around you. Your eyes become a video camera, making a movie about the people who are taking part in the make-believe world your sleeping mind has created.

The hand painting the picture in the dream was not mine. It was smoother and could have been from someone who was much younger. The fingers were long and looked as though they would be comfortable playing a piano or strumming a classical guitar.

As Dayna sat in front of me, she pulled faces and laughed at something I said to her. She then tossed her head back, her hair catching an amber glow from the sun that streamed through the window in streaks of bright yellow light.

And then, the dream changed, and we were on a motorbike, those young hands of mine gripping the handlebars and flicking the levers. I could feel Dayna's arms clasped around me as we leaned into the corners. And then, once we were on a straight piece of road, I slowed down and turned around to look at her. I flipped up my visor to speak to her and she did likewise. Her cheeks were flushed pink with the breeze, and hair which had fallen from her ponytail was tangled between her blue scarf and her red helmet. The dream was so vivid. I could see her smile, I could feel the breeze against my face, I could feel her arms around me. I could have fallen into those blue-green eyes.

As I lay there mulling over what had happened in my dream, I became distinctly aware that the Dayna I had met was definitely the Dayna of the painting. Whatever she said when I met her, I was convinced that she had lied.

Laying there listening to Ellie breathe, I was trembling, my head was spinning with the knowledge I suddenly had. I mustn't have been imagining the connection between us. That bond I felt towards Dayna was real – the two of us were surely linked together by something beyond my comprehension: was it that we *had* been together before – not here, not now, not even in this life, but at another time? From that point, I was sure of it, and that realization swept through my body like a tornado, causing havoc as it reaped its way into every cell. Alongside that realization, I felt an overwhelming frustration – what could I do with that information? I felt enlightened, but simultaneously I felt sick. Was what I was thinking for real, or was it an embellishment of an already confused connection I felt I had with her?

That day, once Ellie had gone to work and I'd taken Jenna to school, I spent a long time sitting at the kitchen table trying to figure out what was happening to me. Thinking about the events of the night before, I absentmindedly gazed out of the window at the coal tits and sparrows, as they expertly negotiated the bird feeder. If it really was true and I hadn't simply had a vivid dream which had merged with reality, then mine and Dayna's ages matched up, and it was quite feasible that I had been with her before. Just not here, not now. If, of course, something such as life after death existed.

I felt vindicated, because I was convinced then that there had at some point in time been a Dayna and me, and everything I was feeling was some residual link from that time. And yet, despite my justification for the connection, and however spurious it might seem, I had an overbearing sense of doubt that I could do anything about it.

Every part of me reasoned that this whole reincarnation stuff was really quite preposterous, especially because I had no religion. I'd been brought up as a Catholic, and then vehemently rejected Catholicism in my teens. At the age of fourteen I came home from school and told my parents I'd discovered humanism in my religious education classes. I told them that it fitted what I was; what I believed. After that, I refused to go to church to sing in the choir, or to go and confess all my youthful sins to the priest – it suddenly seemed to me to be so pointless.

In response, my parents tried to hide their disappointment, shrouding their reaction in a cloud of cotton wool. *There, there, Nate, don't worry, Son* … I imagine they felt it was just a phase. The phase had lasted nearly two decades, right up until that moment on waking that morning – that day after meeting Dayna; the morning my revelations began.

As a humanist, I truly hadn't believed in any supernatural, life before death stuff. I knew about it from having friends whose core beliefs were in Buddhism and Hinduism, and I sometimes wondered about Karma. But since those days at school when the religious education teacher had told us of the existence of non-religion, I had believed that when you were gone you were gone; ashes drifting in the air or dispersing through the ocean, or your body feeding grubs in the ground and nourishing the trees. No heaven, no hell, no afterlife, no revival of your soul into a fresh pound of flesh. Just nothing. That's what I'd thought anyway, and yet suddenly there I was having doubts about everything I'd believed my whole adult life.

So why was I spending my time contemplating this stuff? Why was I even giving the concept the time of day? Was it because deep inside me there was something which told me this was the answer? It wasn't, after all, as I'd suspected, that I had some random attraction to her, it was that there actually *was* a connection between us. Somehow there had been a twist of fate which had led us to one another and to my remembering! I was meant to have found that painting that day in the Yorkshire Dales, I was meant to see her that day at the zoo, and then make the connection to her when I spotted the painting on the antiques programme. All those seemingly fragile links had led me to her. And yet, she had denied it was her.

Why would she lie? I desperately needed to know, and because of that, I knew I would have to see her again. For a couple of months, however, I was somehow going to have to put all of that to the back of my mind as all my mental efforts were going to be fully occupied with getting ready for the exhibition.

At least, that's what I thought I would be doing – but one thing we never seem to take account of when carefully planning our lives, is the power of the mind. We never imagine how much our hidden feelings and thoughts might escalate in the dark of the night. And that ultimately, they can also infiltrate your waking hours.

Chapter 8

A week passed and the dreams were coming to me every night. They were taking over my life and consuming my every waking and sleeping moment. I couldn't focus properly on anything Ellie or Jenna said to me, and those things I said to them felt empty or futile.

Ellie noticed. I suppose she couldn't help but do so. She offered heartfelt concern. Was I feeling okay? Did I have a headache? Was it the exhibition? Was it my work? My work had certainly taken a hit because the only images I could muster were the images of my dreams. Convoluted images I scrawled in the studio were pulled from the easel and surreptitiously burned in the log burner.

I told her that it was my work and worrying about the exhibition that was getting me down, and for her not to worry. I said I was lacking inspiration to work on anything new (and I supposed that, for once, that hadn't been a lie). She seemed reassured by the answers I gave, but for how long?

Each time the subject cropped up she'd nod and say, 'I'm sure you'll get it back, Nate, whenever you've felt like this before, you've managed – and often the things you've created after a spell such as this are all the better for you having had a break.' She was right – I had indeed had breaks in my work before when I'd lacked inspiration, but generally after a few days and a few long walks, things got better – nature was a great healer. It was clear to me with this, though, that what was going on was not the same as what had happened before.

One Friday night at dinner about a month before the exhibition, Jenna offered her version of a solution to all our problems. 'Dad, what *you* need is a dog.' We'd heard this before on several occasions, and as she was getting older it was becoming more difficult for us to fob her off with excuses. The usual ones we gave her were how Thomas and Jeremy would not appreciate having a dog around (even though they had clearly accepted Marc and Christina's dog Bruce), how our lifestyle didn't suit having a dog as they seemed to need much more of your time than cats do, and how they're much more dependent on people.

That dinnertime, however, she was ready with all her answers. 'Well, Daddy, you work from home, and Emma who's in my class, both her parents work at a proper job like Mummy does and they have two dogs and a cat!' She paused, and sighed for what seemed like effect, and I let the comment about a proper job go. 'Anyway, they get doggy day care to come and walk the dogs for them and give them both some biscuits.' She wasn't finished with me yet. 'And *we* wouldn't even need to do that because you're here *all* the time. Also, he can come for a ride in the car with us when you drop me off at school and then when you come back you can take him for a walk before you start working. It will clear your head.'

I noticed Jenna look towards Ellie for approval. Ellie smiled – a suspiciously knowing smile. And then it registered with me what Jenna had just said. Ellie had noticed Jenna had made a blunder.

'Him? Who precisely are we talking about here? And before you answer, what about the cats? Hmm?'

There was a pause while the two of them wondered where to take the conversation next. Ellie, being the conniving adult in this case who'd wanted a dog for many years, decided she would have to chip in and tell the whole story.

'Okay.' She held her hands up in defeat, while Jenna sat still and quiet. A look of nervous, excited, exhausted anticipation fell across her small, sweet face. 'Jenna and I were talking about this earlier today when you were in the studio, and I made the mistake of looking at a couple of rescue websites with her ... and, well, we found a dog who loves cats. His name's Harvey and he's a bits-of-everything mongrel, medium-sized, black and brindle, and he's apparently REALLY friendly and LOVES children.'

We'd always said that if ever we had a dog, we would give one a home from a rescue shelter, and he certainly sounded as though he was a nice dog. 'Look,' Ellie picked up her phone and thrust his image in front of me. 'Isn't he gorgeous?'

The picture in front of me was of a dog who looked as though he was a happy, friendly dog. She showed me a short video of him playing with a rope toy. He had a bit of a dog-about-town, knowing expression on his face, as though he knew the kind of home he wanted. Were we really going to be that home?

'Anyway,' she continued, 'I phoned earlier, and we can see him at ten o'clock tomorrow. Then, if we pass the home check, we can bring him home in a few days.' She was clearly excited at bringing him into our lives, even though it sounded as though I was going to be the one with the lion's share of looking after him. In the end, after all that I'd put them through over the previous few weeks, I gave in, perhaps faster than I would normally have done. I'd been browbeaten into submission.

The next morning, I noticed dark shadows under Jenna's eyes – she'd clearly not slept with all her excitement. I hadn't slept much either, but for other reasons.

Harvey was being fostered by a local family who constantly had three rescue dogs in their care. This was along with their own three dogs, and what appeared to be about ten cats, but it was probably only about five. The house was chaotic with all the animals mingling with four children, and all the kids looked as though they were under the age of ten. *How did this family cope?* I wondered.

Pretty quickly a friendly dog came over to us who we assumed was Harvey, as he was the only one who looked like the picture. He was surrounded by the other five dogs, all of them keen to know what was going on. An overwhelming sea of snuffling noses and leg and tail spaghetti surrounded us. Harvey was in the middle of the tangle of dogs carrying a green ball in his mouth, which he promptly placed at my feet. He really was lovely, and when I put aside the fact that I hadn't played any part in the decision to have a dog, I instinctively knew he was going to become a part of our family very quickly.

He'd been through a tough time. His owner had passed away six months earlier, and although the deceased's daughter had tried to keep him, her own much bigger dog had become insanely jealous and attacked him, even though he was happy with the deceased's two cats having gone to live with them too. The first time it happened they'd thought it was just the two dogs sorting themselves out. Then it happened again, and much more savagely, so the daughter brokenheartedly realized the only solution was for Harvey to go into rescue. He needed to find another home with someone who could take good care of him, without him having the constant fear of being attacked.

The daughter was keeping in touch with the fosterer and would go over to walk him, but he was becoming confused. Each time she visited it was clear that Harvey wanted to go home with her – she was the last connection to the lady he'd lived with for most of his life.

The fosterers thought that a new break with a new family as soon as possible would be good for him. Because of the children in the house, the fosterers were convinced that Harvey had a reliable temperament. The attacks by the woman's dog had resulted in a couple of bite wounds on the right side of his neck, and he'd allowed the fosterer to clean them for him with hardly a whimper. Throughout his time with the family, he'd spent hours happily playing in the garden with the children and the other dogs.

His scars were obvious – you could still see stitch marks around the healed wound. His fur was growing back, and because he was quite a fluffy dog, there would soon be no obvious sign of the injuries he'd sustained at the jaws of his previous adversary.

Jenna gently stroked Harvey on the non-scarred side of his neck, at which he promptly turned and licked her hand – oh, so gently. This dog certainly knew the right buttons to press to lead him into a new home.

After putting a comfy harness on him, we took him for a walk away from the other dogs. He was perfect. His tail was constantly wagging as we walked along, and when we talked to him, he wagged his tail faster. It was warm outside, and as he panted, he looked as though he had a big smile on his face. He was so lovely, I began to wonder whether he had any little flaws that he was hiding away – saving to reveal once he was secured in a nice home with some unsuspecting family. Perhaps he was really a little Jekyll and Hyde. We unfortunately couldn't take him straight away as the fosterer was to come along and do a home check the following day.

The fosterer phoned ahead early the next morning and asked whether we minded if the daughter of the previous owner came along to meet us as well. She said they wouldn't normally do it, but they felt in this situation, and given the circumstances, they were comfortable with it. We agreed.

The daughter's name was Wendy, and when we met her, she was clearly still reeling from the loss of her mother. Coupled with that, she had the upset of not being able to keep Harvey – he was a huge emotional connection to her mother. We served her buckets of tea and sympathy. By the time Wendy and the fosterer left, Wendy and Ellie had struck up some sort of friendship, and the two of them agreed that once Harvey was properly settled in, Wendy could come back to visit him and come out for a walk with us. Wendy cried when she knew she wouldn't have to lose contact with him – that she would always know where he was and that he was okay.

Harvey came home with us the next day – there was no sense in waiting. We'd have taken him the night of the home visit if we could have, but he had to have his final veterinary check before we brought him home. Thomas and Jeremy were not impressed with the new arrival. They spat, they hissed, they raised their hackles. When Harvey didn't retaliate, being expertly cat-savvy and ignoring them whenever they were in the same room, within days they became less angry about having him around. Within a week they were much more curious about his presence and brushing themselves against him. Our new dog had even worked his inimitable charm on two grumpy felines.

While Harvey's arrival quickly lifted the cloud that had been lingering, dogs can't fix everything. There was, however, some sort of renewed sense of peace. Meanwhile, my inspiration for painting had altered somehow, and in the weeks that followed I found myself becoming much more prone to painting animals. Above all else, Ellie marveled at how much better I seemed, adding how she'd always known having a dog about the place would bring positive energy.

I took Harvey into the studio with me each morning after we got back from taking Jenna to school. He lay patiently, alternately watching me painting, or snoozing on an orange armchair we'd put in there especially for him. He stood for a stretch every now and again and then turned around and went back to sleep. When he got fed up because I was lost in what I was doing, he'd come over to nudge me and tell me it was about time we went out for a play in the garden. Within weeks he had woven his way into our lives and routines. Very quickly it became difficult for us to recall what our lives had been like before he arrived.

Those canine-instigated breaks in concentration were surprisingly welcome and refreshing, meaning I could go back to my easels with a clearer mind. It was something I'd never really done – taken a brain-break, but it was clearly good for me. Once he'd exhausted himself chasing his beloved ball, he'd be happy enough to sit inside again for the rest of the afternoon – until the time when we had to drop everything and go and collect Jenna. If it wasn't cold or raining, I tended to park a mile or so away from the school, that way Harvey and I could have a walk. The three of us could then walk back to the car together, all of us getting exercise along the way.

Harvey became popular with the other parents and after-school group leaders waiting at the gates. He relished the fuss he received each day. He'd also found himself a lady-friend in the shape of a rescued black greyhound named Rose Petal – just Rosie for short. Rosie's adopters were Jim and Karl, a couple who had adopted twin girls – Maisie and Martha, and who owned a string of bakeries in the area.

Yes, life had certainly picked up for our Harvey – he even had his portrait hanging in the sitting room with a prime position over the main sofa. Jenna and Ellie had been adamant we should put it there. When Jenna insisted I show a photograph of the portrait to Jim and Karl, they asked me to paint a portrait of Rosie, which they loved. As word quickly spread, I realized that once the exhibition was over it might develop into a side-venture of dog portrait painting.

Amid all that apparently regained domesticated happiness and contentment, however, my dreams had not left me. They'd become much more vivid. When I dreamt of Dayna and me being on the motorbike together, I could not only feel her arms around me and the wind on my face, but I could hear her voice. In the by then familiar dream, we would ride underneath a dark, heavy canopy of trees. At the edge of the greenery, I could see that ahead of us we were about to ride through an old town, then to the left of us there was a large, grey castle which had a metal suspension bridge. The dream then quickly moved on and we would walk hand in hand along the bridge – the bridge became a walkway towards the castle's portcullis.

There was a gentle breeze, and the hot sun was shining down on us. She would run on ahead along the empty walkway, and then turn to call me; teasing me; tormenting me to chase her. But then her voice would fade into the distance and her image would begin to fade as well. As her image waned, she raised her hand and it looked as though she was holding a piece of paper out to me.

In response I would reach out and call out her name 'Daaaynaaa.' I could see my arms – those young arms – reaching towards her. I tried to focus on what the paper said. But her image, and the paper she held in front of her, broke into millions of pieces – dispersing into tiny specs of dust and disintegrating before my eyes.

Gone.

Each time the dream happened I would wake with the by then familiar feeling of emptiness. One night, from the depths of my sleep I must have called Dayna's name out loud. Harvey, who had very quickly decided he was sleeping on the blue armchair in our bedroom, was suddenly beside me, whimpering and urgently licking my hand. It was almost 5 am. 'Are you okay?' Ellie asked, as she touched my arm. 'You called out in your sleep.'

Memories of my dream vivid from the sudden awakening, I was startled that Ellie may have heard me call out Dayna's name. My heart was beating fast, and I quickly denied all knowledge, simply responding with 'Did I?' With panic in my gut, I asked her what I'd said.

'I'm not sure. You woke me up, that's all.'

Relieved she'd not heard me call out Dayna's name, I told her I couldn't sleep and was going to seize the opportunity to take Harvey for an early morning walk. I hoped it would clear my head.

She was already drifting back to sleep. 'Okay, see you at breakfast,' she murmured, and sank back into the pillow. She turned over to curl into a foetal position, clearly grateful of the impending peaceful hour in bed.

So, at 5.30 am, Harvey and I strolled along in the still, chilly early morning air. He stopped every three feet to sniff at the foliage, lampposts, even what appeared to be solitary blades of grass. He was evidently reaping more from our early morning jaunt than I was. I was going to have to do something about the turmoil that was going on in my head. I couldn't carry on the way I was – it wasn't fair to Ellie or Jenna. But what could I do? And then, I had an idea.

Once Ellie was away to work and Jenna safely at school, I got out my laptop, switched on the search engine and typed *r e g r e s s i o n.*

I was bombarded with a multitude of different meanings, many of them mathematical, but the definition I was looking for was the one given by an online dictionary: *Regression: A return to an earlier stage of life or a supposed previous life, especially through hypnosis for mental illness, or as a means of escaping present anxieties.* I didn't feel anxious, or I hadn't felt like that until everything to do with Dayna had started.

I could recall years before having read about a girl who remembered a previous life so clearly that she took her loved ones on a journey to meet the family she said she used to belong to. It all seemed quite outrageous at the time, and yet very convincing. Scientists had tried to prove her wrong and suggest she was just a silly girl making things up and responding to the power of suggestion from those around her. But there were some things she simply couldn't have known – personal things that were verified by those she had apparently loved in her 'previous' life. The more I read about the subject online, and the more stories I read, the more I knew that that was what I was going to have to do. I needed to find out more, I needed to confront this issue. I realized the starting point was to go and see a hypnotist, someone who would finally confirm or refute this for me once and for all.

Looking for hypnotherapists in my area, and more importantly, ones I felt I could trust, was not easy, but eventually I read some reviews for one who was based not too far away. Taking a deep breath, I phoned and made an appointment – I was lucky, they had a cancellation appointment for the next day.

The following morning when I arrived for my appointment, the waiting room was not as I'd imagined it might be. While there was a gentle scent of spring flowers, there were no patchouli-scented incense sticks. Instead, it was smart and professional-looking, with an equally smartly dressed receptionist. I wasn't sure whether I would have preferred a bit of patchouli or jasmine burning away in the corner. I found the sense of order a little officious.

Across the room from me a middle-aged woman with dyed black hair sat with a strawberry-blonde girl of about two perched on her lap. I assumed they were waiting for someone. Right enough, within minutes, a younger woman emerged from the clinic. The door was labeled *Professor Michael Jardine – Hypnotherapist*. I sensed the younger woman was the little girl's mother. She was clearly upset about something, but then I supposed it was unlikely to be people who were content with their lives who ventured into the world of hypnotism.

As Professor Jardine, or Mick, as he preferred to be called, beckoned me into the office, my knees began to feel weak. Each step towards him felt like I was sinking deeper and deeper into a world I could no longer control or comprehend.

Mick was someone I immediately felt I could trust. His eyes were chocolate brown, and his sallow skin was sun-kissed from spending a lot of time outdoors. His hands were worn, his nails cut short and scrubbed clean. Ingrained dirt was embedded around his fingernails. I imagined him relentlessly scrubbing soil from them after having been outside tending the likes of beans and kale in a raised vegetable garden. I pictured him pottering about in a well-stocked greenhouse, nurturing each tender shoot as it emerged from nutrient-rich, dark brown soil. Or perhaps potatoes were his thing, and he spent hours tirelessly digging trenches for them, and watched with eager anticipation as they pushed their leaves through the ground.

After pleasantries were made, despite my apparent immediate trust in him, I felt a sudden pressing urge to get up and walk out of there. This can of worms, this Pandora's box, one I sensed would be better left closed, was bursting. Unknown forces were trying to penetrate the lid, pushing … pushing … pushing. I had an overbearing sense of something priming itself to cause pandemonium in my life.

Mick seemed to sense my hesitation – but he had a persuasive way of dealing with people. I guess that was the name of the game! The power of persuasion – the ability to get inside someone's head and plant seeds, which the person would take away with them and wrap around real events. But I immediately suppressed the doubt – I had to, because this was a chance for me to finally rid myself of my disturbing dreams. I hoped that offloading the story to him would be cathartic, like a valve being released from inside me, as word by word, my entire tale would finally come tumbling out.

I was disappointed when straight away he explained there was going to be no regression that day. He told me that before I went any further, he wanted me to have some cooling off time – a week or two to think about the consequences of going through with the process. He told me that regression sometimes uncovered feelings, thoughts, and memories that we would perhaps have been happier never recalling – and when regression took you farther back than the day you were born into this life, it meant that the knowledge you potentially gained couldn't be undone.

He must have noticed the frustration on my face and went on to explain that, once you discover something, you can't un-know what you learn in the process. Conversely, he added, it could be an enlightening experience as the clock goes back in terms of what someone might know and, more importantly, understand about themselves.

He said that the practice of regression had helped hundreds of his patients do just that, enabling them to rectify something which had been gnawing away at them for years. Only rarely, though, did he take patients into the time before they were born. He reiterated, and much more forcefully, that gaining the knowledge of what might have been before could bring uncertainty – while you hoped the information you gleaned from the experience would give comfort, in the end it could make everything worse.

'In your situation, Nate, I do have reservations,' he warned. 'You have this life you've built for yourself, you have loved ones, you have this living, breathing, wonderful, blessed life that some only wish for and never achieve. Why try to chase something that might simply finish up being a series of coincidences and strange dreams?'

I hesitated before answering him. 'Because it's consuming me anyway; it's taken over my life. What appears on the surface to be a contented household of domestic happiness has become like torture to me. I have to at least try to discover what this is all about ...' I paused, desperately trying to find the words to justify what I was doing, 'so I can let go of it and carry on with my life as it was before this thing started. It's the dreams – I can't control them! And those images, they're seeping into my days. I need help doctor – Mick! I really do.'

He nodded. 'Okay Nate, but I'll still need you to go away and have a cooling off period. You need to be one hundred percent committed to this – and I shall need you when you come along on the day to sign a consent form before we begin. I must protect myself – just in case there are repercussions from what you discover during the therapy. I never know what people are going to find out. It can help with stress, even fears that are possibly linked to a previous life, but you never really know what we are going to uncover until you begin the therapy.'

In agreement, and not really surprised that a consent form of sorts would be involved, I arranged to go back and see him a week later. In the meantime, I had my exhibition to contend with.

A week. That was all I had to wait until I might find some answers. Having that thought to cling to would, I hoped, allow me to progress with the preparations for the exhibition.

I thought that week would take a lifetime to pass, but because I'd finally told someone about the demons in my head, I felt as though my mood had lifted. Ellie and Jenna noticed too, and at dinner one night they told me that having Harvey around had clearly been good for me. They looked at me knowingly, as though their proposal that we should have a dog in our lives had truly been vindicated. I had to agree that since his arrival Harvey had given me a great deal of support – the fella had become integral to our daily routines. He was heavily dependent on us for his care, and in taking him into our home we owed it to him to make sure his life was a happy one.

On hearing us all mentioning his name, Harvey looked up from where he was lying on his bed enthusiastically tearing at a dog chew. He happily wagged his tail. I felt a tug inside my chest and realized the dog I had resisted having for so long had absolutely wheedled his way into my heart. Seeing Ellie and Jenna looking down at him I realized he had done the same to them.

How do dogs do that? I found myself wondering. I had always been a self-confessed cat-person, loving their sense of independence, and there I was pledging my heartfelt love for a dog. There absolutely appeared to be something in this dog-human bond thing.

Chapter 9

It transpired that the gallery owner Joanna was just a little bit obsessed by dogs. I had to take Harvey down for one of my meetings one day when we'd struggled to find a dog-sitter. Joanna immediately fell head over heels in love with him. As a consequence, Harvey was going to end up being the star of the show – my show! His picture was to be added to all the publicity materials that were being produced to remind people the exhibition was almost upon us all, and Joanna insisted we took him to the exhibition on the night. She also requested I paint a picture of him to auction at the exhibition in aid of the charity he'd been fostered by. This, too, would be publicized.

'This is wonderful, Nathaniel. You MUST do this. We can alter the final publicity materials before they go out. Can't we Davey?' Davey Jones was in the process of getting his assistant Alisha (just Ali to her friends) to write something in the pad of paper in which she was hurriedly scribbling.

'Davey?' Joanna repeated.

'It's okay, I'm on it! It's all sorted, don't you fret!' Later, when he knew Joanna was distracted and just out of earshot, I heard him whisper to Ali and nod towards her notepad. 'The dog – make a note about the dog!'

Suddenly having to go against my usual way of working, which had always been based on how I was feeling, and following my own inspiration, rather than painting to the demands of others, I did another picture of Harvey. He politely lay on his orange chair posing. I named it 'Forever Home'. I must admit that in an effort to save time, before I painted it, I had an inkling to take his portrait from the sitting room wall and to present that to Joanna for the auction instead, however, Ellie and Jenna stopped me in my tracks as I stood contemplating the crime. I'd been rumbled.

'But that's OUR painting, Daddy. It's the first one you ever painted of him!' Jenna pleaded.

I tried to justify it on the basis of available time and that it would be for the dogs who hadn't been as lucky as Harvey. I insisted I would definitely paint another one just like it. But, no, Harvey's painting was remaining exactly where it was.

Ellie asked me what would happen if I didn't feel like it at a later date – and that at least with the exhibition approaching I had a deadline; a reason to get it done. She added a 'Hmm?', which I thought was entirely uncalled for. But I had to agree – she knew me too well. I silently admitted to myself I would probably have never done another one if I hadn't had to. Not one just like that one anyway.

And so, a small image of Harvey's freshly painted picture appeared on the bottom right-hand corner of all my reminder-of-the-forthcoming-exhibition flyers, Joanna's web page, and my web page. An additional poster was made, copies of which were circulated around all the local rescue organizations and their supporters. Staff from the local charity were invited to the exhibition to see Harvey raise money for his homeless comrades. Harvey took it all in his canine stride. His presence in the preparations was a welcome distraction because he took away much of the limelight and focus from me, which meant I could try to gather my thoughts and consider what the next few weeks would hold.

I increasingly resented what was going on in my head and wanted to be the person I'd been before the day at the zoo. I wanted to be an artist who could revel in the admiration of the exhibition and enjoy all the attention being bestowed on me by Joanna, Davey, and the rest of the team, but it all suddenly felt so superficial.

What was it all about? I'd always seen beauty in art and seen the point of it all. I'd seen wonder in the pleasure of surrounding your home with beautiful things – in there being something wonderful about giving pleasure to others in the time they might spend interpreting and loving my pictures. But I was having doubts about my direction in life. I suddenly saw them as mere fanciful representations of a world where possessions were often seen as being more important than life itself – more important, sometimes even, than time. You only had to look at some of the astronomical sums of money some artists' paintings sold for – millions and millions! And this was all while so many people in the world weren't even able to feed their own children.

I realized my thoughts about how I was feeling about the world were being influenced by what Dayna was doing with her life – she was making a difference, and how many of us can honestly say that?

I recalled my English teacher at school going into raptures about a scene in *A Man for All Seasons*, when Sir Thomas More suggests Richard Rich should consider being a teacher. Richard Rich responds with: 'If I was, then who would know it?'

Sir Thomas More replies, 'You; your pupils; your friends; God. Not a bad public, that.' Dayna was not after fame or fortune, even notoriety. She seemed to be content with playing her part in quietly working away at saving the world.

I acknowledged I was adding to my existential crisis

and tried to make myself snap out of it, relax, and try to enjoy what was happening in my own career. It was the first time I'd received such recognition, such adulation of my work. Was I secretly relishing the concept of fame?

Each time I thought about the hypnosis session, which was drawing frighteningly closer, I considered what Mick had said about what we know we can't un-know, and that part of what I was embarking on was resonating in my mind. I had so many unanswered questions: What if during regression I discovered something awful that would stay with me for the rest of my life; something I couldn't ever possibly forget? What if my 'soul' itself was bad? What if in a previous life I had done something terrible like murdered someone? What if I couldn't go back, and this thing was never disentangled from my head? What if I had to live with this forever?

What if he regressed me and I entered a world of the unknown, and couldn't actually find my way back?

I figured that of all the worries I had, that was the unanswered question which troubled me the most. Regression still appeared to be a little-known science, and while I hadn't been able to find evidence of anyone who'd failed to come back to their present state, I figured there was always a first time for everything. And that thought terrified me.

The day finally arrived for the exhibition's opening. I nervously headed down to the gallery early so I could do some last-minute checking of labels and check the descriptions of each picture. I'd checked them all the previous evening and a multitude of times during the previous week, but I wasn't taking any chances – there was always that particular part of me that wanted everything to be just so. This was too important an event to allow that obsessive nature of mine slide.

Ellie had taken the day off work, even though she probably couldn't afford the time with that awful child abuse case that was still lingering on. She, Jenna, and the true star of the show, Harvey, were arriving at 6pm – an hour before the doors were due to open. Marc, Christina, and Jacob were coming as soon as they could to offer their moral support.

Wendy said she'd come along to see Harvey's painting being auctioned. She cried on the phone when Ellie called her to let her know we were all helping to raise some funds for the charity who'd taken care of 'the wee man', as we'd all started to unashamedly, and anthropomorphically, call him.

Later on that evening when Wendy arrived, she hugged me and burst into tears again, smearing

131

black mascara all over her cheeks. 'Gosh, look at me,' she exclaimed. 'Excuse me, Nate, I'm off to the washroom to fix my face.' There was a rather large man with her, who I was surprised to find out was her husband. For some reason I'd assumed she lived alone with her tyrannical canine. 'C'mon Arnold, you can wait for me by the door to the ladies.' Arnold dutifully followed, nodding to me, and offering a meek smile as he walked past.

Joanna was in her element. Some people I guess just fall into the profession that completely suits their personality, and in her case, utter enthusiasm, and vitality. I don't think I'd ever shaken as many hands in the whole of my life as I did the night of the exhibition. As much as Joanna reveled in the attention, all I equally wanted to do was get in the car, drive home, and retreat to my studio. But I couldn't, as so much was riding on the event. Just five hours and it would be over. I fixed a smile to my face and began the evening with Joanna dragging me between each group of people, telling them all I was something special.

A lot of them admired my work, and especially the portrait I'd been avoiding looking at all evening. The one of Dayna. My portraits were always transformative, in that even if you knew the person, you wouldn't necessarily know that they were the subject. This was the case for her, but the likeness was probably closer than I would normally have dared to create, hence how Jenna had recognized her. I think in terms of legality I'd pushed this representation of her to the limit. I knew it was her, and I think she would recognize herself too, but in the final stages of painting I had removed her scar and changed the shading of her hair and eyebrows.

I wasn't sure why her painting was drawing so much attention, but looking at her image, I was reminded of how much I'd wrestled over painting her. I'd been desperate to make those eyes the right shade of green, or blue, whatever part of the spectrum they happened to fall upon. That day in the cafe I'd noticed the shade of them shifting, the way our irises often do in the light, and it made me realize why, in her case, I had struggled with it: it wasn't just that the shades changed – everybody's eyes did that to some extent, depending on the light, or whether their eyes were pale or dark. What had been wrong with *her* eyes was that I had been so taken with emulating that shade of green that I had allowed myself no room for error.

A local businessman was very enthusiastic about buying the picture but had noticed there wasn't a price on it. Earlier on I had surreptitiously removed the label when I was doing my last check of the paintings and the information next to each one. In doing so, I'd gone completely against my obsessive desire to keep everything uniform. The truth was, I didn't want anyone to buy it. But when Ellie came over and introduced me to the portly, grey-bearded Terence Sattersthwaite, I had to feign confusion about the label's whereabouts. I meekly suggested the price must have fallen off. My heart pounded as I scanned the room looking for Davey. *How could I prevent this man from buying my painting?*

Ellie spotted Davey across the room and called him over. While he scurried away to look for the price book, Terence asked me, 'How much would you like for it, old fellow?' I imagined the picture adorning some stately home in the southern counties of England, but then he added, 'It'd look fabulous in our holiday flat in Scotland, wouldn't it, My Dear.'

My Dear was Katherine, a tall, thin, stunning and distinguished-looking forty-something with long, shining, dark tresses. She had the smoothest, pale skin, which defied her age. With Davey still looking for the catalogue with its price list, Terence offered me eight thousand pounds, partly for the painting and partly as a commission for me to paint his wife's portrait.

Ellie's eyes nearly popped out of her head. We'd calculated that in the (unlikely we thought) event we sold everything at the exhibition we'd clear forty thousand, and that was with selling thirty-eight pictures. This would be eight grand for just two – twenty percent of what we'd hoped to get all together. Fair enough, I'd still have to paint the commissioned portrait, but that would be easy for me – I think I would have ended up painting her anyway, only in my own way, and not as much of a realistic impression of her, which was what he and Katherine wanted.

What could I say? I agreed the offer and Terence and I shook hands. My precious picture was gone, but the image was still there in my head, lingering, offering me some weird, misplaced solace from the events going on around me.

It was time for the auction of Harvey's portrait. Sitting at the front of the room with Ellie and Jenna, he somehow seemed to understand that this was his special night. He'd received so much fuss from everyone as he'd positioned himself on the laps of people whose shiny jewels had jingled and sparkled as they stroked his soft brindle fur. No one appeared to mind his hairs being left behind on their dinner jackets or evening dresses. This was Harvey's proverbial fifteen minutes of fame, and everyone seemed to want to be a part of his time in the limelight. Where many dogs would have been fazed by what was going on, he took it all in his stride and reveled in all the attention. How much his life had changed in the previous six months since his elderly human companion had died.

Joanna wanted, just for fun, to be the auctioneer of his painting, and as the bids went higher and higher, she seemed to enjoy the drama of it all. As the bid being offered reached eleven hundred pounds, I glanced away from the scene in front of me to the back of the room, where I saw a woman and a man looking at the painting of Dayna. I looked back over to where Ellie was sat with Harvey, and then smiled as I scanned the room again, searching for the eager dog-lovers who wanted Harvey's portrait.

A sick feeling suddenly hit the pit of my stomach as I realized I knew who those people at the back of the room were! I did a double-take – it was Dayna with a man – probably her husband. Dayna was pointing at the picture. She glanced back towards the crowd to watch the auction. Fighting an urge to go and speak to them, I turned to look back over at Ellie, Jenna and Harvey. Ellie looked over at me quizzically. I smiled to reassure her that everything was okay.

'Four thousand, eight hundred and fifty pounds. Is there anyone else? Okay, it's going, going …'.

Someone else raised their hand, and it ended up in a bidding war between two elegantly dressed women. Eventually, Joanna called out, 'Six thousand five hundred pounds, going, going, gone, to the lovely lady in the cerise and jade dress. Thank you, Madam, you are very generous! This will help a lot of homeless dogs.' Everyone cheered, and Ellie hugged tight to Harvey. For the first time, I saw he looked a little unsure of everything. Perhaps this really had all been a bit much for him. I saw Wendy in the crowd – she and Arnold were holding tightly to one another as Wendy sobbed into her hankie. It had been a big night for them as well.

I looked to the back of the room, and Dayna and her husband were no longer there. I scanned the room looking for them, adjusting my position to see past the pillars, but they had disappeared. Marc came over to speak to me. 'It's been a great night, Nate, well done. I'm very proud …'.

'Sorry, Marc, I'll be back in a minute.' With that, I fled out onto the street to see whether there was any sign of Dayna. But there was no one to be seen. Not a person, nor a car making its way down the street, not a stray dog or cat in sight. There wasn't a soul about, and I wondered whether I'd imagined seeing her.

Marc was suddenly by my side. 'What is it, Nate?'

'Oh nothing. I thought I saw someone. That's all.'

'Crikey, it must have been someone important!'

I had to think quickly.

'Um, yeah, weird stuff. I thought it was someone I used to know at university. Strange, huh?' Those lies were dripping far too easily from my tongue.

Marc looked puzzled. 'Hmm. Weird stuff indeed.' I suspected he didn't believe my cover story, but I quickly changed the subject and we chatted about how successful the evening had been. Financially it was going to be a huge boost for us, especially with Terence Sattersthwaite's commission to paint a picture of his wife.

We were all buzzing on the way home – including Harvey, who still seemed to be excited about all the attention he'd received. Jenna spent the journey repeatedly telling him what a clever dog he was for raising money for the dogs who didn't have a family to love them. Secured beside her in his own dog seatbelt, he reached over to her and licked her hand. By the time we got home they were both sleeping soundly on the back seat. If their safety seats hadn't been there, I imagined they would've been snuggled down together, in the same way that Tom and Jeremy always curled around one another.

Chapter 10

As the time for my next appointment with Mick was almost upon me, I began to feel a mixed sense of excitement and anticipation that the problem would soon be over; that I would finally get my head sorted out. The more I thought about it, the more I was sure it had been Dayna and her husband Jackson, at the exhibition – I hadn't imagined it, although it was strange the way they had suddenly disappeared. Jackson was a tall man with salt and pepper hair and round glasses perched high on his nose. Was their presence there some confirmation that the girl in the painting had been Dayna, after all?

When I thought about it rationally, I figured Dayna must have been curious about whether I'd painted her. I wondered what she must have thought of it. It *was* a good likeness of her, despite my efforts to disguise her. I hoped she didn't see the picture as an intrusion on her privacy. Thinking that the picture would soon be in Terence Sattersthwaite's swanky flat made me feel sick – perhaps I should have offered it to Dayna. I pondered over whether I could try to paint it again, but they were never quite the same second time around and once the initial impetus was gone. I thought in any case, that painting her again would quickly have roused Ellie's suspicions, because I rarely used the same subject more than once – apart from Jenna (and now Harvey). I wished Terence hadn't bought it, but I'd had no justification for keeping it. Not one I could share anyway.

I heeded Mick's warnings about the potential emotional risks of being regressed, but I felt that whatever I discovered I would be strong enough to overcome the knowledge – to look at it objectively. It was the not knowing, and the wondering if there really was a time before we are born. That was the problem – it was the mystery of whether my dreams really were significant, or whether I had concocted some strange narrative in my head.

Thinking about it with a new-found sense of logic, perhaps having seen Dayna and feeling as though I was somehow attracted to her, it was that which had been creating the dreams. But that sense of attraction didn't explain the picture and how much like her it was – even Jenna had thought so. And then, of course, Dayna had said it wasn't her. Perhaps because I had wanted it to be her, I created the story – a dream in which it was her, but when she was younger – and I had subconsciously made it so that I'd once been a part of her life, only not as me. When I thought about it too much it made my brain hurt, and I began to tell myself it was all a stupid, humiliating sequence of events, that I should just pull myself together, get over it, and get on with my life.

The day of my appointment with Mick arrived. The day on which I was to find out, I hoped conclusively, what on Earth was going on inside my head? The night before the appointment I had the recurring dream, but it was much more vivid. It always finished at that same point – with Dayna, or who I thought was Dayna, disintegrating before me, breaking down into that fine, fairy dust, and scattering into the darkness as tiny, bright stars.

I hadn't told Ellie about either of my visits to see Mick, or the dreams, for that matter. I felt there was no need as events had escalated too far without her. Perhaps later on I would reveal all and tell her what a silly idiot I'd been – how I'd gone for this stupid regression session, how it had all been an embarrassing experience, and a complete and utter waste of time and money. I would tell her how much I loved her and Jenna, how content I was with my life, and that I was going through some weird early mid-life crisis. However, as Robert Burns prophetically penned in *To a Mouse*: *The best laid schemes o' mice and men gang aft a-gley* ... or ... *the best laid plans of mice and men often go awry.*

Awry – crooked, askew, muddled, amiss, skewed! Definitely not how I had planned everything would turn out as I settled myself onto the hypnotist's dark green couch.

Mick told me he would record my session, so we could sit together afterwards and evaluate what I said. He'd allocated a couple of hours for my appointment. I realized as he peered through the spectacles he balanced on the end of his nose so he could see what he was typing, that whether I wanted to or not, I was going to have to come clean with Ellie about where the money had gone to from our account. Hypnotists didn't charge a cheap hourly rate.

Once we began, Mick said I would start to feel relaxed and that, in very basic terms, it would feel as though I would tune out and not be entirely aware of what was happening. He said some people found that to be a bit of a frightening concept, but if I made myself comfortable before we began, and if I relaxed and tried to open my mind to him, my subconscious would very quickly take over. He told me if I was susceptible to the suggestion of hypnosis, that if once I was under, he felt it was safe to do so, only then would he take me further back in time – to a time before the day I was born.

He said that when he spoke the words 'Sleep now, Nate,' and he touched me on my left temple, I would fall into a state of complete relaxation. He told me that when he touched my left temple again, and he said, 'Wake now, Nate,' I would immediately become aware of my surroundings. I settled myself into the comfortable couch and waited. Once I was relaxed, I saw Mick's hand coming towards my face. He touched my left temple and started to speak.

Like waking from a deep anaesthesia, I was aware of nothing more until his hand was on my arm and I heard him say, 'It's okay, Nate, it's all done.'

Beside me, and with his hand still on my arm, I noticed his face was grave and his brow furrowed.

Chapter 11

Pandora's box was by then gaping well and truly wide open, with potential turmoil emerging from the depths of its bowels.

'Are you sure you want to watch this, Nate?'

I'd apparently been under hypnosis for thirty-five minutes, and Mick told me that during that time I'd said some quite bizarre things. Not sure whether or not I really did want to see the recording, I nodded anyway. 'Yes, I'm sure – I need to know what this is all about.'

The first fifteen minutes or so were made up of Mick asking questions about my life. He then took me back six years to the year Jenna was born, and then seven years to the year of mine and Ellie's wedding. We were on honeymoon in a small white house in an olive grove in Catalonia.

My voice sounded low and gravelly, like some mumbling actor in a film who you wish would speak more clearly. And you wonder whether it is partly to do with the quality of the recording, or some interference from the background noise. But there was nothing wrong with this recording, because whenever Mick spoke, his voice was as clear as crystal, and there was no background noise. There was just Mick, me, and the barely audible

sounds of our breathing. I was slurring my words –
as though I'd had a few gins before going under;
Mick was lucid and calm.

So I wouldn't be alarmed by the sound of my voice
when I heard it, Mick had warned me that my
recording might be like that. He didn't know why,
but he'd seen this happen before with some people.
He'd never managed to figure out any connection
between the cases when it happened and those when
it didn't. He said that most people sounded just as
clear as they do when they're aware of what is
going on around them; others would take on the
voice of someone else, with a different accent, as
though they were rehearsing for a play.

'And what do you see now, Nate?'

'Olive trees, lots of olive trees and a little white
house.' I answered.

'How do you feel, Nate?'

'Happy … and hot. It's hot outside. There are little
black flies everywhere.' I watched the screen in
amazement as I saw myself rubbing at the skin on
my arms and face. Whatever was going on, it
looked as though I was absolutely absorbed in what
was happening to me. And I had no memory of any
of it.

He asked me more questions about being in Catalonia and then said, 'Nate, I'm going to take you back to when you were eighteen. It is September 5th 2004. Describe what you see.

'I'm in a room sitting on a bed. There's another bed in the room.'

'Does the other bed belong to your brother, perhaps?'

'No. No. I don't think so. I don't know who it belongs to.'

'Is there anyone with you?'

'No. I'm waiting for someone.'

'Okay, Nate. I want you to go forward just one hour. Is there someone with you now?'

I hear my voice lighten as I say, 'Yes, it's Andy.'

'Who is Andy, Nate?'

'He's my new room-mate.'

'Ah, okay Nate. Are you at university?'

'Hmm.' My voice sounded a long way off as though I was drifting.

'Nate, I need an answer. Yes, or no? Are you at

university?'

'Yes.' My response sounded much more definite.

He went on to ask more questions about life at university and then took me back to 1991 when I would have been five years old. My voice had developed a higher pitch – a sound I don't think I could replicate in my normal repertoire of sounds. On the screen in front of me my face looked different – almost child-like – and I was shrinking away from the camera, I was forcing my body into the depths of the couch on which I was lying.

'Nate, what can you see now?'

'It's dark.'

'Can you see anything?'

'Not much. I'm frightened.'

'Okay Nate let's go forward five hours. What can you see now?'

'There's light coming in between the curtains.'

'Okay. Where are you and what do you see?'

I giggled, 'In the bedroom. I can see lots of toys and books.'

'Right, Nate. I'm going to take you back to 1986.

What can you see now?'

My voice becomes almost inaudible, and I whisper.
'It's dark.'

'How do you feel, Nate? Are you happy?'

'I'm safe. I feel … safe.' My whispering was so
very quiet. Lying there on Mick's examination
couch, I brought my knees up towards my chest in
something resembling the foetal position. As I
watched the screen an uncomfortable realization
sank through my body. Did he *really* take me back
inside my mother's womb?

'Okay, right Nate, now I want you to go deeper. I
want you to drift deeper into your subconscious and
let me take you back. Nate, we're going to go back
to November 30th 1985. Tell me where you are.'

He was taking me back to a time before I was born.
That was what I had gone there for, but even so, my
heart felt heavy as I waited to see what would
happen next.

There was a long silence on the recording. I could
see that my breathing was becoming much more
forced. My chest was rising and falling faster and
faster, as though I was gasping and trying to get as
much oxygen as I could into my lungs. My
breathing continued to become much faster and

much more urgent and laboured. I didn't respond to his question.

I glanced over at Mick, so he could tell me what was going on. He silently put his finger to his lips and nodded towards the computer. And then I heard his voice again on the recording.

'Okay, Nate. Stay with me. Now go back to 28th October 1985.'

I exhaled slowly, my chest flattening as my knees resumed their relaxed position on the couch. Mick continued, 'Where are you now?'

Mick reached forward and paused the recording. 'Nate, sometimes there are things that are better left unknown. I do this for a living, and I sometimes wish I hadn't heard and seen some of what I've experienced. I truly believe there is something more to this life, and that sometimes it's better just to accept that there are things we can never truly know or understand, however much evidence we might see and experience along the way.'

'Really that bad, huh?' I had already started to feel spooked by what was on the recording, but I'd come so far, surely it was better to know, rather than for me to keep on wondering for the rest of my days? I hesitated before answering. I'd had the dreams, so surely it couldn't be worse than what I'd seen in those. Perhaps I hadn't expressed to him just how awful those dreams had made me feel. I told him it would be all right, that whatever I was about to unveil would be okay. He took a deep breath and reluctantly clicked *play*.

On the recording, an elongated pause followed his question about where I was.

I then inhaled deeply and a voice, the one which emerged from my mouth, well when I spoke, it didn't sound anything like me.

'Help me. Help me!' I was screaming.

'Nate. I want you to calm down and listen to my voice. Take time to have a few short breaths. Okay, good. Where are you?'

'I don't know. It's dark, so dark … and cold. I am so cold.' My voice (THE voice) sounded as though the person (For it wasn't *me?* That wasn't *my* voice) was shivering. In the image on the computer screen, I was tightly hugging myself. And then, I began to breath-hold.

'Nate.'

And then, again I screamed. 'Help! Help!' The voice sounded distant. And then, I held my breath once more.

'Nate.' Mick hesitated and then, much more forcefully, 'NATE! Listen to me, I AM helping you.' And then my chest expanded as I took in air.

Mick continued. 'Stay focused on my voice. I want you to concentrate on the beating of your heart. Listen to it and focus on it. At the same time, I want you to slow down your breathing. C'mon Nate, breathe for me: In … out. In … out. In … out.' He did this for about two minutes. On the screen I saw him shift closer to me. He reached forward and was holding onto my wrist to check my pulse. At the same time, he watched an array of monitors he'd hooked me up to before the process. Initially there was more heavy breathing. And then, my body relaxed.

'Good, Nate, well done. Right, I now want you to go back two weeks to 7th October 1985. Nate, where are you now?'

'On a winding road. There are trees. Low branches. The sea. I can see the sea.'

'What are you doing, Nate.'

'Not Nate.' My head was shaking from side to side.

'Sorry, what did you say?'

'Nate … not Nate.'

'What's your name?'

'Not Nate.'

'I know 'Not Nate', but what *is* your name?'

He asked me this question several times and always, frustratingly, got the same reply: *Not Nate*

In the end, Mick gave up and went down another avenue. 'What are you doing on the winding road?'

'I'm riding a motorbike.'

The voice emanating from my mouth sounded calmer, happier, but it was still not my voice. I sounded younger and I had an English accent. I was still slurring my words, but I thought my accent was from somewhere around the middle of England, the West Midlands – even Birmingham, perhaps? I didn't even know I could talk in that accent!

'Do you recognize where you are?'

'No …'.

I paused as though I was going to say more, but then I began to shake uncontrollably. 'No, no, no!'

Fast and deep, my breathing became erratic, and I looked as though I was struggling for air. The machines he'd attached to me were bleeping. I was holding onto my chest again.

'No! Air. Air. I need air.' In the film I looked as though I was turning my head. 'Nooooo …'. My expression changed as my head continued to turn – as though I was looking at something behind me. My mouth moved but no sound came out. And then I let out an almighty, bloodcurdling scream.

That was the point at which Mick touched me on the side of my face and brought me round.

As I watched myself lying there looking confused, dazed – exhausted – I realized that none of what I'd heard myself say over the preceding forty-five minutes did I have any recollection of saying. I had no memory of anything that had happened during the time from when I'd seen his hand coming towards my face, to the point he brought me round. I was so tired.

Mick turned the computer back towards him while I sat contemplating what had just happened. 'But it doesn't prove anything really does it?' I suggested. 'Except that somewhere in my psyche there's a 'memory' of sorts from before I was born – in my mother's womb … which I feel quite crazy even saying. The rest of it could all have been made up – I guess even the womb thing could have been made up. After all, if you tell me it's in the time just before I was born, then that's where my imagination would take me anyway. And then the wind, the motorbike, the trees, those things could all have been me hooking into my dreams.'

Mick nodded thoughtfully. 'Hmm, possibly, but there's something more here.' He rewound the recording to the last couple of minutes. 'Look here, at the point when you turn your head. I'll slow it down for you. Look, there's a moment when you go to say something. Just after you say 'No', it's as though you turned to look at someone, and your mouth moves as though you're saying the word *day*. But, of course, 'Day' could be short for Dayna. You see? And you know, Nate, I have never seen such a look of desperation, nor heard such a bloodcurdling scream. There's something more here … I'm sure of it.' He sat there silently, gently shaking his head as he rewound and forwarded that part of the recording several times.

As I watched the replays of the film, I felt that by then familiar sickening bolt of adrenaline shoot through me. I wanted to deny that any of this could be real, I wanted to try and look at it in a scientific, logical way. And that can be difficult when you've spent your whole life embroiled in activities as far away from science as possible. 'Okay, but I guess again, my dreams, the dreams I've been having about being on a motorbike with Dayna could have created that?' I leaned forward and held onto my head. Giving a deep sigh, I added, 'I feel so confused!'

Mick's appointment time with me was almost up, and I sensed from the way he glanced at the clock on the wall that perhaps we needed to round this off. 'Where do I go from here?' I asked him. I had no idea what path I should take next.

'We can do this again, Nate, but it has to be your decision. Just be aware that often the more a person does this, the more we dig, the more is unearthed, and there often isn't any conclusion. Many people just have to eventually admit – to themselves mostly – that there are some things we're just not meant to know. I've grappled with that every day of my working life since I began hypnotizing people, especially in cases of before-birth regression.

Perhaps, Nate, you've seen and heard enough, and it's time to go home and get on with your life. Whatever happened before – whether it happened or didn't happen, we'll never be one hundred percent sure, and perhaps the little knowledge that you may have gleaned from today might tell you there *is* something more than this life, without putting yourself through more heartache.'

He paused, and as I sat there close to tears, he added, '… and if you did come back to see me, to what end would it be worthwhile? I don't think you'll achieve anything from knowing more. I fear it would just bring misery.'

I appreciated his honesty – after all, he could have kept me dangling on a string so I would have continued paying him. I thanked him and told him I would go away, think about it, and get in touch if I wanted to try again.

And over the coming months I did go back, not just once, but five times. Each occasion played out pretty much the same as before, only whenever he took me back to the screaming, panicking part, it became clearer I was screaming out Dayna's name.

I began to feel as though I was an addict; as though I was gaining some self-gratification from what I was doing; that the procedure had become like a shot of amphetamines. Perhaps it gave my brain respite from everyday worries and stresses ... and protected me from the nightmares that were stealing my nights.

Perhaps I was actually going quite mad. Maybe I needed a different kind of help?

Chapter 12

Because she knew nothing about it, help was not at that point coming from Ellie's direction. One night, though, she noticed the money coming out of our account for the fees I was paying for Mick's consultations. I hadn't attempted to hide them – it would have been difficult to have done so anyway as our account is a joint one, plus she always did my tax returns for the business account, so had I tried to use that account instead, she would have seen them coming out anyway. I also think that secretly I wanted her to find out. I needed her – she was the missing part in my crazy emotional puzzle. I wanted to share the details of the secret life I'd been living.

One evening once Jenna was tucked up in bed, I came into the sitting room with steaming mugs of mint tea for Ellie and me. An American sitcom played on the TV in the background, and Ellie was looking at her computer. Just before she spoke, I noticed she was checking out the bank account. In anticipation of what was going to come next, I felt my stomach collapse deep inside my abdomen. I wanted to retch; to run and hide.

'Why didn't you tell me, Nate? Why hide this from me?' I was in for it, and I knew resistance was futile. I calmly waited for the accusations to come my way, offering occasional weak lines of justification for my actions.

'I didn't hide it – the evidence is there, right in front of you.' I shrugged, which only seemed to exacerbate the situation. What I found surprising about finding myself in that position, was that I suddenly felt a cloud was lifting from my shoulders.

'I know, but you didn't tell me, you didn't discuss it with me! Why have you been going to see this … this Mick …'. She paused as she scrolled back through the online bank statement to see the name of his business, '… this Mick Jardine guy? Are you depressed?'

'Regression,' I said quietly.

'What?'

'You know, where you get hypnotized and taken back to earlier parts of your life … and sometimes to the times before you were born.'

With a roll of her eyes, she said, 'I know what regression is, Nate,' and added, 'So?'

'So what?'

'So, do you want to talk about it?'

'Not really, but I guess I'm going to have to.'

This situation was alien to us – we generally

bumbled along in our domestic bliss. I had never imagined that it would ever be any other way.

And so, the whole story came pouring out, including the part about my meeting up with Dayna. I deliberately left out the part about appearing to call out her name on each of the recordings. I told her that Mick had woken me each time I'd screamed. Listening to myself, I realized how ridiculous the whole story would sound to someone who hadn't been directly involved in what had been happening.

'So, this woman you appear to be fixated on.' She sounded angry, hurt, and perhaps even jealous, as though she thought I might be embarking on an affair. Although I admit that thought had indeed crossed my mind, so perhaps that had been a fair judgment. 'This woman who you've only met once – twice if you include the day you spotted her at the zoo.' I sensed a hint of sarcasm in her voice. This was not looking good. 'Do you really believe all this about being with her, but in a previous life?'

She turned her head to look out of the window into the dark night. Between the two rowan trees we'd planted beside the path after we moved in, a white, crescent moon was hanging in the sky. I could see Ellie's face reflected in the glass. She looked hurt and worried.

She placed her laptop on the coffee table and stood up. She began pacing backwards and forwards across the room. I wasn't sure whether or not this was a good sign. 'So, based on some feelings and strange dreams you've been having, you've embarked on some weird and expensive therapy? Using *our* money!'

It wasn't good, but what could I do? I just nodded.

Harvey went over to lie in the corner of the room in one of his many dog beds that were scattered through the house. He'd never seen us like that; we'd never *actually* been like that.

She sat back down again, and I could see tears in her eyes. 'Are we in trouble, Nate? Is this, this … thing, whatever it is, is it serious?'

I realized that Dayna herself had known nothing about what had been going on over the previous weeks. She knew nothing of the regression, she knew nothing of what I was thinking; it was all in my head, like some weird, creepy unrequited love.

'Are we okay, Nate?'

'I think so, Ellie. I just need to get through this. I keep on thinking that one more session will finish it up for me; that I'll have a greater understanding of what's going on.'

'And *has* it been helping you? Or is it making it worse?' She was much calmer by that point, and Harvey came over and licked her hand. She absentmindedly shifted her hand to the top of his head and stroked him gently, and then slowly, carefully, down his neck and back; all the time meticulously smoothing his glossy fur. His old dog bite scars were by then barely visible.

'I don't know – it's always the same. Each time he takes me back, there's this moment I reach where I'm screaming. He's tried, but he can't get me away from that point. The last time I was there, he said that next time we could try going forward by just a few days and have that as our starting point. He's never taken me into the time when I'm apparently dead.' I looked at her and shrugged my shoulders 'If, of course, you take the time when I'm screaming and gasping for air as the time of death.'

Ellie shook her head in disbelief.' I just can't get over that you've been doing all this and never mentioned any of it to me. This 'connection' you apparently have with this woman Dayna. Have you honestly not met with her since, or been in touch with her?'

'No.' She looked doubtful that I was telling her the truth.

'No, I haven't!' I reiterated, thankful that for once I

could be truthful.

'I didn't even know you were into this stuff, Nate. You know … the supernatural. After all, you're a humanist! You don't believe in any of this stuff – you've rejected it since the time when you could think about such things for yourself. You know? We live, we die, and our bodies return to the ground, either six feet under feeding the worms and the trees or scattered as ash. The End! You know what? This is the kind of stuff our parents would love to know you were experiencing! My mum would especially take great pleasure in the knowledge that Nate had finally found some kind of religion of sorts – even if it's not the same as hers.'

'I know what you're saying, Ellie, and I *still* don't believe in this stuff – that's what makes it all so bizarre. But it's weird – it really is starting to make dents in everything I've ever believed.' I was shaking my head, and then a spark of panic shot through me. 'And please don't ever tell your mother about this – or my mum for that matter!'

She laughed but didn't say she wouldn't. I sensed things were a little better though. Ellie looked as though she'd had a light bulb moment and sat down again. She beckoned for me to sit by her and then reached onto the coffee table for her laptop. 'Have you looked online?'

'What?'

'Online – you know, for drowning accidents or motorbike fatalities in that year in the Midlands. You said he had a Midlands accent, right?'

She was a genius. This was the professional, straight-thinking Ellie. I was immediately under the spell I was sure she cast on people every day she worked in the courts. I was relieved that at last I had her on board. She seemed to have forgiven me and was obviously intrigued at the story I'd told her. I grabbed my own laptop and the two of us trawled the Internet for more than three hours. We both tried desperately to find some record of an accident that happened in that region circa 1985.

Between us we searched hundreds of different news web pages and obituaries, but all to no avail. Only the main stories seemed to have made their way into the modern online news archives. We looked at Staffordshire, Warwickshire, Worcestershire, Wales, Derbyshire, Leicestershire, Nottinghamshire, and Yorkshire. We found one case where a pillion rider had died instantly near Llandudno in Wales, but it was a young woman. We also found a car-motorbike collision near Matlock in Derbyshire, but in that case the car driver had been the one who had met his demise.

Ellie clearly felt frustrated that we'd not found

anything solid. She sighed – a long, drawn-out sigh, and told me I'd have to go back to see Mick and try to find out the name of the guy on the motorbike. At least then we'd have something tangible to work with and we could search official birth and death records more thoroughly. I noted she said 'we' – she was definitely on my side. I felt relief flood through me, and that night I slept soundly for the first time in months.

Two days later I was back in Mick's clinic. Ellie had taken the afternoon off work to accompany me but was staying in the waiting room during the session. The plan was for her to come in afterwards and view the recording with us. Once inside the consulting room, Mick told me he had his reservations, but I insisted, telling him we had to be open about what was going on – for the sake of mine and Ellie's relationship. I also felt she had to be convinced that I wasn't wasting our money. After her help with searching on the web two nights before, I also felt I needed her mind on this – she might think of something Mick or I hadn't.

And so, with Mick's touch on the side of my face, under I went.

Once I was aware of my surroundings again, I could see straight away the concern on Mick's face. He was shaking his head from side to side. 'Don't let her see what just happened, Nate. I'm married too, and what just happened could destroy the strongest of relationships. It needs to be just the two of us when we play it back.'

'Why?'

'Look, just trust me, Nate. Come back on your own tomorrow and I'll go through it with you. Come at lunchtime as I'm booked up all day – no charge. Okay?'

'But she's expecting to see the recording! What do I say to her?' I felt myself beginning to panic – for mine and Ellie's sakes, and also because I needed to know what was on the recording.

Mick hesitated and then said, 'Look, if it's confirmation Ellie needs, then let's show her the last recording so she can see everything you've already told her. I'll just tell her today's recording didn't work.'

I was sick of lying and dreaded being party to yet another round of abject lies. Reluctantly, I agreed. And so, once Mick had kindly told the lie on my behalf, Ellie sat, fixatedly watching the recording from my previous session. At the point when I started to scream, she clasped her hand firmly across her mouth and turned to me with tears in her eyes.

Her grip tightened on my hand. 'Oh, my goodness, this is awful! Who would ever have thought this could happen?'

She was quiet all the way home, and then as we pulled into the driveway, she asked me whether that was it, whether I was going to call it a day.

'I can't, Ellie.' I need to find out what happened.

She nodded solemnly.

'Okay, I get it. Just don't shut me out. Okay?'

I was grateful for her acknowledgement that I needed to continue. I nodded, 'Okay.'

At the forefront of my mind, though, was what on earth could've happened when Mick put me under. Perhaps the next day I would finally get some answers. Even if I couldn't share them with Ellie – at least I would (perhaps) know more about what was going on.

Chapter 13

The following day when I arrived at the clinic, Mick's afternoon appointment had arrived early. Mick asked me if I'd mind waiting until after he'd seen her. I nipped off for a cup of coffee and sat contemplating what the recording might tell me. Would there really this time be something more tangible, something which would prove without doubt that I'd lived before. With that thought, a thousand voices in my head told me not to be so stupid; I was forever creating unwelcome doubts.

What was happening to me continued to challenge the beliefs I'd held for my whole adult life, and that was difficult for me to contend with. I looked around at all the people in the café and watched those who were parading past the windows; each of them going about their daily business. I wondered whether they had ever considered whether the life they had just now was possibly not the only one they'd ever lived.

The curly-haired bubbly, blonde girl at the till was chatting to everyone, seemingly not a care in the world, but had she ever wondered whether she'd existed before this life? Were there times when she lay at night wondering about her place in this world, whether there was something more, and what that more might look like.

The doddery old woman walking by holding onto a younger woman's arm, did she wonder whether this was it, that the life she had which was coming to an end would be all there ever would be of her? Or did she believe she would meet all her loved ones again in some distant world, before moving on to being someone else?

The ginger-haired boy of about two years old who was being fastened back into his buggy – did he ponder about and dream of a life he'd had before? Was it possible he knew more about this than we did? Perhaps that time before we can properly communicate is a time when we remember, but we don't have the ability to convey that information to anyone in an intelligible way? And then, by the time we can articulate, perhaps there is so much new stuff to learn that the old life is forgotten – stored in the recesses of the mind, never to be discussed?

People, so many people, but do any of them ever remember? I sipped my coffee and mentally retreated to the world I might never comprehend.

Half an hour later, I was glad to be back at the clinic – spending too much time inside my head was not good for me. I smiled and nodded over at Mick as he was saying cheerio to his previous appointment. Once the other person had gone through the door Mick headed straight over to greet me. 'Nate, I'm glad you could make it back so quickly. I've been desperate for you to see this. I think it will help you, and we have a little more time now as my next appointment's not until two o'clock.'

I felt a throb of excitement deep in my belly. 'But why did you not want me – us – to hear it yesterday? Why not Ellie too?'

'You'll see.'

He fast forwarded to the point where we usually met the stumbling block; the point at which I was screaming and writhing.

'Nate, I need you to calm down. Breathe. In … out.'

This hadn't worked when he tried to do it before, but somehow this time, whether his voice was clearer, whether I had become more receptive to the process, I stopped screaming, stopped gasping for air.

'Okay, good, Nate. Well done.' I could hear the relief in his voice. 'Right, Nate.' I want you to go forward.' Forward, why was he taking me forward? Surely that was sometime after I died.

But on the screen, I began to grin. Perhaps there really was a Heaven? I smiled to myself at the irony of all this, given my lack of religious beliefs.

'Where are you, Nate?'

In a wood by a lake.' My voice had resumed the Midlands accent I'd had before the screaming.

'Are you with anyone?'

'Yes'

Who?'

'Dayna.'

'Who's Dayna?'

'She's my girlfriend.'

'How are you feeling right now, Nate.'

'Not Nate.'

'Sorry. How are you feeling now?' He regrettably later told me he hadn't wanted at that point to ruin the thread we'd found, by getting into another debate with me about my name. This was particularly important after so many sessions in which we'd been trying so hard to get me past the scream.

'Okay. How do you feel being there with Dayna?'

I smiled. 'Happy. I love Dayna so much. She's the love of my life. We're soul mates.'

Whoa, he was right about not showing this to Ellie. I think she would have had difficulty separating the words emanating from my mouth from the situation.

'How do you know Dayna?'

'School.'

'Were you school sweethearts?'

'Kind of, I guess, but no, more than that, we were meant to be together.'

'What do you mean, Nate?'

'What?'

'Meant to be together, how do you mean?'

'Like forever, eternity. Like I just said.'

'How do you know this?'

'A letter.'

'A letter?'

I paused and looked puzzled. 'Hmm, the house. The old woman with the message.'

'Which woman, Nate?'

'I don't know … I can't see her.'

In the image on the screen Mick, too, looked

confused. 'Why can't you see her?'

'I don't know, I just can't – I can't picture her.'

Mick continued that line of questioning for several minutes but then gave up. All I would say, on and on, was that I couldn't see the woman and I didn't know who had sent the letter, but that it said something about souls across time. The actual words just wouldn't come.

In the end, Mick decided to go down another avenue.

'How old are you?'

'Umm, er, twenty-two.'

'How old is Dayna?'

'I'm not sure? Younger I think.'

'What year is it?

'Um, er.'

'The year? What year is it?'

'Nineteen, um er, eighty something.' He sensed I was getting confused so brought me back to the place we had been exploring earlier.

'The woods. What can you see?'

'Dayna. She is beautiful.'

'What's she doing?'

'She's looking for something and calling out.'

'What is she calling?'

'I can't hear her. I can see her, but I can't hear her.'

Can you see anyone else?'

'A dog looking out from between the trees.'

'Okay, concentrate on the dog for me. What colour is the dog?'

'Black, with a white blaze on his chest.'

'Does the dog belong to you?'

'No, not mine.'

'Dayna's then?'

'Um, um, erm … maybe.'

'You don't know.'

'No'

'Right. Let's go forward two days. Where are you now?''

'Bedroom.'

'Are you alone?'

'No.'

'Who is with you?'

'Dayna.'

'Okay, let's go forward one more day. Where are you now?'

'Bedroom.'

'Are you alone?'

'Yes.'

'What are you doing?'

'Painting and listening to music.'

'Music? What are you listening to?

'Hmm. I can hear it.' I began to nod my head and hum a tune. And then it clicked in my head what it was: It was a song I was very familiar with - Jon and Vangelis, *I'll Find My Way Home*.

I carried on humming and then Mick interrupted.

'That's a lovely tune, Nate, what is in the picture you are painting?'

'Dayna.'

I glanced over at Mick, who smiled and nodded back towards the screen. There was obviously more to come.

'What else is in the picture?'

'Trees and … and lots of bird silhouettes in the sky… and a …' I waited to hear myself say it. *A fox cub*, but those weren't the words that came out of my mouth.

'A swan … at the edge of a lake.'

'A swan and a lake? Are you sure?'

'Yes … no, no, wait, there are two swans! One is in the water.'

Knowing about the picture back home, Mick was desperate to clarify this. 'Is there a fox or a butterfly in the picture you're painting?'

'No. No, there's no fox, no butterfly.' On film I seemed to be getting agitated and confused, and my voice was expressing how irritated I was becoming. And then, without being prompted, the tone of my voice was adamant. 'Two swans, mute swans!'

'Okay, I now want you to go forward in time, just two weeks. It's a Tuesday.' Mick kept a handy link on his computer which told him the actual day of the week of any year with the pressing of a couple of buttons. He said he wasn't sure whether knowledge of the actual day helped in the regression, but he felt if it helped just with one piece of information, then it would be worth it.

On the screen I could see myself beginning to breathe deeply and then hold onto my chest. My hands moved to my throat, and I looked as though I was choking. And then I held my head as though I was in pain.

'Okay, Nate. Nate. I want you to come back to me now.'

I watched myself as I continued to clutch my head. Time was ticking by on the timer at the bottom of the screen – a few minutes passed. Worrying sounds began to emanate from the back of my throat as though I was choking. Mick's voice became more urgent, and on the screen I could see his normally calm demeanour turning to panic. As he reached forward and touched me on the side of my head, I could see my eyes were wide and flickering from side to side. My brow was furrowed with deep lines of concentration. This went on for what seemed hours but was probably only a couple of minutes or so.

And then, finally, with a huge intake of air, I came round.

As he switched off the film I said, 'Wow, did I nearly not come back that time?'

'I have to admit you had me worried there, Nate. I've seen a couple of people who've been reluctant to come back before, but none in such a violent way as you were then. I spent last night going over old notes and so on, and the only explanation I can come up with is that I just happened to catch you,' he corrected himself, '… the apparent previous you, that is, in the throes of dying.'

Feeling rather shocked by what I'd seen, I asked 'Where do we go from here, do you think?'

'Given what happened, I'd be reluctant for us to go through this again, Nate. But perhaps there's enough information available now for you to work with. You have some evidence, some deep-seated memory of sorts, of you with her, in a wood, with a black and white dog, some letter of some sort, and a mysterious woman.'

'One I couldn't see.' I reminded him.

'Hmm,' he agreed. 'And then, of course, there's the painting. It might not be the right painting, but it sounds as though he was an artist, and there are similarities between the descriptions of the paintings – a girl on a bench at the edge of a wood, animals.'

I sat opposite him, trying to take it all in; attempting to understand what had just happened. 'I think you're right; I think I'd be reluctant to go through anything like that again.' I paused while I considered what my next steps were going to be. 'I'm going to have to see her again, aren't I?'

'Probably. At least if you're going to resolve this once and for all anyway. But if she's not willing to offer more information, then I guess you just have to move on and try to forget about this. You know, perhaps it's time to put it, and her, behind you.'

Before I left him, I promised I'd let him know what happened. He seemed almost as desperate to know as I was.

That night Ellie, Jenna, Harvey, and I had been invited to Marc and Christina's for dinner. Once we finished eating, we sat down with the two dogs lying beside us. They lay sprawled on the rug together; their canine friendship apparently already as firm as that of their human companions. Jenna and Jacob were settled in the other room trying to teach one another how to play Monopoly. We'd offered to have a game with them, but, no, they wanted to play their own version; a version which, quite frankly, sounded rather corrupt on Jenna's behalf. I don't think the banker is allowed to take an extra £100 note each turn! Jenna was definitely going to turn out to be a successful young lady if she could pull that one off for a whole game.

I settled back into the sofa and felt, for the first time in a long while, quite relaxed. I was glad we were staying over so I could have a glass or two of beer, and Ellie her much-loved tipple – sweet Somerset cider. The people next door to us (the ones with Marmalade, the terrorizing ginger cat), were going to give the cats their evening meal and check on them for us.

While I'd avoided talking about it all evening, once dinner was over, the conversation turned towards my recent goings-on with Dayna and Mick. They listened intently as Ellie relayed the story – or at least it was the story as far as she knew it. She still had no idea about my lunchtime meeting that day with Mick. She had no idea that inside I remained on the brink of something which could have far-reaching consequences. For her, Jenna, and me.

While they listened, Marc and Christina sat with their mouths agape, both of them wide-eyed and apparently speechless, until eventually Marc turned to me and asked, 'So what happened when you met her, this Dayna woman?'

I hadn't been expecting to have to embellish the conversation with more detail. Stumbling over my words, I thought fast. 'Well, um, she said the painting wasn't her.'

'But then the dreams began, yes?'

'Hmm, yes.' I looked to Ellie for some help, but there was none forthcoming. It seemed she, too, wanted to hear more. Perhaps there was an element of her wanting to know the current version of the story and how I would tell it to other people. It was possible she thought I might give more information than I previously had. Maybe she realized there was more to tell, and she secretly thought I might slip up, and she'd discover something I'd not already told her.

I'd noticed couples doing that, avidly listening to a story the other one was telling and correcting parts of it; even claiming a different version of events or suggesting that wasn't the version they'd heard the first time the story was told. There was often an implication that somehow the story had been inflated for effect, or, as in this case, watered down to minimize interest. I tried to keep the story straight, lest I trip up and let on that I'd been back to see Mick, and, more importantly, that I planned to see Dayna yet again.

I was deliberately not mentioning Dayna's name, though – mainly because I was desperately worried I'd give something away about what I was going to do next. 'Pretty crazy, huh?' I offered, hoping that would be the end of the conversation.

But Marc was like a tiny terrier tearing at a dog chew fit for an Irish wolfhound. 'So, when did all this start?' He wasn't letting this go.

'Oh, about six months ago.'

'So, around Christmas time?' Mentally recalling my festive distractedness, I felt again that he was onto me. I was starting to resent the way people began questions with the word *So*, whenever they were quizzing you about something. His eyes were narrowed, and his brow furrowed with intent curiousity.

'Oh, er, yes, about then anyway.'

'Nate, of course it was. It was that day at the zoo,' Ellie interjected, looking puzzled. She rolled her eyes and shook her head at me. 'I'm sure that was just a few days before these guys came over for dinner, wasn't it?'

I nodded, stumbling over what to say next, but children and dogs have ways of providing a timely distraction. As I scrabbled for words, Harvey stood up, arched his back, and began retching. This culminated in him bringing his dinner up right there on the floor next to Bruce, all over Marc and Christina's yellow and red rug. In response, Bruce decided this was a great opportunity to consume some of Harvey's lumps of regurgitated dog food. *Dogs, you've got to love them,* I thought, as everyone became sidetracked. I would be forever indebted to my four-legged friend. I promised myself that the next time he and I were on our own, I'd stop by the pet store and get him a new toy – one of the fluffy ones he loved to carry around in his mouth or have us throw for him to fetch.

Amid the unexpected mayhem, the moment, and more importantly the cross-examination, was indeed lost, as we fumbled about to clear up the mess. Two overly-inquisitive children arrived to join in the commotion.

'Is Harvey poorly, Dad? Is he going to die?'

'No, he just threw up his dinner.'

'Oh, good, that's okay then. Why did Bruce eat Harvey's sick?'

'Because that's what dogs do.' Ellie replied. 'Dogs do that because they really don't like to waste food – and if you think about wild dogs, they regurgitate food for their young all the time – it's just natural.'

There was a pause.

'Regurgitate? What is THAT?'

I chipped in. 'It's when one animal eats the food and stores it in their stomach and brings it up later. It's often to feed to another animal once they get back to them. It's all part of animal survival – it's normal for some animals!'

'Urgh! That's like forcing someone else to eat vomit. That's gross!' The two of them exited the room making retching sounds.

I'd escaped. For the time being anyway – but I suspected that that wasn't going to be the end of it.

Chapter 14

I lied to Ellie again. I told her I was going to stop chasing whatever the thing with Dayna was. I said I'd had enough and didn't want to pursue it any longer. She seemed relieved, and I felt awful about saying that and going on to pursue Dayna anyway. Lying temporarily got me out of the woods, allowing me to chase this thing without any more hurt. I didn't like the person I'd become, but the thoughts, the dreams, they were not going away. They were controlling me in a way which had made me desperate to know more.

I eventually plucked up the courage to email Dayna and told her I had to urgently meet with her again. Her reluctance to meet up was evident from the tone of her reply, particularly when she insisted once more that the picture hadn't been her. In the end, though, she agreed to meet me again in the cafe the following Friday morning. Same time, same place – a naïve part of me saw it as being a date. From another, more stable point of view, I could see that if I wasn't careful, the police might come knocking at the door and charge me with harassing her. I really had become the stalker of Ellie and Jenna's intense conversations.

I'd been deliberately vague with Dayna about what I wanted to talk to her about, simply saying I just had a few more questions, if she could spare the time to meet with me again. I insisted it would be worth her while our meeting again – that I had some information about the picture that she would find interesting.

For our second cafe rendezvous I didn't take the painting – it was just me and my new permanent sidekick Harvey. The cafe was dog-friendly, and a waiter willingly gave me a table in a quiet corner away from all the hustle and bustle. While we waited for Dayna to arrive, Harvey dutifully lay down on the blue and grey paw-print dog bed beside my chair, gnawing away at a long-lasting dog chew.

Dayna was late – twenty-five minutes late in the end. I'd been about to get up to leave, when there she was. She looked windswept from the fresh autumn breeze, and yet elegant. 'Sorry, Nate. I got delayed. Gosh, and Harvey. How are you?' She reached down and carefully stroked his head. 'You really are a very handsome boy, aren't you?'

As far as I was aware she'd never seen him before – unless that really had been her and Jackson at the exhibition, when Harvey was having his fifteen minutes of fame. I let the moment pass but felt that it was evidence that there really was something more between us, and more importantly, that she felt it too.

After we'd ordered two black coffees, I decided I should cut to the chase and tell her everything that had been going on – including the regressions and dreams and so on. I began right from the beginning with how I felt the first time I saw her at the zoo.

Once I'd got over my initial embarrassment at the seemingly preposterous nature of what I was telling her, I realized she really was concentrating on listening to me. Her intense interest was overpowering, compelling me to explain everything in detail. She occasionally smiled an awkward smile; a few times I saw her eyes begin to fill with tears; other times she sat there with her head slightly cocked to one side, focusing on every single word.

When I'd finished the whole story, leaving no stone unturned, including stupidly adding that I felt this deep attraction of sorts to her, she sat in front of me, seemingly dumbstruck.

I reached down and stroked Harvey's head, thankful for his presence and, once more, his offer of distraction.

Eventually, she gave a deep sigh and spoke, 'I really don't know what to say, Nate. That is some story.'

I felt shattered. Was she really going to deny any of what I'd told her? Even after my having bared my soul to her.

'But …'.

She raised her hand to indicate I should say no more, that the conversation was over, but I hadn't gone that far for the whole experience to be dismissed as being a story; some tale I'd concocted in my head.

'No Dayna, I need to get this over and done with – for the sake of my family. Are you telling me that there was never someone in your life who loved you when you were younger, who rode a motorbike, who painted, who …' I hesitated before saying it, 'who died in an accident?'

She took a while to answer. 'No, Nate. There was no guy who died in an accident.' She emphasized this and for a fleeting moment I sensed she was lying, perhaps protesting too much.

'Okay, let's put all that to one side. Let's forget that we may have met before. Do you feel any of what I feel for you? Can you feel the connection I experience when I'm with you? The link I felt as soon as I saw you. Have you ever felt that too?'

She immediately shook her head, 'No, Nate, I

haven't. And even if I had done, what would you want me to do with that? Run away with you and live a disjointed life away from the people I love?'

'So, you *do* feel something?'

'Nate, you are a very handsome young man, what fifty-something wouldn't be utterly flattered by any attention you gave them?' She hadn't answered my question and I was getting nowhere. I felt so very frustrated.

'But the picture? In my regressed state I talked about a pair of swans and a lake, but there are no swans or any water in the picture I showed you. What is it with the swans? And the mysterious letter? What about that? And Jon and Vangelis, eh? Why did that song come into my head? What about all those things?'

I saw a glimmer of something in her eyes when I mentioned the picture of the swans, but then she sighed. 'What? Nate, I have no idea what you're talking about.' Her voice was slightly raised. I could sense that people around us were starting to notice. 'Look, I don't think you should contact me again.' She got up to go, and put ten pounds on the table. 'My turn,' she said with a weak smile, nodding towards the money. 'Go back to your Ellie and Jenna, Nate, and have the most wonderful life.'

She reached down and stroked Harvey on the side of his neck. 'Look after him, Harvey.'

And then, without turning to look at me again, she walked out of the cafe and out of my life.

Part Two

Then

Chapter 1

Rachel had known about the crush I had on Pete a long time before the day we saw him in the park playing tennis with his older brother, Ade.

'Whoa, get a look at those legs!' She suddenly called out at the top of her voice so everyone and their dog would hear. She followed her shout with a loud wolf whistle. I immediately looked away in embarrassment, and was horrified to discover my large, goofy, black and tan dog Buddy was happily digging in the flowerbed. The one the parks staff spent ages planting up every spring, and lovingly tended through the summer and autumn.

Leaving Rachel to her own wayward devices, I gratefully headed over to retrieve Buddy. Seeing a sod of grass fly up in the air, closely followed by a half-grown daffodil still nestled in its bulb, I screeched, 'Buddy! No! Please stop digging!' I raced around the flower bed and grabbed hold of a disgruntled Buddy's collar. 'Buddy, you do spoil yourself sometimes. Look at all the other dogs having fun, and now you're going to have to stay on your lead!'

I attached Buddy's lead, and surreptitiously glanced around me to check there wasn't a park keeper on the prowl. I patted the sod of grass back in place and pushed the daffodil back into the hole out of which I thought it might have been dug. I stood up, brushed the soil from my hands, and trod the sod of grass down to make sure it didn't look out of place.

As my foot pressed hard on the turf, I looked behind me to see what Rachel was doing. My heart sank when I saw her standing next to Pete and his brother. She was talking to them both through the chain-link fence which surrounded the tennis courts. She twirled her hair around her finger as I'd seen her do many times before. It had become a habit of hers since we were at school, and we shared an article from a *Jackie* magazine about how to attract a new boyfriend. Her head was cocked on one side as she intently listened to what they were saying, something else the article had suggested we do in pursuit of a mate. I sighed – she was so transparent.

I reluctantly walked towards them and as I got closer, I heard them talking about music and how awful it was that Dead or Alive's *You Spin Me Right Round* had got to number one. Pete said he hoped the new Phil Collins record would soon make it to the top of the charts instead.

He loved listening to music, I already knew that. When I was still at school, I would divert my route to deliberately walk past his house every day, and I'd hear all sorts of loud music blasting through the open window – mostly rock music. I sometimes wondered, hoped perhaps, whether he had it playing loud for my benefit because he knew I was walking past, but would then chastise myself for being silly.

I loved him. I'd loved him since I was fifteen years old, and he smiled down at me when he opened the door to the art department to let me go through the doorway first. He was seventeen at the time: a sixth former; tall and slim with long, dark brown, straight, floppy hair. I'd blushed to the core and my heart had leapt. I used that art lesson to ruminate with Rachel about what had just happened – had that gorgeous guy smiled at me? Did he like me? I was worried he might like her, but she swore she would never in a million years ever go after someone like him. Not that there was anything wrong with him, he just wasn't her type, she added!

The art teacher told us off for our frivolity, and added, 'You girls need to get on with your work or you'll miss your break!' We must have been annoying him, because he was usually one of the more fun teachers. We both obediently shut up and couldn't look at one another in case we burst into fits of laughter. Later on, we giggled all the way to the science block, having persuaded the art teacher that we couldn't possibly do without our break as we needed to visit the ladies.

In the following couple of years, I'd thought about

Pete all the time, always hoping for chance meetings. He was always with a group of lads, sometimes girls too, and it seemed my unrequited love was hopeless.

Often in the evenings I'd walk Buddy past Pete's house in the hope I'd catch a glimpse of him, always hoping Buddy would pick up a particularly good scent on the lamppost outside Pete's house. Poor Buddy was taken out in all weathers. 'It's only water!' I'd shout back to Mum as she'd call from the sitting room that I would catch pneumonia if I went out in that pouring rain. 'We'll be fine, we'll dry off.' I wasn't even sure that was how people caught pneumonia, or at that time, even what pneumonia was. I figured it was just something dramatic she said to frighten me.

Pete's bedroom window was invariably left open, even when the weather was chilly. Each time I walked past his house, I would try to hear what he was listening to. He tended to listen to the same song over and over for days on end. I used to imagine him reaching for the needle on the record player and delicately placing it back on one of the dark black bands on the album, which indicated the start of his latest favourite song.

If I figured out what he was listening to, I'd take the money from my paper round into town the following Saturday and find the record. There were times when in the music shop in town I would sing a line or two to the tousle-haired boy who had a Saturday job there. Usually, he would know right away which song I meant, meaning I could pay for the record and head home as quickly as possible to listen to it. Other times, I would stand there humming the tune over and over until someone in the shop got which record it was. This was usually when the shop was a lot quieter.

I often wondered whether the Saturday assistant and his boss were having a good laugh at me once I'd left the shop. One time I stood there telling them the story of a song I'd heard on the radio, which I heard again as I walked past Pete's house (only I didn't tell them the bit about walking past Pete's house – I didn't want them to think I was strange or anything!) 'You know,' I said defiantly, as the two of them looked at me in that curious, almost polite, yet meditative way. 'It's got something to do with coins or money?'

'Something like that anyway.' I said, meekly responding to their by then blank expressions.

'Money?'

'Yes?' I smiled, pleased that they were taking me seriously.

'No, I mean is it *Money*, by Pink Floyd?'

Now it was my turn to look blank. 'No, I know that one, it's called *Money*. I wouldn't need to ask about that one if it's already called *Money*.' I stopped myself from rudely rolling my eyes at him.

'I guess not,' the younger one of the two said.

And then I remembered a key piece of important information. 'Oh, and it's by a woman … or at least it's a woman who sings it?'

They both stood there with fresh blank expressions etched on their faces. 'Abba! *The Winner Takes It All*?' the younger one asked with an element of doubt now in his voice. It wasn't the style of music I usually bought.

'Nooooo!' I laughed and flung my arms up in the air in frustration. That eye roll was becoming harder to resist from doing.

Eventually the older one of the two, the one who looked a bit more worldly-wise, said,' I know, I know what it is, The Pretenders, *Brass in Pocket*.'

'That's it!' I exclaimed and began to sing it, much to the amusement of the other customers who'd lined up behind me, and then added, 'I'll have one of those on a forty-five please.'

Then came the bombshell,' I'm afraid we don't have it on a forty-five … it's been a couple of years since it was out. We have this, though!' And he produced a far more expensive LP and thrust it in front of me.

They had a debate with one another about whether it fitted my usual genres of music. I didn't care whether it fitted or not, it was certainly what Pete had been listening to. And that was good enough for me.

I grudgingly handed over all the money I had in the world and left the shop, hoping all my effort had been worth it.

Whatever music I'd bought, once I was safely in my room, I would sit on my bed with Buddy at my side and dream of a time when Pete and I would sit huddled together listening to the dulcet tones of Jon Anderson from Yes, the coarse, jarring music of ACDC, or the deep and meaningful lyrics of Pink Floyd.

There were times when, out and about outside of school, Pete would be out walking his own dog, Jess, and we'd pass by one another and say 'Hi.' Those were perhaps the most infuriating times, because if I saw him heading my way, I would always fumble to think of something clever to say. The best I ever mustered was, while nodding across at Jess and smiling at her, 'She's a lovely dog.' At this, Pete would just grin and say Buddy was too.

I once sent him a Valentine's card and signed it: 'Roses are red, violets are blue, I have a dream, and it looks just like you.' My hands were shaking, and my legs were like jelly as I walked Buddy over to Pete's street and delicately put the card through his letterbox early on Valentine's morning. There weren't any lights on in his house, but as the card dropped on the mat, I heard Jess offer a short bark. I froze to the spot and listened to make sure she didn't bark again. I held on to Buddy to make sure he didn't respond to her. I could see he was desperate to do something, but instead he gave a tiny whimper. Thankfully Jess didn't bark again, almost as though she wasn't sure whether she'd heard anything or not; she was simply protecting her charges just in case.

Later that Valentine's Day evening, I was doing my homework but couldn't concentrate, due to the butterflies that had taken up residence deep in my belly. I wondered whether Pete had realized the card was from me. It was about 6.30pm and I was watching through the dining room window into the dark, wintry cold street, when I saw Pete's brother's car pull up outside my house. My heart pounding, I watched from behind the net curtain as Pete eased himself out of the passenger seat and raced up the drive to my front door. I could see he had a card in his hand.

Once the car had zoomed away leaving a trail of blue smoke in its wake, and I had retrieved the card from the hall mat, Mum stood next to me as I read his words. She hugged me and I immediately burst into tears.

On the front of the card was a cute cartoon dog and inside he'd written 'Love from P'. Underneath his message he had put two small kisses. He loved me! At last, I knew he felt the same about me as I did about him. That night I slept with the card held tight to my heart.

In the year that followed I found my dream job working as a trainee nurse in a local veterinary surgery. One day a few months after I began working there, I was walking home from work and noticed there was a purple Austin Allegro moving slowly beside me. I'd seen kerb crawlers in the red-light district in another part of town and quickened my pace. But then I heard a loud toot of the horn. I bravely glanced towards the road. My heart did somersaults when I realized it was him – Pete. He wound down the window and pointed to the spare seat in the front of the car. 'You want a lift home?'

My heart leapt again, and I felt the heat rise in my face. 'Yes, yes, of course – thank you.'

We chatted about my job and his course at the local college. He said he'd be heading off to university a few weeks later. He asked after Buddy, and I asked how Jess was doing. But then, all too soon, we were parked outside my house. He told me he was going to the local pub later that night. I hesitated and wondered whether that was it, whether he was going to ask me for a date. He paused, and then added, 'You know, a few of the guys are coming over.'

My heart sank, but I smiled and got out of the car. I said I hoped to see him soon. When I got inside, I went to my room and cried for three whole hours. While I wailed away to myself, in the background Pink Floyd's *Wish You Were Here* album played several times over. My parents were out but my younger sister, Hannah, sat beside me and stroked my arm. But I was inconsolable. 'Guys, they're not worth it …' she said. She was echoing the words I'd said to her just months before when her first boyfriend, a boy named Ben who was in her year at school, had two-timed her.

I thought of calling Rachel and asking if she wanted to go to the pub later that night but decided it would be too obvious. I wondered whether he said he would be there so I would go there too, but in the end, I backed out and stayed home, wallowing in my self-pity.

And so, several years later, there Rachel and I were in the park. Strangely, after the Valentine's card and car incidents Pete and I had never really spoken to one another – perhaps out of embarrassment and not really knowing how or even whether to progress things. This was to the extent that my subsequent walks with Buddy had been deliberately in the opposite direction to Pete's house. I didn't know why I suddenly felt embarrassed around him. It could have been the remnants of some teenage angst. The sort of stuff Rachel and I used to read in all those teenage magazines. And yet, after all those years, there I was, finally about to talk to him again.

I took a deep breath and approached the three of them. I felt that familiar surge of butterflies passing through me. My feet heavy, my nervous legs carried me over to the fence that separated the tennis courts from the rest of the park. Pete immediately smiled his big wide smile and crouched to put his fingers through the chain-link fence to speak to Buddy. 'Hey Buddy, how're you doing old fella? I haven't seen you in ages. You're going a little grey around the old face there.' Those feelings I had suppressed about him came rushing back to me. I still thought he was lovely.

Rachel and I chatted to them for half an hour or so. We then sat on the bench outside the tennis court to cheer them along as they finished their game. Poor old Buddy was still attached to his lead following his earlier border-digging misdeed. I didn't dare let him off again because I'd noticed the park keeper was on the warpath.

Once they'd finished their game, with Ade winning three sets to two, the four of us took a frustrated Buddy for a walk around the perimeter of the park. The trees were pushing promising leaf buds through their branches and fine stems, the birds were delivering their hopeful song for the impending mating season, and there was still a cold nip in the air.

I pulled my scarf around my neck and zipped the front of my thin, blue anorak. Pete smiled and offered his own jacket that he was carrying. He said he was still warm from his game, and he had a few layers on anyway. His muscular legs were by then covered by his jeans and he'd pulled a hooded sweatshirt over his T-shirt. Happy that he was warm enough and not simply being chivalrous, I gratefully accepted the extra layer.

His jacket was huge on me, but it smelt of him, and I snuggled into it. It was a new, unfamiliar smell, and one which was comforting. Rachel walked ahead with Ade. Perhaps there was something going on there, too? I doubted it though because she'd just started dating the latest 'love of her life', Dave The

Rave, a local disc jockey. It was more likely they were giving Pete and me some space, which I was grateful for, so Pete and I could talk without any interruptions. It dawned on me that I was actually chatting to him properly for the first time.

Buddy was finally forgiven for his earlier crime, and I let him off his lead while we walked to the edge of the park. Despite having been granted clemency, I was watching him how a hawk watches its prey before pouncing on it. He, however, was desperately attempting to keep us all together by weaving in and out of the trees and between Rachel and Ade, and the two of us.

Us. How many times through the previous years had I dreamed of an 'us'? Deep inside, I questioned what was going on between Pete and me. I wondered whether the events of the day would actually lead to anything. I hadn't seen him for so long, but we were older, no longer school kids. Even so, were we wiser and better able to communicate how we felt? I had a sick feeling in my tummy that perhaps he was simply being friendly. He might even have already been dating someone.

Pete was dutifully picking up and throwing a saliva-soaked tennis ball he had donated to Buddy. As Buddy jumped up and down to get the ball, and Pete threw the ball as far as the eye could see so my big dog could chase after it, I remembered why I had loved Pete so much from afar. Years before, shortly after the event at the art room doorway, I'd seen him in the park, enthusiastically throwing a ball for Jess, and my unrequited love for him had flourished.

About fifty yards from the huge, black, ornamental iron gates to the park, I attached Buddy's lead. As we walked along the busy streets chatting to one another, I realized that all too soon, Pete and Ade would be heading off in one direction, and Rachel, Buddy, and me in another.

The crossroads which included the corner of my street, that's where we would say our final farewells, and then, I thought, perhaps we'd not see each other again for ages – years even. There could be a moment in the minutes that followed which would change the fate of my life forever. I fell silent, wondering how, once we reached the impending parting place, that afternoon would end. I wondered what he would do. Would he lean forward and kiss me on the cheek? Would we hug? I chastised myself for my silly thoughts and stupid expectations. I was no longer that fifteen-year-old schoolgirl who had admired Pete from afar; the girl who blushed every time I passed him in the school corridors. Blushing which, of course, had been aided and abetted by Rachel, who'd eagerly nudged me every time she spotted him.

When Rachel and Ade reached the corner of my road, they stopped and turned around to wait for us. Rachel had the widest smile on her face. Because he knew her so well, my closest confidante, Buddy, started whining and pulling on the lead to go and see her. He was desperate to get to her as quickly as possible. Cherishing every precious passing second with Pete, I thought *Whoa Buddy*, *don't go so fast.*

Pete finally spoke and his words came out in a rush. I sensed he, too, was possibly racing against time, against the fifty or so steps we had until we caught up with the other two. 'It's Sunday tomorrow,' he said quite matter-of-factly. 'Do you want to take Buddy and Jess out for a walk?' Looking briefly ahead and then quickly back at me, he added, 'you know, just the two of us?'

Something deep inside me flipped and I felt almost sick with excitement, 'Yes, definitely! What time?' All those old magazines would have suggested I was too eager, too keen to react to the offer of a date, I should have appeared cool, but all that so-called advice had long before gone out of the window.

Only about twenty more steps to go before we caught up with them.

'I'll walk over with Jess, and we can leave from yours at, say, one o' clock?'

I was so happy. We had finally made it; finally got together and arranged an actual date. Up until then I'd felt I'd known him so well, and yet that day we spoke more to one another than we had in the five years since he had opened that art classroom door to let me through.

Fate is a strange thing, and on that day, my heart sang with joy at the possibilities in front of us. I wondered why we hadn't got together before but lingering on those thoughts for too long was futile. We'd finally got there, and that was all that mattered. I danced into the house, unhooked Buddy's lead, and the two of us went upstairs. I put my new Meatloaf *Dead Ringer* album on repeat and sang my heart out.

Several Meatloaf album cycles later, Buddy and I grabbed our respective dinners, and then curled up together on top of the bed and fell asleep. We were both exhausted and seemed satisfied with the day we'd had. At about 3am I woke and realized someone had closed my curtains for me the night before. They'd also placed two thick blankets over Buddy and me. *Thanks, Mum*, I thought, and nuzzled into the warmth of my beloved dog. I told him we were going to have great fun later that day and that he'd better get plenty of rest for a nice long walk with his new friend Jess. The two of us drifted back to sleep until six in the morning. When I woke again it took me a while to register what that knot lingering deep inside my tummy was. When I realized, I shot out of bed and raced to the next room to wake my sister Hannah.

Chapter 2

At breakfast I couldn't eat, and when lunch time came and I still couldn't find an appetite, Mum handed me a glass of orange juice, a banana, and some ginger-nut biscuits. She told me I had to eat something, or I'd waste away – I apparently couldn't live off love alone. 'Muuum!' I appealed to her, while my six feet four inches, seventeen-year-old brother Jack sniggered into his post-breakfast/pre-lunch banana and peanut butter sandwich. When would he *ever* stop growing? My parents were often prone to asking him when his legs would stop being hollow.

I spent the entire morning pulling all my clothes out of the wardrobe, trying them on, and then parading in front of Mum, Dad, Jack, and Hannah. Only Mum and Hannah were still interested by the time I was on the tenth outfit – Dad and Jack sidling out of the room to go and 'look at a broken fuel pipe' in the garage. In the end, I tried on practically everything I owned, finally settling for a pair of faded jeans and a black round-necked jumper, which had frustratingly been the first set of clothes I'd tried on. At five to one, having added my blue denim jacket, a purple print scarf, a pair of blue baseball pumps, and a lilac beanie hat (this being added at the last minute by Mum in case I *caught pneumonia* or *froze to death out there*), I opened the door before Pete had a chance to ring the bell.

Depriving me of any level of decorum, Buddy lunged forward as soon as he saw Jess standing on his doorstep. Pete laughed as Buddy leapt around Jess in excitement; Jess was much better behaved and stood there calmly, politely wagging her brindle tail.

With Buddy beside me, I quickly guided Pete to the end of the street, so we'd be out of the way of prying eyes peeking from behind net curtains. Once on the corner, we had the option of three directions. Pete turned, smiled at me, and asked, 'Where do you want to go?' The early springtime sun was reflected in his deep blue eyes, and for a moment I couldn't speak. It was a moment I had yearned to happen for years, and once it was there, I became tongue-tied. He was so lovely, and all the times I had imagined that moment had not given me false hopes. With a quizzical look on his face, he smiled, cocked his head to one side, pointed a finger, and indicated straight on.

I looked to where he was pointing, wondering what he meant. And then it dawned on me.

'Yes. Oh gosh, of course.' Then, not wanting to seem as though I had nothing to say, I suggested, 'We can go through the park and then perhaps over the railway and on to the canal bridleways.' It was going to be quite a long walk, but I wanted the afternoon to last for as long as possible. Because of the dark nights and extremely cold winter I hadn't taken Buddy to the canals since the autumn, he would be glad of the extra-special long walk. 'Will Jess be okay walking over the bridge which goes over the railway? You know, just in case a train goes by?'

'She'll be fine, won't you Jess?' Her ears pricked up at the sound of her name and she wagged her tail. I couldn't believe it; I had found someone who talked to his dog, just like I had long chats with Buddy. Pete could do no wrong.

Once we were in the park, we let the dogs off their leads to run free for a while. I warned Buddy to leave the plants alone and not go digging up any grass, but he was completely oblivious to anything I said; he had a new playmate and that was the most exciting thing in the world to such a boisterous dog. The two dogs gamboled over one another and made up their own chasing game. Pete and I walked along behind them, laughing as the two of them burnt off lots of energy; energy which, if they'd realized how far we were going, they would have saved for the long walk ahead of us.

As emerging leaves and flowers overhead caused

soft, shifting dapples of light to scatter across the ground like kaleidoscope confetti, we chatted about our families and friends. When I laughed at some comment Pete made about his younger brother Julian having liked me for ages, Pete laughed too, and then he, oh so naturally, took hold of my hand in his. Sparks of warmth travelled from my hand through the whole of my body.

That feeling.

That was what I had spent so many teenage nights dreaming of.

We didn't talk for a short while after that, instead we simply strolled along hand in hand, smiling at the dogs, smiling at passers-by – feeling comfortable and enjoying the warmth of the moment.

All too soon, it was time to put the dogs' leads back on because we were heading out onto the footpath for about a mile, before we'd reach the bridge across the railway and then onto the canal. Once we got to the tow path it would be safe enough to let them off again, just so long as there weren't too many people around. Both dogs came bounding over with their tongues lolling out of their mouths. Their chests heaved as their lungs tried to take in as much air as possible.

We'd had to let go of one another's hands to attach the dogs' leads, but any innate yet unwarranted fear I had that we would never hold hands again were unfounded, because as soon as we were safely on the footpath with the two dogs attached to us, our free hands were comfortably drawn back together. In such a short space of time it had become something natural.

As we walked over the bridge a passenger train thundered along on the tracks beneath us. I gasped, and Pete held tighter to my hand. We laughed. Both dogs were surprisingly unperturbed by the sounds and vibrations which reverberated in the air. They were both pulling on their leads because they could see the canal walkway just a hundred yards or so away; the place where I was sure they both sensed their freedom awaited.

Once at the edge of the tow path we did a quick scan of the way ahead, to make sure it wasn't too busy to let the dogs off again. There was an elderly man away in the distance walking with his collie dog, but other than them, the path appeared to be empty.

On the canal, a brightly painted barge chugged along. The family aboard waved as they went by, and we cheerfully waved back. Once they were safely past, we let the two dogs off their leads. Just as though they hadn't just half an hour earlier been exhausted, the two of them went bounding along the path.

The topic of the Valentine's cards came up and my heart sank with embarrassment. I felt my skin flush pink. 'I really wanted to ask you to go on a date, you know?'

I looked up at him, 'You mean on the day you gave me a lift home from work.'

'Yeah,' he nodded,' 'but you know it was my friends who tormented me in the end, and I guess I should have been stronger with them.'

'What do you mean, your friends?'

'Well, you know …' he seemed embarrassed now, 'I guess it goes back to when we were at school and with me being a couple of years above you, they used to tease me about liking you.'

So, for all those years I hadn't been imagining any of it. 'It's okay, at least we're together now.' I smiled up at him and held tighter to his hand. I then added, 'You know, maybe back then it wouldn't have worked. We're older now, perhaps this way we'll stand a better chance. Back then you might have finished up getting bored with me.'

'Never!' he smiled, and I thought he was going to

kiss me. Our first kiss! But then the two of us simultaneously noticed the two dogs were harassing the old man and his collie dog.

'Sorry, so sorry!' We both called out, as we chased after our wayward dogs and rescued the collie from Buddy's unrequited amorous advances.

'You're not meant to do things like that, you've been neutered!' I told Buddy, and then turned and apologized once more to the disheveled old guy, and his equally unkempt, black and white dog.

Arthur was the old man's name. He seemed lonely and as though he wanted to talk to us for a while, so we stayed to chat to him. 'Excitable dog you've got there!' He nodded in the direction of the now-leashed Buddy. 'Youth on his side though. Yes, indeed, youth on his side. Not like poor old Eric here.'

'Eric?' I said, 'what an interesting name for a dog.' I was feeling curious about Buddy's advances on a dog named Eric – he'd never been inclined to be that way with male dogs before, only females.

'Ah, yes, old Eric. Got him from the rescue place thirteen years ago, I did. He was such a skinny little runt – reminded me of someone I met in the war. Eric Guthrie.' He paused to chuckle to himself, and Pete and I exchanged a smile. 'Soon as I saw scrawny old Eric here, I knew there was only one name I could give him. The wife thought I'd gone bonkers, but she got used to calling him by that name.' He paused, and Pete and I waited, instinctively suspecting that he hadn't yet finished with his tale of the two Erics.

'Yes, Eric … lost his life in 1944 at Normandy – Eric number one, of course.' He paused again, this time apparently waiting for a response, but before we could say anything he added, 'You know, the D-Day landings.'

'That's awful! I'm so sorry.' Pete offered. 'Were you there too?'

'Oh yes, I was there. I held Eric against me as he died, and then, once the war was over, I made the trip to Lancashire to see his missus. Distraught she was, and her with four children to take care of an' all. She'll have got her widow's pension, mind, but I'm sure it wouldn't have been enough. I think she had designs on me filling his place – a bit desperate I think …'. He paused and indulged in another short chuckle to himself. 'But I had to be firm with her and tell her that I had my Betty waiting for me at home.' His expression changed to one much more serious as he went on to tell us his Betty was sick, and he was worried he might be losing her.

What could we say? We both stood there and

nodded in sympathy.

'You two?' Arthur asked with a nod of his head in our direction. 'What's your story?'

Pete and I shifted a little uncomfortably, and then I smiled, 'It's actually our first date.' I felt the colour rise in my cheeks and smiled over at Pete, who was grinning back at me.

Arthur took hold of Pete's arm and said, 'You take good care of this one, young man. The years will fly past and you don't want to look back and regret that you didn't do the right thing in staying with her. I knew as soon as I saw Betty that she was *The One*. I've seen many a man regret not grasping happiness when it was staring him in the face. The grass is never, ever greener, you take my word for it. Fate leads us to be with the ones we are meant to be with.' He smiled and chuckled to himself again. 'You mark my words, young fella! My Betty has been there for me through the toughest of times, and me for her too. But now, well, I imagine what will be will be!'

We sat on the bench and stayed a while longer to talk more about our dogs and Arthur's time in the war. Old Eric the collie was apparently a bit of a character and went everywhere with his cat toy. Arthur reached deep into his coat pocket and revealed a ragged, chewed up old black and white toy in the shape of a cat. The head was hanging off and it was covered in mats of dried dirt and saliva, but as soon as it came into view, the old collie lifted his head and stood up, excitedly wagging his fluffy black and white tail. He danced around in a circle and then jumped up and down on all four paws, something collie dogs were often prone to doing. I noticed Buddy's eyes light up at the sight of the toy. I kept a tight hold of him, for fear he would snatch the cat from old Eric's jaws.

Daylight was dimming, and so we told Arthur we'd loved talking to him and we hoped we would see him again. I stroked Eric on his wise old head and looked deep into his opaque, cataract-filled eyes. 'I hope to see you again soon, old Eric.' Holding hands, Pete and I headed back along the banks of the canal before it got dark.

On the way back through the park we got talking about music and I confessed how I used to often walk past his house when I was at school. He admitted that the day he held the door to the art room open for me that he'd worked out that I had art the session after him, and that day he'd lingered in the small lobby until he could see me walking along the corridor.

He laughed when I told him about the times I sang to the guys in the music shop. I told him there was one time I was singing *Whisky in the Jar* by Thin Lizzy to them, and they had started dancing around the aisles. One of them had come and grasped hold of my hands and danced me around the shop. Pete laughed again and said he'd never known. He'd seen me walking past his house a lot but hadn't known I was on some sort of pilgrimage to find out what he was listening to – he simply thought it was my regular route.

With the Thin Lizzy song in our heads, we began to sing it together. Although there were people still rushing along over on the other side of the park, in the dying light and by the yellow hue of the streetlamps, we began dancing around the trees, singing the song out loud. There was no one else nearby. It was just the two of us along with our confused dogs, who were both excitedly following us in and out of the trees and along the paths.

'… *There's whisky in the jar-o* …'

Chapter 3

Monday at work, I could hardly concentrate. Pete and I had agreed to meet that night after evening clinic was over. That morning in the operating theatre as I passed the instruments across the drapes to Tomas, the Dutch locum vet who was fixing a fractured femur on a middle-aged spaniel's hind leg, all I could think about was that that evening I would be seeing Pete again. Nevertheless, I manipulated the dog's foot and lower limb as Tomas instructed. Finally, happy that the stainless-steel pin was in place and would stabilize his leg until the bone was healed, Tomas set about suturing; first the muscle, then the subcutaneous tissues, and finally the clean, pink skin. The leg would later have extensive purple bruising from all the manipulation during surgery.

Tomas had brightened the practice with his boogieing around the operating table to whatever was playing on the radio, his favourite songs being like those Pete, and I would listen to. That morning, I was suddenly called back from my thoughts by his twirling around and doing a strange little tap dance once he'd applied the final suture. 'That's another one done!' He was a confident vet who was in the country for just a year. He was covering for us until we could fill a permanent post and had been with us for ten months. We wondered whether he might stay. In the time since he arrived, he'd helped to see me through the stresses of my final veterinary nursing exams, jollying me along and quizzing me with random anatomy questions whenever he was operating. Until that weekend and meeting up with Pete, I'd thought Tomas was rather nice and that perhaps he was someone I'd like to spend more time with. Sally, one of the other nurses, an older woman with three kids, had teased me that she thought he liked me too. How quickly the heart can change its allegiance! I smiled to myself as I thought of mine and Pete's Thin Lizzy rendition the previous day.

Tomas came up to the spaniel's head end where I was checking his gums to make sure they were nice and pink, and checking the eye reflexes and eye position to check his level of consciousness. We'd switched off his anaesthetic and were making sure he was well enough to go through to the recovery kennels. Tomas checked him too, to make sure he was satisfied with how he was doing. 'Okay then. All good on The Western Front for Stan the super-spaniel!' He then hesitated and looked at me across the operating table. 'So, Stan-spaniel's doing good, but are *you* okay?'

Oops, I thought, he'd obviously sensed I'd been a little distracted. 'What, me? Yes, I'm fine,' I answered, perhaps a little too enthusiastically. He smiled that smile which, on the Friday before I had thought to be quite cute. I responded with a wide, happy smile, but inside my smile was lying to him.

He seemed relieved. 'Okay then, let's lift this lump of a dog through to the recovery room for Sally to look after, and we can go onto the next one – a terrier spay, is it?'

'Uh huh. A little dog named Meg.' I agreed and helped him lift Stan-dog through to the recovery room.

I don't know quite how I got through my work that day, but that evening was only the second of so many dates Pete and I had. In those early days we often reflected on the time we'd missed and wished we had dated sooner, but I guess fate has a way of dealing you a certain set of cards – and it was what it was.

Just a couple of weeks after our first date I was invited over to his house to meet his parents. Just like the first time we'd gone on a date, I spent hours getting ready. Pete was picking me up in his car, and as 6pm approached, I checked the mirror for the hundredth time. I'd seen his parents from a distance on my frequent excursions past his house when we had all still been at school, but this was for real, and I so wanted to make a good impression on them.

Tomas, Sally, and one of the head vets, Carla, had

teased me all week about the 'meeting the parents' event. Tomas had been fine once he found out I was dating someone. The gossip machine at work was never going to miss this new snippet of information. When Sally told him about it in a jokey way in front of me, he joked back that he'd missed his chance and that he'd been hoping to ask me for a date the next week neither of us was scheduled to be on call. I blushed, feeling flattered, and he laughed. I wasn't sure whether it was all just a part of the teasing they were all investing so much time in doing.

Meeting Pete's parents was quite an experience. His Mum wore flowery dungarees and a lime green vest. Because it was still quite chilly outside, she'd covered her outfit with a long, fluffy, red cardigan. Her greying hair was tied in a ponytail with a yellow and red, floral headscarf. When Pete and I walked into their dining room, through the window we could see her outside in the heated greenhouse picking herbs for dinner. She looked up and waved, before wafting through the French doors. She rushed over and gave me the tightest hug. Recognizing me from all our recent trips out, Jess jumped up to join in the embrace. Once I was released from Pete's mum's grip, Jess nudged at my leg to get her own individual 'Hello,' perhaps wondering where Buddy was.

'I'm so happy to meet you at last! Just call me

Helen! I hate it when people have that awkward 'What should I call her?' conundrum, so definitely, absolutely, Helen is just fine!' She offered a wide Cheshire cat grin and grasped hold of my arm, tugging me away from Pete and Jess, 'Come, follow me through here and I'll introduce you to Pete's dad, Jeff.'

Jeff was stood next to a radiator in nothing but his underpants. He seemed not to have noticed we'd arrived and was shaking the creases out of a pair of stiff jeans he'd just taken off the radiator. He came over to me and shook my hand. Grateful that he hadn't attempted to hug me in only his graying Y-fronts, I glanced at Pete, who offered an apologetic smile and rolled his eyes.

Jeff released my hand from his ungainly grip and lethargically pulled the cardboard jeans over his Y-fronts. He then reached for an equally stiff and wrinkled orange and green striped T-shirt, which had also been flung over the top of the radiator. Once on, he stretched the T-shirt downwards in an attempt to eliminate some of the creases, and said, 'There, that'll do! Who needs an iron anyway?' He chortled to himself – and I couldn't help but warm to him.

The four of us set about preparing dinner and I thought of how Mum would have had everything ready to plate up whenever we had visitors over, but it was fun chopping vegetables and mixing a cake. Helen said the cake would take until about midnight to be ready to eat, but we could just eat it warm if we had to.

We finally sat down to eat at nine o'clock. Pete's younger brother Julian had emerged from his room and seemed bemused by the whole situation. Pete had told me Julian was now over me, having met a girl at the local youth club. About half an hour after we started eating, Ade arrived home from his work at a local photography studio. He and his boss had spent the day printing the pictures from a wedding the previous weekend and from a christening the day before.

Helen got me to sit opposite Pete. Over dinner it was clear there were some 'in-jokes' which had to be explained to me – some of these stories went back some way into their family history. Helen and Jeff had some tales from when they got together in the early sixties. They pointed to photographs on the wall, ones which demonstrated their early family days with their young boys in the time of love, peace, and flower power. Pete and both his brothers joined in with their stories, and at times it was like watching some strange sitcom playing out in front of me. I felt warm inside and as though I had known those people for my whole life.

They talked about their beloved camper van, and Helen promised to give me a tour of it after dinner. It was a converted ex-ambulance, and blue and white with flower stickers along the side. In the window was the archetypal worn CND sticker. The van was a little rusty here and there but looked so very cozy inside. It was obviously well-used and much-loved. It was apparently road worthy and legal, but Helen admitted she would no longer trust taking it out of the UK. 'You and Pete should take it for a holiday in the summer! I'm sure Jess would love to have a holiday too – and your dog Buddy – what a lovely name for a dog by the way. I can't wait to meet him; I've heard all about his antics.' She smiled at me and winked, before pulling me back through to where the guys were clearing away the dishes.

I'd noticed she had a habit of winking, usually at Jeff, and I figured some of their stories were tales which had grown arms and legs and been elaborated on over the years. Or perhaps there were some things that the rest of the family were not privy to – some secret back stories.

'Pete, you should go off on holiday with the dogs this summer?' Helen suggested.

Pete looked over at me. 'Would you like that?'

'Absolutely!' I answered. 'Maybe a group of us

could go and we could take a couple of tents as well.'

'Sure, that sounds fun – Ade you have to come along too.'

'I'm not going, that sounds gross,' Julian interrupted. 'I've got better things to do with my summer!' He groaned.

'Ah, that's okay, don't worry about it, Jules, you probably wouldn't have enjoyed it anyway.' Pete smiled across at me – he seemed relieved to not be having to have his younger brother tag along. Ade, though, he was close to Ade and I'm sure he wanted him to be there. Ade said he'd think about it – perhaps he wanted to wait and see who else was going along.

By the end of the evening, I was exhausted. On the way home in Pete's car, I wanted to know what he thought about the concept of Rachel and Ade as a couple. 'Maybe,' he said, 'but I think he's still smarting from a relationship he had with an older woman who had a kid. They were together for two years and he loved the little girl as though she was his own. Then out of the blue, the woman went back to her husband. That was about a year and a half ago and he's had a couple of dates since, but I think he's got trust issues.'

'Oh.' I said, trying to hide my disappointment.' For a few moments I mulled over what he'd said. 'I guess when I think about it, they're not terribly well-suited anyway. Ade's quite quiet and Rachel tends to go for outgoing types like Dave The Rave. I don't like him, but I suppose he's not for me to like or not like. I just don't trust him – I think he'll break her heart!'

Pete laughed as he pulled the car into my street and stopped the engine. It was almost one am, and so, after exploring some more the likelihood of Rachel and Ade as a viable couple, we agreed it would be better to leave everything to fate. 'Since Ade and Martha broke up, he's thrown himself into his work – perhaps our camping trip will give him a chance to relax. He'll maybe feel it's time to move on – we can hope!'

Pete reached over and kissed me, and then I touched him on his nose, at which he wrinkled it up like a rabbit. We were developing some of the crazy mannerisms like those of his parents. I told him I loved him and went inside to steal Buddy from Hannah's room, before heading off to bed.

As I lay in my bed, I figured at some point with the way things were going with Pete and me that we would need to get a place of our own. It was quick, but then we both felt as though we'd known each other for years. Holding that thought, I curled up next to Buddy and buried my face into his fur, inhaling his wonderful, comforting canine smell. I fell asleep with the image of me and Pete living with our dogs in a little cottage next to a wood.

Chapter 4

The summer that followed we spent travelling around Scotland in the camper with Rachel, her new boyfriend Jake (she'd successfully ditched Dave after he was discovered in the ladies' toilet with another friend of Rachel's). We also had with us Ade and my ditsy, flame-haired sister Hannah. Somehow, we'd all managed to free ourselves of any real responsibilities for a couple of months. I'd been saving since I began my job – I'd never even been sure what I was saving for, but this trip seemed to be the right thing on which to splash out my hard-earned cash.

I could have kissed my boss Carla when she said she would get in a locum veterinary nurse to cover for me while I was away. It felt as though the six of us were somehow seizing an opportunity that would only happen then, in that time before we all got caught up in our careers and settling down – and perhaps even bigger responsibilities like having kids.

With Jeff and Helen helping us, we did some work on the camper. And then, one sunny day in late-June, we headed off on our travels north. Hannah, Jake, and I had never been to Scotland, so the road trip felt as though we were going to some distant, far-off country full of Celtic mystery, amid rolling hills and mountains.

Pete and Ade knew Scotland well, because the family and the camper had travelled there many times over the years, so the two of them shared the driving. The two dogs squashed in beside us all, both seeming happy to be joining us on our adventure. Our respective parents were equally happy, as it meant they could do what they wanted for the summer, rather than having to look for suitable dog sitters.

Our aim was to head north to Scotland via the north-west route, entering Scotland just past Carlisle at Gretna Green. We planned to then drive up the west coast, along the top of Scotland, and come back down via the east. We had our map of Scotland stuck onto a piece of card to stiffen it and had circled all the sites of interest and possible campsites for our overnight stays.

We had heaps of pre-recorded cassette tapes that each of us had been avidly recording onto with all our favourite songs. We left from Pete and Ade's house, and once their parents had hugged us all several times, we pulled away in the camper and waved to them. It felt as though we were heading off on some school trip. But it was no school trip, we'd all grown up and were heading on a real grown-up holiday. I felt a sense of excitement deep inside me – how much all our lives had changed. This was the beginning of something big for all of us. It felt like some transition, a rite of passage into true adulthood.

Pete had put together a compilation of Pink Floyd, Rush, Yes, Led Zeppelin, and Nazareth songs. We'd heard the songs so often that we sang our hearts out, all reminiscing about the first time we'd ever heard *Dark Side of the Moon*. For me, it had been in a friend's basement (and strangely not, as the others might have imagined, emanating from Pete's bedroom window). There were about ten of us left there at the end of a party and someone put on the whole album. I'd never heard anything quite like it. I immediately went out the following weekend and bought it. For Pete, it had been Ade who introduced him to *Dark Side of the Moon*. Everyone seemed to have memories of when they'd first heard it, or who played it to them first.

After a couple of hours, we stopped at a service station to get some refreshments and take the dogs for a walk around by the trees. A couple of hours later as we passed the border from England into Scotland, we cheered; our holiday in this land full of castles, mountains, and the home of the Loch Ness Monster was finally a reality.

That first night, after about four and a half hours of

driving, we decided to stay in a campsite just outside the small village of Rockcliffe. Once the tents were up, and we'd eaten beans and baked potatoes we cooked on a small fire, we took the dogs down to the rocky, sandy beach for stone skimming competitions. No one could beat Jake as his stone bounced on the rolling water fourteen times. Once we were bored with that game and it was obvious no one had a chance of beating fourteen bounces, we threw the frisbee for the dogs for a while. Then we sat on the beach until the sun had disappeared from the pastel pink and purple sky. All feeling weary, we headed back to the campsite.

At Caerlaverock Castle the next day, Jake and Rachel initiated a game of hide and seek. Later, we continued our castle tour and went to Threave Castle outside the small town of Castle Douglas, where we walked the dogs up through the forest. Next on our itinerary was Dunskey Castle in Portpatrick, which was perched on the side of a cliff. While the rocky cliffs were unsafe, we managed to see it from the path along the top of the cliff. For hundreds of years those castle walls had gradually been falling into the Irish Sea. I felt in awe at the concept of our ancestors having built the castle there in the first place.

Later that night we sat at a campsite near Troon and

had a few beers. Jake hadn't really said much so far on the holiday but after a couple of drinks he became emotional. He told us he was grateful to be spending time with us all and that he normally struggled with groups. He said he wouldn't have tagged along, except for Rachel insisting he joined us. I could imagine the conversation they must have had – she could be very persuasive.

He told us he'd had a tough time growing up after his mum died when he was only seven years old. He said he, his brother and his dad had muddled through for several years, and then when he was eleven his dad met someone new. She turned out to be the archetypal wicked stepmother. She had two children of her own and favoured them in everything they did – even at mealtimes. If his dad noticed, Jake said he never acknowledged what was going on.

At sixteen, he left home after managing to get a local joiner to take him on as an apprentice. The joiner had a small flat above his premises and let him use it rent-free until he got himself sorted out. Once qualified, he bought himself a small, terraced house – he was a few years older than the rest of us. By the end of his story and on his third beer, we were all feeling emotional. He ended his story by adding, 'I love you guys already!'

That night I lay awake in the tent thinking about his childhood and couldn't imagine my own mum not having been there when I was growing up. He was such a nice, sensitive guy – I just hoped Rachel wasn't too much for him.

The following day we walked along Troon beach and then headed off in the camper along a network of country roads. It was still only just after one pm when we spotted signs for a charity garden fete someone was holding in aid of the local hospice and animal rescue shelter.

'We have to go and support it.' I proclaimed to the others. Meeting no resistance, Pete shrugged his shoulders and followed the signposts. About five hundred yards away from the car park for the fete, we spotted yellow and red bunting waving in the breeze. But then with a chug, chug, thud, the camper van came to a sudden halt. Pete thought he had simply stalled it, but no, it wasn't going to re-start for anyone.

We piled out of the van and, with the dogs peering through the back window at us, pushed it to the side of the road. Ade opened the bonnet, and he and Pete stood in front of the engine, scratching their heads. I began to wonder why we'd brought such an old wreck of a van on holiday but didn't say anything. The camper was Pete's family's precious heirloom.

Ade pulled out the dipstick and checked the oil level, examined a few other parts I couldn't name, and then shook his head. 'I have no idea what's wrong with it.'

We were close to a small cottage and could see an elderly lady working in her garden. Pete went over to ask to use her phone to call the car rescue services. They were going to take two and a half hours to get to us, so we asked the old lady if there was a garage in the village – she said the nearest one was over thirty miles away.

Disappointed we were going to have to hang around for the afternoon, we decided some would stay with the van and wait for the car rescue person, while the others would go on to the fete and take the dogs for a much-needed walk. Pete said he'd stay with Ade and the van.

Leaving them at the side of the road on two deckchairs to sun themselves while they waited, the rest of us went on to the fete with the dogs. Jess happily trotted along beside Buddy and me, and I felt warm inside.

In the end, though, the fete was somewhere I should perhaps not have gone that day. We can't re-write history, but what happened in those next few hours affected all six of our lives in one way or another.

Chapter 5

There are those in this world who seem to possess some kind of inner power to see things that aren't tangible or visible to the rest of us. Many would say that those people have some element of what could be described as a 'sixth sense.' I suppose that when it came down to it, Rose-May was one of those people.

After paying our fifty pence entry to the fete, we had a browse around the cake stalls, buying a few bags of tray bakes to share back at the van later on. Buddy and Jess made it their mission to beg as many treats as possible from passing admirers. Jake won a stuffed toy rabbit in a throw the hoop game and gave it to Rachel. I worried how long it would last once Buddy noticed it in the camper. We paid five pence to guess Teddy the teddy bear's birthday and dropped some money into the guitar case of a young guy who was strumming a guitar, singing his heart out in a great rendition of *American Pie*.

It was Hannah who noticed the yellow caravan in the corner of the field before the rest of us. Leaning against the outside of the caravan was a painted sign which said:

'My name is Rose-May. Cross my palm with a donation and I'll tell you your future.

All proceeds will be split between the local hospice and the animal sanctuary.'

Underneath was a small disclaimer saying that Rose-May wouldn't be held responsible for how people might interpret what she told them.

'C'mon.' Hannah squealed as she pushed her way between Rachel and me. She grabbed our arms and dragged us over to the caravan. 'It'll be fun.'

I sighed, and looked over at Jake, who rolled his eyes and then laughed.

One man was waiting outside the caravan. The four of us formed an excited queue behind him, eagerly waiting for our turn to go in. He turned and looked at us with a serious expression. 'She's really good at this you know, Rose-May. She should have done this for a living but instead she works as the local doctor's receptionist.' That brought us all down to earth a little. He must have noticed the disappointment etched in our faces and added, 'Don't let that put you off though – as I said, she is really good! When my wife was only a few weeks pregnant she predicted we'd have a girl, and she was right!'

I wasn't that impressed as I figured she'd kind of had a fifty/fifty chance of being right there, but then he continued. 'She also said we'd be going to

Australia for a year, which we did.'

Hmm, I thought, that could have been the power of suggestion. But then came the convincing double-whammy, literally. She apparently went on to predict that he and his wife would have identical twins when their daughter was two years old, and they'd be a girl and a boy. She also told him he'd be forced into having a change in career because an accident in the engineering company where he worked would mean he'd have to change to an office-based job. All of this had apparently come to be. He said he was waiting for his son, who was in the caravan having his own shot at his life being foretold.

He hadn't finished with his attempts to convince us of what we had in store. 'People are astounded by what she says and her insight. She sees things you see. You know, apart from this she also talks to dead people.' A wry smile crossed his lips.

That was all much more convincing, and I began to wonder whether seeing Rose-May had been the right thing to do. I felt a sudden bolt of apprehension and thought of how Mum had always told me it was better to leave these things alone. Perhaps she was right.

And then, before we could talk some more, the son – a boy of about fifteen – emerged from the caravan. The two of them went off together, heads close as the son confided in the father about what his future would hold. Meanwhile, we four had to decide who was going in first!

We had a tossing of the coin championship while Rose-May stood in the doorway of her caravan. Her curly red hair was pulled back into a thick ponytail and she wore a red and gold patterned dress, which swamped her slender figure.

Rachel won the coin toss. Before they went in, and to save time because a queue had gathered behind us, Rose-May told everyone waiting that she couldn't be held responsible for anything she said in the caravan. She said that once she was in a trance, she wasn't always aware of what she was saying. Rachel nudged Jake and giggled, just a little too loud. With a disapproving look, Rose-May beckoned for her to follow her into the caravan.

Rachel remained in there for fifteen minutes, after which she emerged, pallid and a little shaken. Rose-May had certainly worked wonders on her. I'd won the second toss, so I didn't have much of a chance to speak to her before I left Hannah in charge of the dogs and ascended the metal caravan steps.

I crossed Rose-May's palm with silver (the fifty pence charge that was on the sign outside) and gave her a timid smile. I was unsure what I'd been expecting, but she sat watching me for a while. She then took hold of my hand and closed her eyes. And then she began to speak. 'I see animals, lots of animals. You'll be thinking to yourself, *ah, yes, but you just saw me with the dogs outside*, won't you dear. But no, a lot of animals, not just dogs – you take care of them. You have a good heart but be careful that you don't overdo things – it can exhaust a person.'

She breathed deeply and entered what I can only describe as a trance state. And then she continued, 'I see a ring, and then she frowned and turned her head to one side … hmm … perhaps two. And you will have children. There will be great sadness, but you will find happiness.'

And then she gripped my hand tightly. 'Tell him *No, don't go*! You must tell him it's not safe.' Her brow was furrowed and her eyes flickering beneath her eyelids as though she was in REM sleep. And then she began to sing: '*It's raining, it's pouring, the old man is snoring ... he went to bed with a bucket on his head ... and he couldn't get up in the morning …*'

With that, she lifted her hands from mine and held onto her head. She stayed like that for a minute or more. She was silent. And then, easing her head from her hands, she turned her head to one side so it looked as though she could be looking out of the caravan window, but her eyes were tightly closed. A strange grimace contorted her face as she added, 'on a day not sunny like today, and not so very distant from now.'

I was suddenly terrified.

I thought she was finished, but still with her eyes closed, she gripped my hands again. 'We live a hundred lives or more, but chance, yes chance, can change the way.'

She didn't say anything else and came around from whatever trance state she'd been in. I was shaking and asked her what she'd meant when she said I should tell him not to go, and what had that been with the nursery rhyme – and the chance thing? What was it all about?

'I'm sorry, my dear, I have no idea. I don't remember a nursery rhyme or anything else after what I said about the animals. The words come from a connection between us, it's like some state of being from within us that's beyond our usual thought processes. Once I come round again, I have no recollection of what I've said, sometimes it's the future, often links to the past and present, but only the individual can work out what it all means. Most of my ancestors used tarot cards or read tea leaves, but when I was young, I realized I had this gift … if you could call it that, because sometimes it's a curse … for being able to tell someone's fortune from touching them, like some kind of seer, I suppose. However, it sometimes gives more information than I'd like.' She must have seen the look of disappointment and worry fall across my face. She took hold of my hand and told me she was sorry.

I must have looked in a confused state when I left the caravan, and I brushed past Jake as he was about to climb the steps. He seemed keen, but then he hesitated and looked back at me before taking the final step into the caravan. I simply shrugged and smiled, desperately trying to process the meaning of what Rose-May had told me.

Outside, Rachel and I shared our stories with Hannah. Rachel had been told that she was with a guy who was not the one. We were sure the woman had no idea Rachel and Jake were together. She told her she would eventually meet someone from a foreign land with whom she would be happy. She had a spirit guide and should listen more to her instincts – she didn't need to always be the wild person at the party. She would travel widely and eventually settle in a place far away.

'That's crazy!' Hannah laughed. 'So, you're going to split from Jake and …'.

'Shush, not so loud, Hannah!' I whispered. 'Jake

will hear you.'

She turned to me. 'And how on Earth did she know you work in a veterinary surgery? That's bizarre stuff – she couldn't have got that from just seeing you with the dogs. I know she didn't say about the vets in so many words, but it was close enough – there can't be that many people in this world who spend their days caring for animals.'

'I know, and that's what scares me, because what about the two rings?'

'Oh, she probably means that when you're old and grey, in your nineties, and you've outlived Pete, you'll find some crotchety old fella in a nursing home and marry him! Or perhaps because you and Pete are so lovey-dovey with one another, you'll be one of those sickly couples who retake their vows after twenty-five years or something! Just don't worry about it!' Rachel laughed.

I told them about the strange nursery rhyme and the warning, but again Rachel laughed it off and said to just not think about it – it was a garden fete after all! We all laughed – but inside my heart was pounding.

Jake emerged from the caravan with a worried look on his face. 'You okay, love of my life?' Rachel asked him. He gave a half smile and said he was okay, adding that it was really all a load of rubbish.

Hannah began to look worried. 'Perhaps I'll not go in. We've taken up so much time – and look at everyone who's waiting!' She turned and indicated the queue of about six people behind us.

'No, you're going in!' Rachel insisted as she shoved her towards the door. 'It'll be a laugh – go on – it's not for real!'

Hannah looked at me for support and I shook my head and laughed. 'Go on, Hannah, you'll be fine!'

Hannah's reaction to her meeting was nonchalant, unlike the rest of us, she came out smiling. 'That was soooo much fun,' she said as she jumped from the caravan steps and leaned forward to hug the excited Buddy and Jess.

'What did she tell you?' I was curious to know what she'd been told.

'It was crazy, honestly, she told me she saw me in nature with lots of flowers and trees – how did she know I'm going to horticultural college after the summer? I just don't get it at all!'

Hannah was three years younger than me. Since the two of us were youngsters, we'd loved being outdoors, only my path had led me more to caring for animals, and hers to plants. She had helped mum in the garden from when she was little and had carried her own kid-sized gardening tools and gloves in a blue metal bucket, which had a rainbow on the side. She even used to take them when we went visiting so she could help unsuspecting relatives with their gardening.

'Did she say much else to you?' I asked her.

'No, not really, although it was strange actually because she said that same thing she said to you about saying no to someone. She also began to sing that nursery rhyme, but because I'd heard you talk about it, it didn't really affect me in the same way it did you. Strange though, huh?'

'Oh, you're right, that's weird. She can't even know that we're sisters because we don't really look alike.' I wondered what on earth that whole 'no' thing was about. I thought about going back in and crossing her palm with more silver to see whether she could find more information for me, but the others were desperate to get moving to see whether the van was fixed. And there was that ever-lengthening queue. Poor Rose-May would be exhausted by the end of the day.

On the way back to the camper Jake enlightened us about his session in the caravan. He was told he'd have two children and that he would have his own business and move to a land far away. He said she started to speak in French, but he could only remember something about a *chateau* and a *jardin*. 'It's all a load of rubbish anyway,' he said, and then tickled Rachel around her rib cage. She screeched and ran along the dirt path, exciting the dogs so they wanted to chase.

Looking over at Hannah I said, 'She knew a lot of stuff that no one could possibly have known – and she certainly seemed to enter some strange state when she was talking. It's all very peculiar!'

Hannah shrugged and nodded.

As the camper came into sight, we could see the road rescue mechanic was putting his tools back in his van. Pete gave us the thumbs up and grinned that wide smile I had admired from afar for so many years. I felt a sinking feeling in the pit of my gut. What had Rose-May meant? Perhaps Jake was right, though, maybe it really was a load of old rubbish, after all, she told both him and Rachel that they would live far away but had told Rachel that Jake wasn't 'the one'. I tried to push the warning to the back of my mind.

With a fixed alternator on the van, we headed north to Oban via Loch Lomond and The Trossachs. We would arrive late, but we called the campsite we were staying at from a phone box. They said they'd have the reception open until eleven – and there was a small shop where we could buy some essentials. If we were late, they said to just set up camp to the left of the fork in the track, and they'd see us the next morning.

The scenery was beautiful, with mountains like I'd never seen before. Purple heather and grasses of every shade of green and yellow poked their way out of the crevices between the grey and purple stones. I saw a group of five wild goats grazing on the mountainside, hooves strangely stable on the rocks and ledges, yet at the same time they looked as though they might topple and tumble down the face of the mountain.

As we drove alongside a river in the Cairngorms, we spotted an osprey approaching the water – its legs and feet extended to catch a fish. As his feet kissed the water a huge splash temporarily obscured our view of him, and then he reappeared and flew to the sky, his prey securely locked in his talons.

We were all quiet for a few minutes, until Ade broke the silence, 'I think I'll remember that moment for the rest of my life! Never, in all the summers we spent here with Mum and Dad did we ever see anything like that.'

Chapter 6

Darkness was falling by the time we reached Oban, so we pitched our four tents in a circle next to the camper. Exhausted, we sat on some rugs on the cooling grass and pooled the food we'd bought at the garden fete. After a thrown-together supper of crisps, nuts, bananas, and some dark chocolate crispy rice bakes from the cake stand at the fete, we said our goodnights and settled down for a welcome sleep.

The chill of the morning air woke me at about five o' clock in the morning. I lay watching Pete as he slept, relishing the quiet moments with him by my side. I still couldn't believe that we were actually together. Things had moved so fast once we'd decided that we couldn't be without one another. It was strange to think how different my life might have been, had he and Ade not been playing tennis in the park that cold day when I was there with Rachel and Buddy. I would still have been on some path with no particular direction – perhaps I would even have been going out with Tomas from work. The thought seemed alien; Pete and me, that was how it was always meant to be.

My mind drifted to what Rose-May said – what *was* that with the whole trance thing anyway? It was likely it was all just a performance for the event. I wished she'd told me more though; that everything hadn't been quite so vague.

What had she meant about that whole 'No, don't go' thing? There were too many possibilities. 'No, don't go,' could just as likely be 'yes, go!' Either way you've got a fifty/fifty chance of making the right decision, haven't you? I wished I'd never gone in to see her. It all seemed incredibly irresponsible for her to let us leave with such open-ended instructions. But perhaps that was the idea – you could always apply what she said to something and think to yourself *well, she was right, wasn't she?* With all of us there were potential repercussions because her words would always be there, hanging in the air with the power to influence our lives.

The trance-like state she entered appeared as though she was talking in tongues. It had felt as though I'd witnessed a strange, unexplained phenomenon. And unfortunately, however much I wanted it to be fake, what happened with her had seemed to be anything but that.

Pete stirred in his sleep and must have sensed I was lying there watching him. His eyes opened and he smiled; that smile I had fallen for that day back at school. I loved him – and whatever fate had in store for us, we would overcome it, just go with it, and seize the day. *Carpe diem* – just like we were doing with our friends; riding the tide and allowing ourselves to seize the opportunities that came our way. Two rings, though, that thought was not going to leave me in a hurry.

We spent a few days in Oban and then drove up via Fort William and Eilean Donan Castle to The Kyle of Lochalsh. With each of us clutching a bag of chips, we took a boat from there to Kyleakin on the Island of Skye. On the deck, a local man who'd been to the mainland to collect a secondhand car, pointed to some rocks about a hundred yards away. He handed Hannah and me his binoculars so we could see what he'd been looking at. Gathered on the rocks were about forty puffins. I'd never seen a puffin for real before. They looked smaller than I'd imagined, but I was in awe at their beauty.

Very quickly, it was time for Ade to drive the camper off the ferry onto Skye. I felt a great sense of adventure that we were in a place so full of history; somewhere even my parents and grandparents had never been. It was as though we were in the middle of our own Enid Blyton adventure 'Five Go Mad on the Isle of Skye', only in our case there were six people and two hyper-excitable and less than clever dogs. I was glad I'd brought along a couple of sweaters as the temperature was a good few degrees cooler than back home. Mum had reminded Hannah and me about the 'catching pneumonia' thing before we left, so we'd dutifully squashed them into our already tightly packed rucksacks.

After stocking up on food we set up camp and took the dogs for a walk on Camas Ban beach in Portree. To get there, we had to make our way down a steep slope. Despite the chill in the air, once on the sand we all took off our shoes and ran around the beach putting sand down the backs of each other's T-shirts.

We threw pebbles into the sea for the dogs to chase. The stones formed perfect rings on the unusually calm sea as they hit the water's surface, providing a useful target for the dogs to dive into. As they leaped into the air, and splashed down into the water for maximum effect, Buddy and Jess pushed their faces deep into the waves. Creating a swirl of sand with their antics, they seemed fascinated at how the stones we threw vanished once they were submerged. They were mesmerized at the disappearance of their quarry, once the pebbles had hit the ocean floor and couldn't be distinguished from others lying there.

They looked over for reassurance that we'd actually thrown something, and that we weren't playing the 'fetch' trick where you only pretend to throw the ball. Tired once more, we headed back to camp and promised ourselves we'd visit the same beach again before we left to go back to the mainland a few days later.

The following day, we headed up the northwest side of the island to Dunvegan Castle. Dogs were allowed in the gardens if they were on a lead, and so the six of us and the two dogs explored the manicured gardens. They were tightly packed with shrubs, bushes and trees of every shade of green, and flowers of every colour imaginable, each leaf and flower contributing to the palette of nature's rainbow.

Hannah was in her element amid the ground cover plants, testing herself on the plant names she'd been teaching herself in preparation for her horticulture course. 'Now, is that an *Aubrietia*, or a *Campanula*?' she said quietly as she walked across to touch some small flowers that were cascading over the top of a grey stone wall, like thousands of bright purple stars. On closer inspection she knew straight away, 'Hmm, it's a type of *Campanula*! See, it has much more of a bell-shape than …' she scanned the rest of the wall, 'this one, which is *Aubrietia*.' I smiled to myself, thinking of the Latin names I'd had to learn in my veterinary nursing training.

'They're so pretty,' I said. She nodded and smiled,

her face lighting up with enthusiasm.

We got chatting to some other tourists who were walking around the gardens with an old German shepherd cross named Maxi. While we made a fuss of her, Buddy and Jess crowded the poor dog, enthusiastically trying to make friends with her. Maxi wasn't interested, and through opaque cataracts affecting both eyes, she simply stared into the distance, unperturbed and indifferent to the advances of our dogs. The couple told us they'd just come from some fairy pools nearby and suggested we shouldn't miss seeing them.

We were intrigued, so after a short drive we left the camper parked at the edge of a road and traipsed across rough ground to find the pools. After half an hour, there in front of us was the most beautiful sight. It was later in the day by the time we got there, and the dying light cast our shadows across the rocks which surrounded the crystal-clear, turquoise-green water. The pools were being fed by charming, cascading waterfalls, and at the first pool we sat for a while on the rocks, each of us silent, listening to the water crashing from the rocks into the pools below.

Further on, we came to a deeper blue pool, its rippling water inviting us to plunge into it. Although it was summer the water was freezing, but it was the most beautiful day and I think I was the happiest I'd ever been. As day began to turn to night, the reddening sky gave the pool a deep lilac hue. If there was a heaven, I imagined that place was how heaven would be.

The days that followed we explored, ate, and slept, each day discovering more and more about this magical island. We loved Skye so much that we stayed longer than planned, but eventually we knew we would have to leave. And so, once back on the mainland, we continued our journey across the top of Scotland.

When all too soon we reached John o' Groats, I felt overwhelmed that, for the first time, I was standing on the grassy cliff at the far north-east corner of our mainland. Overcome at the beauty of the open sea, I fought the urge to cry silly, emotional tears. Despite my efforts to fight them back, the scene became blurred as the water welled in my eyes. Pete came over and stood beside me. He put his arm through mine – I looked up at him and smiled. And then, in my peripheral vision I suddenly saw something moving out in the sea. I turned my head in the direction of the movement and squealed with excitement as I pulled my arm from his and pointed out towards the horizon. Realization at what I'd seen flooded through my body. 'Oh, my goodness, look, look, over there!' I turned to call the others.

'Look, everyone, quick!'

Out in the open sea about a hundred yards from the peninsula on which we were standing, was a pod of ten or twelve dolphins. One by one, they leaped into the air, deftly demonstrating their agility; beauty; magnificence; absolute wildness; their freedom. For a whole hour or more they danced their graceful dolphin waltz. The dogs lay beside us – even they seemed in awe at what was happening in the open sea.

And then, finally, the dancing dolphins headed off into the distance, eventually becoming one with the deep blueness of the ocean, which was by then tinged with orange reflections from the sunset. Only widening ripples in the water remained as evidence that they had ever been there.

Chapter 7

Our dolphin experience fueled a desire to see more, and so, a few days later we stood with a group of about forty people on the sands at Chanonry Point, looking out into the Moray Firth, desperate to see more dolphins. After an hour of waiting and scanning the ocean, we caught sight of them, and we spent the next hour watching them ducking and diving in their search for fish. Eventually, just like their cousins further north, they made their way away from the shore and back out to sea.

The dolphins augmented the magic of the time we had there: the six of us and our two canine companions. For me it was like an awakening, we had so much to gain from being young and living in this amazing world. As I looked around at my friends' excited faces, the awe I felt was mirrored in each of them. There, then, in that moment, I felt I needed to do everything I could to defend the naturalness of the world. I'd always loved animals and had been the one passing petitions around at school to stop seal clubbing and end animal experiments and so on, but I wanted to do more.

Back in the camper having some lunch, we talked for hours about how we were going to change our lives and make this world a much better place. It felt silly that we'd all been so inspired by seeing some dolphins catching their food, but we were all serious – our eyes had been opened to the importance of defending something so sacred. For me, it felt as though I'd experienced some sort of revelation. This was my life – I really had to do something good.

The next morning on the two-and-a-half-hour trip down from Inverness to Inverurie, we were quiet, having exhausted ourselves with the possibilities of how our lives could be. We were all deep in thought and for once not debating about which tape to play.

We stopped by for a quick look at a mediaeval Pictish stone. Standing in front of its carvings I wondered how many others had done the same – stood there and pondered at the meaning of the symbols. To those who created it all those centuries ago, the symbols would have meant something. The more I considered it, the more I found my world getting larger, and my own self becoming much less significant.

From Inverurie we travelled down through the magnificent, yet eerie, Cairngorm Mountains and took a detour to the town of Saint Andrews. The old grey buildings of the town hid tiny nooks where small cottages hinted at stories of times long ago. The golden beaches were just a short walk from the shops, giving the dogs a fresh chance to race along the sand and splash in the frothy waves they'd come to love. On the horizon, where the ocean met the sky, it seemed as though the sea came to an abrupt end, and that a boat we could see in the distance might fall from the edge of the world into oblivion. For a moment I felt I could believe our ancestors' theory that the earth might be flat.

Although it was summer, there were some students wandering along the cobbled streets, some of them sporting their university gowns. Depicting the stage they were at in their studies, gowns were either placed on one shoulder and off the other shoulder, others wore the gown hanging loosely around the back of their shoulders. It made me long to be a part of their community, to perhaps leave my job and go back to studying, not necessarily there, but somewhere. What would I study? Zoology seemed a good idea, but I also cherished a new desire to learn more about what had come before us. Before we humans had taken over the world. Palaeontology or archaeology, perhaps? My world suddenly felt as though it was full of opportunities.

On our final morning in Saint Andrews, we headed back down to the golden sands. The wind was blowing in from the sea, whipping up the fine grains of sand into a zigzag frenzy just over a meter high. Buddy had never encountered such a thing, and as the sand blasted against his face, he suddenly darted

258 of sand into a zigzag frenzy just over a meter high.

across the sands to me with his tail between his legs; Jess close behind him. We put them on their leads and led them away from what was turning into a bit of a sandstorm. Realizing the mini sandstorm was changing into something altogether more violent than a bit of a sandy breeze, we ran as fast as we could to get beyond the sand dunes to the van. Once there, we grabbed some tissues and blew the coarse sand from our noses, and wiped sand from the corners of both dogs' eyes. We sat there, exhausted from the sudden bout of exercise, and laughed as we shook our hair to rid it of the gritty grains.

Downhearted that we couldn't walk along the beach again that day, we went shopping for gifts to take home and to my Aunt Cathy's in Yorkshire where we were staying for a night on our way home. The journey was going to take us about four and a half hours.

Just in time for tea.

Still with salt and sand-filled hair, we arrived at the home of mine and Hannah's Aunt Cathy and Uncle Bertie. Tired and hungry, we piled into their huge Georgian house and, much to Jess and Buddy's joy, we were overcome by three more dogs: Henry, Hattie, and Horace. Watching in the distance from the top of a large, antique display cupboard, was the longhaired tabby and white feline, Jasper.

Chapter 8

My aunt was my mum's sister and sixteen years her senior. Mum was the accident their parents had never anticipated having. Cathy married Bertie, big, burly Uncle Bertie, quite late on in life. It was too late, they said, for them to have considered having any children. Bertie was a kindly man with a big brown and grey beard and shining hazel eyes. The two of them spent their days travelling the length and breadth of Britain trailing their large caravan, taking their dogs, and sometimes cat too.

They doted on their canine and feline companions, but they seemed to equally thrive on the company of any of their eight nieces and nephews. They'd been keen that Hannah and I didn't miss this opportunity to see them just because we had our friends with us. They were desperate to meet them – but especially Pete because they'd been told so much about him.

Straight away the five dogs formed some sort of hierarchy with bossy little Hattie, the corgi-cross with the overshot upper jaw, putting them all in their place. But no dog was any match for the fearsome Jasper the cat, and Buddy and Jess immediately picked up on his superior position. As soon as Buddy saw Jasper, he playfully barked at him from six feet away. Jasper simply looked at him, turned his back and lifted his paw to wash himself; all the time waving his tail in that threatening motion that often precedes an attack. Jasper was hardly fazed by the presence of a lunatic dog that was three times the size of the three dogs he was used to: the 'H-Team', as Cathy and Bertie referred to them.

My aunt was old-fashioned and preferred that we stick to all-male and all-female sleeping arrangements. We'd expected it to be the case but had hoped in their massive house she'd have let us choose. Putting our disappointment to one side, we all tucked into a massive vegetable and bean casserole and the finest chunky potato fries I'd ever encountered. As we ate our meal, we told Cathy and Bertie the tale of Rose-May from the garden fete in Scotland.

As I finished my own version of what Rose-May had in store Cathy's face suddenly became pale, making her inhale deeply. She reached over to grip Bertie by his arm. 'Bertie! Bertie! What did I say to you this very morning?'

Bertie hadn't really been listening to the conversation. His mind was still fixated on the technical reasons why our camper might have broken down on the day we were telling them about.

'What did you say, my love?' He looked puzzled, and just a little alarmed at the sense of urgency in Cathy's voice.

'This morning, Bertie, do you remember I was recalling the day I met the old grey woman all those years ago. Well guess what happened while they were all in Scotland? That's right, they met a woman who foretold their fortunes. Gosh, what a coincidence that you should be telling me this today after I was only talking about such things this very morning!'

As we all sat listening intently, Cathy told us the story of the time she'd come across her own prophesizing lady. A knock at the door one day years before had revealed a small, thin woman with long, grey curls. She bore a thin, pale face and hollowed cheeks. Her image had haunted Cathy for some time afterwards.

The woman was selling heather door to door one afternoon when Cathy was twenty-six, and her sister Juliette (mine and Hannah's Mum) was about ten or eleven years old. Cathy had a sixpence in her pocket and handed it over. The old woman looked into her palm and then over to Cathy with cold blue eyes, which changed to a warmer sea-blue when she smiled. She took hold of her hand and told her she would meet a man from the north and the man would work with wood. When Cathy met Bertie, he had worked in the steel industry, but when he was made redundant from the local factory he went back to college and re-trained as a carpenter. 'So, you see,' she raised her palms to the skies and looked around the room to us and our friends, 'you see, you should all take this as a warning! There's something in these prophesies!' She nodded to reaffirm her faith in the power of some people to foretell the future.

Rachel immediately broke the silence. She looked puzzled. I tried to warn her with my eyes not to say anything. But then, she tossed her curly blonde fringe away from her face and said what we'd all been thinking. 'Hmm,' she began 'but what about the power of suggestion? Surely at some point you told Bertie about the whole carpentry thing, so perhaps that embedded itself in his mind and, hey presto, when he was made redundant, he thought to himself, *I know what I'll do, I'll go and re-train as a carpenter, just like the woman told Cathy*! It would have been a bit more convincing if he'd been a carpenter to begin with! You know, when you met him?'

Rachel paused for effect and really didn't seem to be picking up on everyone's body language. We were all telling her with every look, every posture, to shut up. And so, she continued. 'And as for being from the north, Sheffield's only a bit north from The Midlands – you could have bumped into one another on a train or something. It's all a bit far-fetched really, isn't it?'

She paused and looked around us. She'd shattered all Aunt Cathy's long-held mystical illusions in one fell swoop and we were all speechless. Perhaps sensing the atmosphere in the room (but I had my doubts with it being Rachel), she added much more feebly, 'Don't you think?'

My aunt's expression was a mixture of annoyance and embarrassment. I doubted whether Rachel would ever be invited back. There was a pregnant pause as none of us knew what to say, nor dared to breathe, but then Bertie broke the heavy silence, 'So, would anyone like some fruit salad and strawberry and mango sorbet?'

Once the crockery and oven dishes were washed up and put away, we headed out for an evening walk around a small part of Roundhay Park. It was a little cooler for the time of year, and we were all glad of our warm clothes. The coots, ducks, geese, and swans were paddling along in the lake with their still-young offspring splashing along behind them. The juvenile birds ducked and dived, mimicking their parents' search for edible water-dwelling greenery or little beasties.

Pete searched for my hand and held it tight. I caught Bertie's eye and he smiled. He'd always been my favourite uncle, and I was glad he approved.

Exhausted, after midnight we all headed off to bed. The house was cool as we made our way up the winding staircase. On the landing as I kissed Pete and said goodnight, I felt myself shudder. I shivered and Pete sensed something was wrong. 'You okay?'

'I think so, probably just tired. It was weird, though, I just felt as though all my hairs stood on end.' I shrugged and smiled at him. He seemed a little worried. 'I'll be fine,' I added.

The two dogs followed me into the room that had been allocated for Hannah, Rachel, and me. Pete seemed a little disappointed that his faithful hound preferred to spend the evening with us girls. He called along the landing, 'That's loyalty for you, Jess,' just as her long tail disappeared into the girls' bedroom.

Chapter 9

In the opulent room allocated to us three girls, Hannah, Rachel, and I spent the first half an hour complaining that we'd had to be separated from the guys. Hannah said she was glad because she'd felt during the holiday that there'd been a sense of her being paired off with Ade. 'I know you've not done it deliberately,' she said, 'but, you know? It's Ade?'

'What's wrong with Ade?' Rachel and I chorused – perhaps a little loudly but we were quite safe as Pete, Ade and Jake's room was on the other side of the house. In fact, we couldn't have been bedded down farther away from them.

We all laughed at the prospect of Ade and Hannah getting together, not because there was anything wrong with Ade, just that the two of them couldn't have been more different to one another. Hannah with her plants and trees and feeling at one with nature, and Ade with his being married to his work and spending ninety percent of his time shrouded in red light in a dark room. Hannah was quite whacky in her bright vests and psychedelic dungarees; Ade was more comfortable in a polo shirt and a pair of black trousers – a stark contrast to his parents. 'Oh well,' Rachel laughed, 'opposites do sometimes attract you know? Perhaps one day! Did Rose-May not predict anything about your love life?'

Hannah's smile turned to a look of concern. 'Well, no, she didn't actually. There was nothing like that – just the stuff about the flowers.' She looked puzzled. 'Perhaps she couldn't see so much with me? I suppose it's possible I was blocking her out … or something? Especially after seeing you lot coming out with terrified expressions!' She waited for us to respond.

'Oh, I wouldn't worry, Hannah,' Rachel said. 'She predicted doom for me and Jake. She implied I was with the wrong person. God, I'm missing him. Do you think your aunt will mind if I scoot along the corridor and smuggle him out of the house for a little romantic rendezvous in that huge garden of hers?'

'No, Rachel, she'll fling us all out onto the street!' I warned her.

'Anyway,' Rachel retorted, 'I'm glad the three of us are together in here and that we've got the dogs with us – I find this house to be awfully spooky! Do you two not feel it?'

I had to admit I did. The house was built in the 1830s and had huge rooms with multi-paned sash windows and high ceilings. Original ceiling roses encircled elaborate, crystal-laden lighting, and picture rails separated the lavish deep blue and gold wall coverings from the cream of the ceilings and tops of the walls.

The room had two guest beds with an extra mattress placed between them. I'd lost the flip of the coin and had the mattress. I didn't mind though, Cathy and Bertie's house was like some luxurious, lavish hotel. But even with the abundance of rich features, there was certainly something amiss. The atmosphere didn't feel quite right.

One by one, we eventually drifted off to sleep – the dogs first, closely followed by Rachel, Hannah, and then me. My body settled into the mysterious kingdom of dreams. Pete and I were holding hands and walking along a bridge. A long, grey bridge with vast metal beams which reached high into the sky. He turned to say something to me. As he did, his face became blurred. I called out to him, 'Pete, Pete, come back!'

But then we were all awoken by a whimper from across the room. What *was* that? I called out Pete's name. But then I remembered where I was.

Hannah reached beside her and put on the bedside lamp, which cast a soft yellow glow from her side of the room. As my eyes adjusted to the light, I could see Buddy over by the cupboard door. He lay on his haunches, hyper-alert and defensive. He alternately reached forward to sniff at the bottom of the cupboard door and then turned to look at me, offering gentle whimpers. Jess was lying at the bottom of my mattress; her ears forward in that way that dogs position their ears when they see something they're curious about. Her head cocked to one side as Buddy reach his head forward towards the cupboard door and growled.

My body turned to jelly as I looked at my sister and best friend for advice about what we should do next. Both their expressions suggested we should pull our blankets up over our heads and hide from whatever it was that Buddy could sense. Apart from playful growls, none of us had ever before heard Buddy make such a sound.

Jess suddenly leapt from the bottom of my mattress and went to stand beside Buddy, who was by then standing with his hackles raised. Her hackles came up as she, too, sniffed at the bottom of the cupboard door. Then, simultaneously, they both suddenly shifted their gaze to look over to the side of the room where Hannah was lying. They both growled. Deep, warning growls. Following their gaze, the three of us could see they were not looking *at* Hannah, but at the space above her.

For a minute or so and as we tried to call them over, they seemed to be intensely watching something, but then they turned their attention back to the cupboard door. This time they both offered quieter grumbles in the backs of their throats. Jess's hackles were starting to flatten, but the line of her fur was still ruffled from the fright she'd clearly had. Buddy was still on high alert.

There was suddenly a harsh knocking at the door. 'Girls! Are you okay?' It was Bertie; he sounded concerned.

I offered a meek, 'Yes, I think so.'

'Shall we come in?' Our aunt was now there. I imagined the two of them stood outside the door in striped pyjamas and matching night caps.

'Um, okay!'

The door opened and the two of them stood in the doorway, my aunt in a baby-pink chiffon nightdress and cream satin dressing gown, her hair in rollers; Bertie in, as I expected, striped pyjamas. The dogs went over to them, by then much more submissive and tentatively wagging their tails.

Chapter 10

We headed downstairs, where Bertie made us hot chocolate and gave us a heap of biscuits to choose from. Together, he and Cathy told us the story of the old woman who used to live there. They bought the house twelve years earlier, after reading about its ghostly happenings in a newspaper. It was thought by many that it was a haunted house which would never sell. Some had thought the article was a clever plan by the people who owned the house for a few years after the old woman's demise in the early 1970s, to sell the house as something worthy of a ghost hunter's curiosity. Cathy and Bertie finished up in a bidding war with another two families. And won.

They'd never been bothered by the ghost – Annie, as they'd named her. They felt she wasn't harmful – just a little eccentric. They said she behaved a little like a poltergeist, seemingly moving things. They admitted they weren't sure whether the goings-on were ghost Annie's, or perhaps their own eccentricities, and they'd simply bought into the idea of living in a haunted house. They'd never before told Hannah or me about their wayward phantom, mainly because they hadn't wanted to stop us from visiting. Even when we'd previously sensed things, they'd never come clean. But why now? Why would Annie suddenly make an appearance now?

And why had Buddy and Jess had such a reaction?

Cathy thought we should head back upstairs to search in the cupboard that had caught the dogs' attention – perhaps there was a mouse in there making a bed out of some old blankets? The guys heard us all on the landing and came out to see us. Even with his messed-up sleep hair and tired middle-of-the-night washed-out, weary face, Pete was lovely. All eerie happenings temporarily forgotten, I felt that now-familiar fluttering in my tummy. I never wanted that feeling to go. He walked over and held my hand, 'What's going on? Are you all okay?' Lines of concern were etched on his forehead.

We all piled into the room. There was no evidence that anything had been amiss. The dogs were no longer perturbed at being there and went to curl up on the mattress on the floor. Cathy opened the cupboard to check for any visiting rodents. Inside, there were three pairs of shoes, a pair of boots and, tucked in the corner, a small wooden box.

The box was just visible, far away at the back of the cupboard. Cathy stretched her arm right in and pulled the box out. 'I've never seen this before.' Looking up at Bertie she asked, 'Is it yours?'

Bertie had an odd expression on his face, he shrugged his shoulders and shook his head. 'Nope, not mine.' I noticed him turning his gaze away from her towards the door – was he looking for an escape? I wasn't sure, but it seemed obvious to me that he *did* know something.

Cathy shrugged and looked around at all of us gathered around her. She carefully lifted the lid; its hinges creaked. The box was made of dark mahogany and rosewood. A floral design was carved into its lid. It was small, only about four inches by three inches. Once it was open, only Cathy could see what was inside. 'Oh!' She exclaimed and held something up for us all to see.

In her hand were three sheets of paper, covered on both sides with a meticulous, tidy script.

A letter.

Intrigued to hear what it said and with all of us wide awake, we all descended the stairs. Bertie made more drinks, while the rest of us gathered in the sitting room waiting for Cathy to read the letter to us. She read some of it to herself, and then with a furrowed brow, carefully placed it back in the box. Even Rachel was silent as we all waited in quiet, excited anticipation. Fresh mugs of hot chocolate warming our hands, we settled back to listen to what this person had to say. Deep in my heart I hoped this was not going to be an anticlimax – this was such a fascinating turn of events for the end of our holiday.

As Cathy began to ease the lid from the box once more, Bertie made a strange cough sound. It appeared as though he was clearing his throat ready to say something.

'Cathy, my love, perhaps we shouldn't,' he eventually offered.

'What? Do you know something about this, Bertie?'

'Well, not exactly, Dear.'

'What do you mean, not exactly?'

The situation was becoming much more interesting. I looked around at the others, and they were just as captivated by this unfolding of events as I was.

'Ok, I have a confession, well, sort of a confession anyway.'

Even more fascinated, we looked from one to the other as though we were watching a game of tennis.

'Does this have something to do with you, Bertie?'

'No, Dear, not at all.' He seemed to realize he was on dangerous ground and decided to come clean.

Bertie explained that when they moved into the house he had come across the box. It was wedged beside a piece of wood inside one of the built-in kitchen cupboards. He said he was alarmed by the contents of the letter but had felt it would be wrong to throw it away – he was frightened it would bring them bad luck or something.

In the end, after reading the whole letter, he'd carefully placed it where he thought Cathy would never find it. He said he was worried she would never settle into the house. He'd put it in a place where he knew he could find it if ever the situation arose where it seemed appropriate. He finally added that perhaps because of what had just happened, that this was the time. As he said that, he glanced at me, and then quickly looked away. I frowned at him. What was this? What on Earth was going on?

'Wow, that was some revelation, Bertie! So, do we all want to know what's in here? Especially as Bertie already seems to know!' Cathy seemed to be a little put out at not having been privy to Bertie's long-held secret.

We all either shrugged or nodded. With that, she carefully eased the lid back from the box, its hinges creaking once more. She cleared her throat as she smoothed the creases from the paper.

And then, she began to read aloud.

Chapter 11

August 6th 1953

To Whom it May Concern

I'm writing this in the hope that at some point in the future the words will make sense to someone; that somehow what happened today will be something which enlightens those who dwell in this house after me.

Despite the beautiful sunshine of this day, the house is unusually cold just now, and I feel frightened. I know this house – I feel the stone, the bricks, the trees in the garden, they are all a part of me. I have never felt threatened here. I inherited the house from my mother when she died in 1944. I have known this house for the whole of my life; I was born here in 1898.

In 1916, I married my beloved Tom. Within weeks, he had to leave for France to fight in the war, and he never came back. When I lost him, I lost my everything and have never remarried. I couldn't.

And so, this fear is not normal for me. I'm used to living alone. I'm used to the creaks and scrapes of the house, and the draughts which make me shiver even when there is no window or door open. A cardigan usually makes me warm again. But not today.

And so, to what has happened and why I feel I should leave some note; some indication in case anything happens to me. Perhaps my words will help to make some sense of it all.

Today something unnerved me. And I must share it. This might not be important to me or to my extended family, but from what I was told today it may be important to those who exist in the future. Even writing that makes me feel as though I'm being ridiculous, but I have to offer this information, and I hope that one day it makes some sense to someone.

Earlier today I was in the garden tending my vegetables. I heard a knock at the front door and headed down the alley between the houses to see who was there.

On the steps in front of the house was a woman – a peddler of some kind. She wore black, funereal clothes; a green and blue shawl was placed around her shoulders. Her face was narrow and wrinkled. There was a deep scar across the right side of her neck – it could have been a birthmark.

I reached up and touched the scar I had on my neck. It was from a fall I'd had when I was eight years old and crossing a river on some stepping stones. I'd almost reached the riverbank and slipped and reached out for a branch, but another branch had almost impaled my neck. Like a skewer it had penetrated the right side of my neck and almost gone right through to my mouth. I'd been lucky because it hadn't damaged any major blood vessels, only a salivary gland which I had to have removed. The doctors did a good job of repairing the other internal tissues and the underneath of my tongue, but on the outside, I was left with a visible scar of about an inch and a half. I still had numbness where there was some nerve damage. The odd thing was that it had penetrated an area where I had a birthmark, a small, narrow port wine stain. A double whammy.

At the mention of a scar, Pete and Hannah looked at me, but didn't say anything. They both seemed enthralled. I was too, but in the bottom of my belly I felt sick. What *was* going on? I glanced over at Bertie, but I couldn't gauge the expression on his face. The beard didn't help, but it was clear that he, too, thought the letter was about me.

Cathy seemed oblivious and continued with the rest of the letter.

Thinking the woman might be a traveler because there was a camp nearby, I reached in my apron and held out some money for her. She refused and pushed my hand away, saying that wasn't why she had come. And then her expression changed. She took my arm and told me it was important I pay heed to what she had to say. She had come to me with a warning.

Cathy stopped and looked at us all, before taking a breath and continuing. What was this thing that was going on with us and fortune-telling women? She looked at Bertie, whose eyes were pleading with her to not continue. She ignored him and carried on. He sighed and gently shook his head.

The warning was such that I couldn't understand what I was to do with the information, hence my letter now. I only hope it will be of some use to someone, sometime in the future. she was adamant that this message does not relate to me.

I don't fully remember what she said, but this is the essence of it:

'When time has passed and your life has become as mine was then, listen to the words of one who knows - tell them not to go into the night shadows. Our lives are entwined as one. We must reach inside ourselves and prevent our worlds from drifting, for if we drift, we cannot reunite. You must believe in him and not give in to envy.'

Reader of this message, please forgive me if you don't understand, for I have tried to recall the words as they were spoken. I hope this makes sense to you and that someone, somewhere, is helped by this warning.

The experience has unsettled me, but I shall try to respect the woman's warnings and place this note in a box where it might be found. If you know for sure this message does not relate to you, can I ask that you place it back where you found it so that eventually the words can be interpreted by the person to whom they refer.

One final word, though, and I think this may be even more important. Once the woman had turned to walk away and was halfway down the garden path, she turned and smiled, and whether this was intentional or not, this was the point at which I felt somewhat intimidated. She raised her hand and looked as though she was striking something in the air between me and her. She then touched the right side of her neck. 'Tell them to look for the mark! I must find him again – we must be as one.' She looked up at the grey storm clouds above and added, 'On a day like today.' As she turned and walked away, I could see she had tears in her eyes.

Yours faithfully

Annie Ryan

Annie – the lady who Cathy and Bertie assumed

was haunting the house. We thought that was the end and relaxed back in our seats, exhausted and ready to try to make some sense out of what we'd heard. But then Cathy spoke again, 'Ooh, not yet Folks, there's another piece of paper here. It was written in … when? Goodness, this one was written almost seventeen years after the first one.'

27ᵗʰ July 1970

I never saw the woman after that day. I'm now old and getting tired. I've thought a lot about what she said to me, and I think it has had an adverse effect on my life. I think perhaps because I live alone, the impact of that day was intensified – someone with another to talk to about it would probably have fared better.

In the years since she turned up at my house, I have kept my doors locked, even during the day. I have spent a lot of time sitting at the table behind my curtain; watching out for her; obsessing. I felt unnerved by her and wanted more information. I needed to know what she meant – I even searched the streets for others who might have had the same mark on their neck. But, alas, it was not to be.

I hope when the message meets its intended recipient that all I've endured through these years will have been worth it.

Cathy looked over at Bertie, her face etched with her impending question. 'When we researched this house's history to try to find out who our ghost could be, did we not find out that Annie died in, I don't know, 1971? That was shortly after she wrote this extra note.'

'I'm sure you're right, my love. I'll go and fetch the house folder.'

My head was spinning. It felt as though, after my experience with the fortune teller at the fete in Scotland, that this message was for me. I could tell the others thought this too, because no one would make eye contact with me. Not even Pete, even though it was possible the message was for both of us.

Chapter 12

We sat up for a couple more hours attempting to decipher the message. Eventually Rachel, of course it would be Rachel, said what everyone was thinking – that it had to be a message for me. With an array of expressions engraved on their faces, they all nodded their agreement. Some seemed curious, some bewildered, some anxious. Pete looked incredibly worried. He squeezed my hand to tell me all would be okay, but inside I had never felt quite so vulnerable and alone.

But what *had* the message meant? It was full of suggestion, with nothing concrete said for us to work on. What had the woman meant when she said about not going into the shadows? What about lives being entwined and if they didn't respond to the warning the recipients' worlds would drift? Was she really referring to me? But why? And was the other life Pete's? Was this some kind of after-death communication? But why me? And why now? And why did she, just like me, have a scar on the right side of her neck?

We came to no conclusions, and I felt awful for Annie Ryan, who had spent so many years of her life looking for the woman who'd given the warning. For someone living such a solitary life it must have been extremely unsettling.

What force had allowed the message to come through when we three girls and the dogs were in the room? People say dogs have a super-sense which makes them more liable to seeing and hearing things we humans don't. Many people have felt alarm when their dogs suddenly go quiet and gaze at something in a room, which no one else can see? What Buddy and Jess did was exactly that, only on some much more impressive and disturbing scale.

If there are such things as ghosts, and if, as people also say, spirits can attach to objects, then perhaps some residual energy attached to the letter was strong enough to come through that night. This strange, mysterious force was then detected by the dogs. I suppose the need by the sender was particularly urgent, as she *sensed* the intended recipient was lay sleeping there in the room. I was exhausted thinking about it.

At around four am we decided to go and try to get a little sleep. My head hit the pillow and I was gone, my slumber providing temporary respite from the night's disturbing events. When Rachel opened the long tapestry curtains at eight thirty, the light streamed in, forcing Hannah and me to wake. 'Morning, Girls!' she sang, far too cheerfully. Hannah buried her head under the pillow, blocking the sudden emergence of daytime.

At breakfast, it was as though there was a huge, great elephant in the room. It was clear that some had been pondering over what had happened, had wondered at the importance of the message, and whether it was at all significant. And yet, no one was talking about it.

We all made polite conversation, until I could no longer hold onto my emotions. 'C'mon Guys, it's just a whole series of coincidences, let's just move on from it and enjoy our last day away.' I sensed they were all glad I'd broken the mood, but inside I felt sick. What right did these so-called fortune tellers have to meddle in people's lives? To mess with your head and plant seeds which made people think they needed to live their life differently? Desperate to change the mood, I said 'What shall we do today?'

Cathy was quick to answer. 'Do you all want to go back to Roundhay Park? We could go in through a different entrance, walk past the larger lake and head on into the wooded areas. The dogs would love it!' The vote was unanimous. It would be a perfect end to our holiday.

With the events of the previous night temporarily forgotten, we all piled into our camper and Cathy and Bertie into their estate car with their own dogs. It was a beautiful, fresh summer's morning. As we got into the van, blackbirds and sparrows were chirruping in the deciduous trees above us. The giant weeping willow's branches waved in the breeze; the fine leaves cast dappled, dancing, rippling shadows along the driveway.

The park was warm, but that gentle breeze prevented us and the dogs from becoming too hot. The dogs raced on ahead, only turning occasionally to check we were still behind them. We walked for two hours and then stopped to buy ice lollies, while the dogs took themselves for a welcome drink at the edge of the lake. It was a perfect morning.

Back at the house, we devoured a table full of nutty and beany salads and baked potatoes, followed by coffee and lemon-chocolate tray bakes, all rounded off with herbal tea. With full bellies we had to say our farewells and head off on our way home; some of us were working the next day.

All packed up and with the dogs peering out of the camper windows at us, on the driveway Cathy quietly handed me something. 'Just in case you ever need to refer to it – I'm sorry! If you need to, then just burn it. I would do it for you, you know I would, but the decision's not mine to make.'

My heart sank.

I felt the texture of the paper in my hand, and

through the envelope she had put it in I could smell the mustiness of the pages. I'd thought I would be able to push the contents of that letter to the depths of my mind. I didn't want it, but what could I do? It was of no use to Cathy and Bertie. All those years it had clearly had a message to deliver to someone. And it seemed as though that someone was me.

Pete noticed the letter being handed to me. He didn't say anything, but he must have been wondering since the previous evening whether the note referred to him and me. And if so, what did it all mean?

I nodded to Cathy and took the note, secreting it deep in the inside pocket of my blue and orange cloth bag. I pushed it right to the bottom, beneath my purse, my keys, my hairbrush, my make-up. Out of sight, out of mind, but I knew that at some point I would have to confront its contents again.

I don't know whether there was some subconscious intention for Cathy to absolve her and Bertie of some responsibility, in that by passing on the note, the thing that had haunted their poor ghost, Annie, they were giving Annie the peace she had craved: some eternal tranquility.

In the months and years that followed, there were no more reports of ghostly happenings at their lovely big house. And actually, in my heart I was sure when we left their house that day that the recipient was meant to be me, but I just didn't know when or how I would ever use the information.

After us all giving my aunt and uncle hugs in heartfelt gratitude for their wonderful hospitality, the six of us headed off towards the motorway – our journey to home, and some sense of normality.

I was determined that the few hours in the camper were not going to be tainted by the note that was in the gloomy depths of my bag. As Ade drove, and the rest of us resumed our favourite pastime of playfully debating about which cassette tape we would play. Once the tape was decided, we'd debate again about which songs we should play, rewind, and play again so we could hear them the most. Pete was in charge of the cassette player and patiently fast-forwarded and rewound the tape to play the songs we wanted.

'Play something by Rainbow.'

'No, Yes or Rush! Play, I don't know, *Spirit of Radio*.'

Pete fast forwarded to *Spirit of Radio* and the rest of us head bobbed in the back of the camper.

'Play Status Quo!' That had been Jake's request for the holiday.

'Noooooo!' The rest of us groaned.

'Pink Floyd.'

'Led Zeppelin.' And so, the Rush tape was pulled from the machine, and we all sang *Stairway to Heaven* at the tops of our voices, closely followed by the whole of Pink Floyd's *Dark Side of the Moon*.

As we entered The Midlands, Pete put on one of his most recently purchased and much-loved tapes, Marillion's *Fugazi*. We all tried to learn the words ready for the concert we had booked to go to see them in the winter. As the music blasted out around us and through the open windows of the camper, we all sang at the tops of our voices.

Was that the happiest I was ever going to be? That pure, uninhibited joy that comes from feeling as one with those around you – at having that shared experience which you would remember forever, before your world became full of responsibility? How do you maintain that utter happiness? How could we stop the clock and freeze that moment when the world was something we felt we could grasp and keep?

The time for us.

Ours.

Chapter 13

Life resumed a sense of normality but those bonds we'd forged were there and we all met up every week. That elephant in the room was always there, though, and I felt that no one, not even Pete, truly understood the ramifications of what had happened on that last night of our holiday.

Back at work the day after we returned, I couldn't concentrate. A turmoil of emotions raced through me. When I'd arrived home the previous evening, I went straight to my bedroom and gingerly removed the letter from my bag. Standing in the middle of my room, I held the musty-smelling paper in my hand and circled the room several times wondering what to do with it, where I should keep it. I considered finding a match in the kitchen drawer and heading outside to burn it on the patio, as Cathy had suggested. I was scared that it could be a curse, however, and that if I destroyed it, instead of ridding me of it, it would exacerbate the problem. Perhaps burning it really would make things much worse.

In the end, I found an old purple and silver box I'd inherited from my late great-grandmother. I carefully folded the note and placed it against the lilac velvet bottom of the box. Easing the lid back on, I realized I still had the problem of where I should keep it.

Having put the letter in my great-grandmother's box, I realized that whatever the consequences, I'd subconsciously made the decision to keep it. Glancing at the paper basket beside my desk, I understood, then, that all ideas of destroying the letter had been eliminated from my mind. In desperation, I walked over to my desk, opened the bottom drawer, and placed the box right at the back. I hoped I would never need it again. I hoped that with it being out of sight it would allow me to get on with my life, devoid of coincidental spooky witchcraft, and prophesizing old women.

At work in the operating theatre, we were doing routine neutering for most of the morning. The local cat rescue had brought in eleven cats to be neutered, four of them feral. As we started with the more placid cats, Sally and Tomas seemed concerned that I hadn't come back to work full of the joys of my holiday.

Later, while we took a break before the onerous task of sedating the feral cats, Sally took the opportunity to ask me what was wrong. I gave her a quick summary, while she stood opposite me with her mouth open, her face aghast. She went on to tell me about predictions that had been made about her own family, and that not all of them had ever come true.

'Honestly,' she reassured me, 'you don't need to worry – it's something and nothing. This stuff is just designed to play with our heads!'

Over the coming months life fell into a regular routine. Hannah had grown into a beautiful young woman and our holiday away had seen her becoming much more confident. She was doing well on her horticulture course and, if I'm honest, had let some of her new-found confidence go to her head. She became flirtatious, even, sometimes, flirting with Pete. He brushed it off when I told him I'd noticed. 'It's you I love,' he reassured me.

He'd often come to meet me after work, and we'd take the dogs out of the city to the forest. Together we watched as the summer faded, and autumn arrived with all its copper and red glory. Hannah would sometimes ask to tag along. I became a little annoyed with her but couldn't refuse.

I was looking forward to the time when Pete and I could be together in our own home – we were saving hard, but it was probably going to be a couple of years before we could afford to do anything about it. In the meantime, we had a short holiday in North Wales to look forward to. The six of us were going, and I felt excited that we could all echo the fun we'd had that summer.

The week before we were due to go, Pete arrived

unexpectedly at our front door. He had a surprise for me and told me to close my eyes. He led me down the path to the garden gate, and when I opened my eyes, there in front of us was a huge black motorbike.

'Oh, my God. It's amazing!' The chrome of the bike was gleaming, and you could see your face in the shiny black paint of the petrol tank. Flung across the seat were two jackets, and hanging from the handlebars were two helmets, one black, one red.

'You want to go for a ride?'

'Yes, yes, absolutely.' I was so very excited. I wondered how much it had eaten into our house-buying budget but let all those worries go as we mounted the bike. He gave me a quick lesson in how to ride pillion; something I was glad of, or else I fear I would have fallen off when we were leaning into the corners.

Pete had passed his motorcycle test at about the same time as he passed his car driving test. He hadn't ridden for a couple of years but had spent a few days familiarizing himself with this big bike. It was great fun, and we headed out of the city along country roads, finishing up at a pub in The Cotswolds – in a little place called Long Compton. After a lemonade each, we mounted the bike again and headed home.

Ade had already agreed with him that for the trip to Wales he would drive the camper and take Hannah, Rachel, Jake and the two dogs. While I was excited at the idea of travelling to Wales on the bike, I felt we'd miss out on some of the camaraderie of being in the camper, but Pete was so excited, I went along with what he wanted.

We couldn't stay in Wales for longer than four days, mainly due to various work commitments. Once there, however, we fell into the ways we'd had during our summer in Scotland. We stayed in a cottage – a huge step up from our camping under the stars. The cottage had a television and a VHS player, along with thirty or forty films, including Top Gun, Karate Kid, The Empire Strikes Back, and Terminator. The first night we voted and decided we'd watch Flashdance as a double bill with The Dark Crystal. Jake hated Flashdance, which made us want to watch it even more, especially as he'd still not got over his obsession with Status Quo.

We were staying not far from a huge castle – Conwy Castle. On the Saturday, we took it in turns to go in as dogs weren't allowed. Jake, Rachel, and Ade went in for a tour of the castle in the morning and Hannah, Pete and me in the afternoon … whoever was not on castle touring was walking around the town with the dogs.

Hannah remained in the castle gift shop, while Pete and I walked along the suspension bridge. Alone, just for a little while, he said we should get married, and what did I think about that.

'Was that a proposal?' I asked.

'Do I have to do the bended knee thing?'

'Of course.'

And so, right in the middle of the suspension footbridge, he got down on one knee and proposed. We kissed and I told him I would. That was how it was meant to be, the two of us together forever. We'd become indivisible, and wherever one of us was found, you'd usually find the other. We even sometimes finished one another's sentences, and we had a way of knowing what the other was going to do next. Or at least I thought that was the way it was.

Later on, we made a huge dinner with some food we'd taken with us. Pete and I told them that when we got back home, we'd go and find a nice engagement ring. None of the others seemed surprised, and Hannah and Rachel argued over who would be the most senior bridesmaid. There would be no such argument about the best man – we all knew it would be Ade.

All heaped around the room on cushions and having flipped coins to see who got the comfiest seats, after dinner we sat down to watch Footloose. I felt so warm inside. Life was wonderful – how much more perfect could it have been? I was there with the people I loved and who loved me; I had my handsome dog lay down at my feet; his best friend Jess lying with her toes companionably touching his.

Pete seemed restless and got Rachel to pause the film. 'Look, we're out of bread, I'll go down to the local store and fetch some before they close. I pulled a face – I was enjoying the film. 'But the film?' I said.

'I'm not really enjoying it, and I won't be long. They'll be closing in half an hour, so I need to go now if I'm going to get some ready for our breakfast.'

Before I could say any more, Hannah jumped up and asked if she could go with him. What *was* she doing?

Pete, my ever polite and helpful Pete, looked a little awkward, but said, 'Okay, Han.'

Han? Since when had she been known as *Han*?

And then, to make matters worse, he nodded over at

297

me and said, 'She can borrow your stuff, can't she?' What could I say that wouldn't come out as being jealous or obstructive? And anyway, if she was going, then she'd need some protective clothing.

'Er, yes, okay.' I glared at him. He quickly looked away.

'Great!' Hannah said, and clambered across everyone to reach for my jacket, helmet, and gloves. She glanced at my bike boots, but then remembered they'd be too small for her. I felt a little triumphant spark of selfishness, and then immediately worried about her jeans-only covered legs and flimsy pump-covered feet.

The rest of us went out to wave them off. Low, quickly gathering clouds almost obscured the already-visible moon. A persistent drizzle filled the air. Autumnal leaves cast an eerie glow due to the light from the kitchen door. As I watched them mounting the bike, I glanced at Rachel. She offered a weak, sympathetic smile and shrugged. It wasn't like her to not have something to say. I was being unreasonable, I knew that, but inside I felt my heart was breaking.

As the engine throbbed, I suddenly felt sick. I looked to the grey sky; I touched my scar.

Part Three

29 Years from Now

Chapter 1

The world has changed much since I first met Dayna.

Twenty-nine years have passed since the day at the zoo. The concept of a better world which was craved by so many of us was not completely unfounded, and I suppose that in the end the good in the world overrode the horrors that came about in the years following our meeting. The 2020s brought wars, disease, famine, environmental catastrophes. There was no part of the world unaffected by what was happening.

The years have gone by, and while it's been a struggle, the world has emerged as a more peaceful place. It has been nature which has united us; the mutual understanding that we must protect the Earth, all who live on it and the wild places, has become an integral part of all our lives. The thing that as a species we neglected and almost destroyed, we now treasure.

The situation is, however, a long way from being optimistic: climate change predictions which began way back in the mid-1900s have happened – no one can say that we weren't warned! The sea level has risen due to the melting of icebergs and ice caps, and subsequently some low-lying islands and mainland coastal settlements have tragically been lost to the ocean.

The destruction of wild spaces continued to be relentless until, finally, it was that destruction which tipped the balance, and governments across the world panicked to find a solution. The global population consequences of this have been such that there are now lower birth rates and fewer people. Resources we have are limited because we have taken and taken from the land and seas. There remains, of course, some countries which have fared much better than others.

Amid the chaotic environmental disarray, other species have suffered – how could they not have? Most larger wild animals are no longer truly free and reside either in reserves or sanctuaries. The world is a large place, however, and I like to think that with our deliberate rewilding there have been opportunities for animals to break free and live natural lives; as they did a hundred years ago, before we humans messed up the planet. Just as people have lost their lives through climate change, so, too, have many animals.

Dayna was instrumental in helping governments to agree treaties specific to wildlife. Recognizing the threats that climate change was having, she and other key zoologists relocated many animals away from harm – this was the only way that some of the species specific to affected areas were going to avoid extinction. She, and others like her, were saving as many animals as they could – not only primates, but other species too.

In 2034 I saw an article which described how, when being involved in the rescue of a pack of painted dogs, she and her team located a group of villagers who'd managed to survive the adverse weather conditions by digging underground tunnels. While they had lost more than a third of their population, when the painted dog rescue began, the sixty-odd remaining villagers had come out of hiding.

They had been lucky enough to gain access to a small but significant underground sandstone aquifer, which had provided them with ample water to enable them to survive. Food sources had been running out as little would grow. The presence of Dayna and the other wild dog rescuers resulted in dual rescue efforts and resettling of humans and dogs. The rescue was not easy, and once the people were flown out in Chinooks, Dayna and her team remained. They relentlessly trapped and caught, one by one, the family of wild dogs, before transporting them to their new home in the lowland plains of northern Germany.

Mine and Dayna's paths never really crossed in the

years that followed our last encounter. I kept up to date with what she was doing from afar. I saw her a couple of times in passing, but only from a distance. She was always with her husband. I didn't know whether she'd ever told him about what happened between her and me.

I sometimes went to hear her speak about the environment, and I think she saw me in the audience once or twice. She spoke with the great passion she had when I first met her that day in the café. As time passed, there was an increasing level of urgency in what she was saying. I always left before the talks were over. I had long ago received my orders from her to stay out of her life and was never going to disrespect that.

There were times when I felt she was watching me too, but I managed to not obsess about it. In the years that followed since our meeting, and after that first sighting of her with Jackson at my first big exhibition, I once thought I saw her looking through the window of another exhibition a couple of days before the opening night. Another time, I was distracted by one of the gallery owners and felt as though someone was looking at me from the other side of some large pillars. When I looked again to where I thought she had been standing, whoever had been there was gone. I often pondered about why she was showing as much of an interest in me as I was in her, when it had been her who'd been so clear about our never seeing one another again.

There's no doubt that I was influenced by having met her. She unveiled in me something which made me want to make the most of my life; to try to use the resources I had to make the world a better place for Jenna and future generations. It sounds so corny, and yet it was the most important thing we could do; something we, as humans, had to do to prevent our world and all who made it their home, from environmentally imploding.

While my painting style was the same, what I painted had changed. My portraits began to reflect more greatly what was going on in the world – people starving, people fleeing, pictures of people and animals surrounded by destruction. We had to make everything we did matter and there emerged an urgency in what I did. I pulled together a book which had all my environmental pictures in it. When it sold well, I anonymously donated the proceeds to Dayna's charity – knowing she would use the money to do good things.

Everything now is based around community and helping one another to survive. I don't want to portray an image of optimism across the board, for we still have those who flout the laws and live illegal black-market lives, but I imagine criminals will always be a part of human society. You hope that eventually the good will outweigh the corrupt.

Amid the changes there have been huge advances in technology, and computers are now able to diagnose within minutes all sorts of diseases with a tiny drop of blood, urine, skin, or tissue on a small hand-held sensor. Each machine has its own built in solar-powered software so it can be used anywhere in the world. Medical advances, too, have been substantial, and fully functioning organs can be made, tailored to each patient's needs.

As a result, life expectancy for many people is likely to be more than a hundred. It is not a rare thing these days for centenarians to still be spritely and looking forward to their next fifteen or twenty years. The improvement in global diet due to a lack of processed foods has helped, along with the necessity for using the land for growing crops, rather than rearing farm animals. The concept of eating animals has become something we look back on with a sense of horror. The oceans were ravaged almost to the point of devastation through fishing and ocean noise, but now except for the transport of essential resources across continents, the water is pretty much left to its own devices to repair and exist for its own good. I hope nature will find a way now we are leaving the sea alone.

While carbon dioxide has filled our atmosphere and changed the pH of our oceans, altering complete ecosystems, the race to find ways of capturing carbon from the air has so far been successful. It's not a long-term solution by far, but for now much of the excess carbon is extracted by huge tree-like filters which extract the carbon from the skies and store it underground. The problem lies in such storage, in that there will be a limit to the amount of carbon we can store. Some scientists say we have enough of this storage space for fifty years or more; some believe we could do this for as long as a couple of hundred years without difficulty; more pessimistic scientists consider we have only twenty years to find other solutions. Planting more trees has helped, but some regions now have such scorched earth that it's made it impossible for anything to grow there.

I suppose what we *have* done with all these measures, is to have bought ourselves time to take stock and think about where we go from here. Ideas of abandoning this planet and going to find another planet to destroy were discarded in favour of pulling together in an attempt to mend the one we have.

The one thing we haven't managed to do is beat the rise in drug-resistant microorganisms. The emergence of particularly determined resistant strains of bacteria and viruses has been something which has resulted in a lot of people and animals dying. Many more are expected to die in the coming years; hence we are careful when we do get ill not to mix with others and to just wait it out, hoping our immune system will kick in.

In the end, Dayna contracted a resistant strain of bacteria. I read that she was working in the Congo Basin rescuing a group of bonobos that were posing a threat to the people in a local village. Whether she caught the infection from the people or from the bonobos, or even from something she'd encountered in the environment, no one was initially very sure, but she developed an illness which quickly spread through her body. Her immune system could not cope, and while being flown back to the UK, she died of sepsis in an isolation chamber.

The bacterium is an as yet unknown anaerobic one, and scientists still working in The Congo are busy taking soil samples and trying to find its source. The story in the press report suggested she wounded herself on a nail which was protruding from a transport cage they'd just put a bonobo into. It was something as simple as that which contributed to ending her life. It's thought the bacteria entered her bloodstream via the wound and, similar to tetanus, produced a dangerous toxin. In her eighties and still fit and working hard, she'd had so much left to give to the world.

In the reports about her death, it said she had been so busy she'd forgotten to wash the wound. It was such a rookie error for someone of her experience and knowledge, but it's thought the bacteria behaved in such a virulent manner that it's unlikely washing with an antiseptic would have helped anyway. At first it was thought it was a new, emerging primate disease, but samples taken had proven the bonobos were okay. As planned, they were moved to quarantine and are awaiting entry to their sanctuary home.

Now when people die of unidentified and potentially transmissible diseases, they are frozen in case their tissues are needed in research of other illnesses that have manifested in similar ways. The body is sometimes kept by the government for years afterwards as there's a constant fight to keep up with the evolving and emergence of harmful microorganisms.

We have walls of remembrance, where people's names are engraved onto plaques, and trees are planted in memorial gardens. Those trees and plaques can be anywhere the family wants them to be. Her family planted her tree at the edge of a wild animal sanctuary near their home. Zoos no longer exist – in this new world no one wants to ogle at animals for fun – where animals are displaced, they are taken to sanctuaries such as that one, where rewilding has taken place.

When I found out about her death I was devastated, and the urge to go and see her remembrance tree was strong. I had to say my own farewell to her – to reflect on what had happened all those years before.

I told Ellie that Dayna had died and what I was going to do. She knew why. She understood that I needed some closure. She offered to come along with me; but this was something I had to do alone. The whole thing became less strange to Ellie over the years – but whether she ever came to truly understand, I imagine I'll never know. For a year or so after my meetings with Dayna, Ellie and I both felt that something was amiss in our relationship. There was the sense of an 'other'. It was something huge; something which had the potential to drive a wedge between us.

Time healed, and we both realized that what we had together was not worth losing. And so, like so many whose relationships are affected by other influences, we had to work at it. It was as though I had had an affair, but without the personal relationship that goes with such a thing. In time, we got to a place where we were happy again.

Chapter 2

In the memorial wood near to the wildlife sanctuary, I walked for a mile or more before finding her tree. It was a ten feet tall pear tree, which would be filled with pure white blossom come springtime. Beneath it her ashes would eventually be scattered by her family.

I had with me a few spring flower bulbs and some wildflower seeds – it had become customary for anyone visiting memorial trees to take seeds, bulbs, or plants to plant around the edges of the cemetery. The plots for planting were always highlighted by the caretakers of the grounds. The flowers would eventually provide food for the bees and other pollinators, who would visit the blossom in spring and summer. There was something pretty special about visiting memorial gardens in springtime and seeing the array of pink, white and cream blossom, and witnessing the arrival of the first bees and butterflies busy about their work.

Smaller plaques than the ones on the remembrance walls were placed under each memorial tree. The writing on them would eventually fade, just as the memory of the life that once was, would dwindle into nothing once their loved ones, too, had passed on. The plaque would gradually crumble to the ground, becoming part of the earth.

As I scored the earth to sprinkle some seeds by the hedgerow nearby, I heard chatter and footsteps getting closer to me. In the distance, I saw three people walking along from the direction I had come. I strained my eyes to see them and thought I recognized one of them. I looked away to give myself time to think where I'd seen that person before. It was an elderly man with two much younger women. And then I realized. It was Jackson, and those were probably his and Dayna's daughters, Pieter, and Lottie.

'Nate! The spritely, bespectacled old man reached out his hand as he approached. 'I'm glad you're here.'

His daughters introduced themselves. It was clear they all knew who I was. I was bewildered. Jackson smiled. 'We don't live far from here and we've been up here every day since we planted the tree. It's beautiful here, isn't it?' His question rhetorical, I simply nodded. 'I imagine you're wondering how we know you?' I nodded again, silently dreading but simultaneously feeling a knot of excitement at what he was about to say.

'Dayna told us about you all those years ago, about what happened, and I'm really not surprised to find you here. It disturbed her for some time, what went on back then, but eventually she realized she had to let go of it. And so, Dayna being Dayna, she put everything into her work. Before she did that, she parceled up some things and told me that if ever you turned up once she was no longer around, then we were to give the parcel to you. Have you got time, Nate, today, to come to our house and we'll give it to you? Like I said, we're not far from here – just a few streets from the main entrance, in fact. We moved here about ten years ago – Dayna had become very attached to some of the animals in the sanctuary and wanted to be near to them.'

I finally found my voice. 'Of course, Jackson. Um, yes, whatever – that would be good. Thank you.'

Jackson nodded and smiled. The three of them helped me to plant the spring bulbs and the rest of the wildflower seeds. And then the four of us – three people who had known each other forever, and a complete stranger, strolled familiarly along the road back to the car park.

I gave them a lift back to Jackson's house. The house was a large, Victorian-style villa, and as Jackson pushed the door open, five dogs of various shapes and sizes came rushing to greet us. But then I noticed, two of them weren't dogs at all, they were pigs. How very Dayna to have pigs as companions.

Pieter offered me a cup of tea – part of me wanted to just take whatever it was they had for me and go, but the rest of me was keen to linger and experience a little of Dayna's life. I wanted to cherish some moments with these people who she had clearly loved so much. I gratefully accepted and took a seat at the breakfast bar.

The dogs and pigs were all eager to be around me. One of the dogs was keen to put his head on my lap and receive the maximum amount of fuss that was available to him. He had long, wiry hair and resembled something of a deerhound. He was nothing like our old Harvey who had passed away many years before at the grand old age of eighteen, or any of the other dogs who had come along after him, including our Jack Russell types Trudy and Trixie back home.

'Shall we take these drinks onto the terrace?' Lottie suggested. 'It's warm for the time of year.'

Outside there was a soft breeze, and wispy, white clouds gently drifted across a background sky of deep blue. It was, indeed, warm for the time of year. It was late October and in years gone by we would have been wearing coats. The terrace overlooked a long garden which had wildflowers and fruit trees at the bottom. Some trees were laden with late fruit still to be picked. Pretty much everyone grew food of some sort – usually a variety, with everyone working on the theory that if one crop failed, others would survive.

We chatted for a couple of hours about Dayna, her work, their work, my family and work, and the state of the world. I felt like I did at home, that I could talk to these people forever. I wanted to spend time with them, and hypothetically fix all the world's problems. We all avoided the subject of why I was there.

Perhaps it was for the best.

As I got up to leave, Pieter told me to wait – she had remembered the package. I was glad she'd recalled why I was there; I would have been embarrassed to have had to ask for it. She came through holding a large, flat, almost square package. And I knew instantly what it was.

'Mum wrapped this for you years ago and told us that if ever you came here, you must have it. I'm afraid it smells a little musty. Mum opened it and added bits and pieces now and then.' Pieter smiled and handed it to me. I took it with both my hands. It was precious, and it was something I knew would hold the answer; the solution to everything that had happened all those years before.

With the package tucked under my left arm, once I reached the door, Jackson took hold of my right hand and peered at me over his glasses. 'I hope this finally provides the answers you need, Nate. I don't know whether anything would have been different if she had given this to you all those years ago, but I'm glad you finally have it – I wish you well.' He nodded and smiled.

Along the stony driveway to the car, I felt my legs had turned to jelly. Each step felt as though I was lifting my feet through infinite time; immersing them in a terrain that would exist for long after all us mortals no longer existed.

So many years had gone by, and all the time I'd thought I'd never know what the story was between Dayna and me. I never expected that one day I would know more. I truly hoped I would be vindicated for all that had gone on between us when we first met. Once in the car, I turned and waved, before driving back to the car park at the memorial garden.

With the car still, the silence was eerie, until a male blackbird flew to a nearby hawthorn, and sang his latest repertoire of mimicked song.

Chapter 3

Taking a deep breath, I tentatively began to open the parcel, which I knew without a doubt from the shape of it, was going to contain a painting. I carefully peeled back the paper and wondered if it really would provide the answers I had longed for.

Once I could see the top corner which had the canopy of a forest, I felt a rush of excitement, of acknowledgment. This was it. This was the moment I had hoped for. The shades of green on the top of the picture gave way to the unmistakable blue-green and brown shades of a lake. And there, swimming on the lake, was a swan. At the edge of the lake, just as in my regression, was another swan. Beside them, sitting on a bench, was the young Dayna. This was absolutely the image I'd described when I was regressed all those years before.

I was right ... for all those years I had been right.

The enormity of that realization was overwhelming, and I felt a sob rise in my throat. The consequences of this were huge; this was much bigger than just me. There was no way I could have known about the painting. No way at all.

There was more in the parcel than the painting. A bundle of photographs was tied together with a purple ribbon. Untying the bow, a heap of images fell to my lap. Apart from Dayna there was no one I recognized in the photographs, although I could see that most often stood next to her was a young guy much taller than she was. He looked in his early twenties and had shoulder-length hair. They looked so very happy – carefree, spirited.

There were other pieces of paper in with the painting – many of them were flyers from my exhibitions … there was also what looked like a long letter from Dayna, along with a shorter letter, which, it would seem, was not written by her. I scanned over it, but it didn't make any sense, I noticed it was dated a long time ago. I put it to one side, and instead began to read Dayna's letter.

Dear Nate

If you're reading this, then I'll have left this Earth and gone to the place where our bodies become dust and our souls are liberated once more … if that is, indeed, what happens to us.

I owe you an explanation and, I guess, to let you know that some of what you said was right all along. I don't know how that happened; how we happened to cross paths, and in such strange circumstances. Was it chance? Were we actually meant to be in one another's lives for eternity? Somehow, anyway, even if we were not together? Was it so we'd know that the other was okay? For we've not done so badly with the cards we've been dealt, have we, Nate?

When I saw you that day in the zoo, as you did with me, I, too, felt a sense of familiarity about you ... it's such a cliché, isn't it Nate? But, yes, it was as though I really had seen you before - I had a deep sense of déjà vu. Are there really ties that connect us across lifetimes, Nate? Are we destined to keep on meeting ones we have loved before, without ever resolving the issues of the past? That day, and in our subsequent meetings and the months that followed, I began to doubt what was real and what was fantasy.

I thought that would be the end of it, just a fleeting, mysterious moment that would never be unraveled; just like so many a person has in their lifetime. But when you contacted me about the painting, I felt compelled to meet you, to come and see it, to go behind Jackson's back and go down an avenue I wasn't comfortable exploring. It was all so difficult for me. Can you imagine the sadness we would have caused if we had continued down some surreal path into the unknown? It would have been catastrophic for all the people you and I loved.

Time has passed by so quickly; the years feel only a whisper since the day you came to me bearing spiritual yearnings, but I don't have any regrets

about the decisions I made when we met. I feel,
however, that you really do deserve to know the
truth, and in particular that the details of your
regression struck a chord with me. Things you said
that day have resonated inside me since the day in
the cafe, and while I don't regret it, I feel heartfelt
sadness that I didn't tell you there, then, that much
of what you said was true. There was no reasonable
way in which anyone, but those of us who were
around in those days so long ago, could have known
the things you told me.

There were things you said – about the motorbike,
and, of course, the paintings. I don't know how you
could possibly have known about the picture with
the pair of mute swans in it – or the things you said
about my dear Pete. He is the tall guy next to me in
many of the photographs.

I reached for the pile of photographs in front of me
and looked at him. I felt nothing. There was no
eureka moment, no bolt of lightning flashing
through me. Disappointed, I picked up the letter and
carried on reading.

You mentioned a dog, and I guess that could have
been some weird coincidence, but there was another
dog, beyond the ones we had living as part of our
families. I imagine I'm not really making sense,
Nate, but please bear with me as I hope all will

become clear.

On our first date, Pete and I met an old man named Arthur. He was out walking by the canal with his dog Eric. Arthur was a survivor from the Normandy landings in the Second World War, and after that first meeting Pete and I used to often bump into him, and he would tell us tales of the horrors of war. As the months went by and Arthur's wife died and his health deteriorated, we used to take Eric out for Arthur, with our two dogs Buddy and Jess. You mentioned a black and white dog in your regression, and even though there are millions of black and white dogs in the world and any connection might seem spurious, I was sure the dog you spoke about was Arthur's dog. He was a black and white, fluffy collie-type. The reason for feeling sure it was him was how you mentioned the black and white dog in relation to the woods, and that he had a white blaze on his chest.

One day Buddy and Jess ran off into the trees and I was calling them back. Perhaps it happened more than once as they were quite naughty when the two of them got together, but there was one time when sweet old Eric was with us when we were searching for them. On that particularly memorable day, we'd put the three of them in Pete's car to take them to the forest on the edge of town, and my sister Hannah decided to tag along. My unruly dog Buddy inspired Jess to go chasing squirrels with him. As Pete, Hannah, and I wandered the forest looking for the two of them, good old Eric ambled along beside us, seemingly oblivious to the mischievous wanderings of his canine friends. We eventually found the two of them, excitedly doing vertical jumps beside an old oak tree. They were trying to catch a grey squirrel that had no doubt long ago leapt from one tree canopy to another. It was that woodland which inspired Pete to do the paintings.

You told me that in your regression you felt as though you'd come off a motorbike, and that you felt as though you were drowning. We'd spent the day in Wales at Conwy Castle. I don't know whether you ever figured it out, but I'm convinced that was the scene you somehow managed to describe from your dreams. I don't know whether you've seen it but it's a magnificent castle with a metal bridge. On that bridge Pete proposed to me.

We were all staying in a cottage nearby, and one night while the rest of us watched a film, Hannah and Pete went for a ride on the bike. They were only going a few lanes away to fetch a loaf of bread ready for breakfast. Pete and I had had a bit of a disagreement before they left. On their way back from the grocery store along the dark, wet country roads, on which it was by then raining hard, they skidded as they were going around a sharp bend.

Pete landed in the river and banged his head, while Hannah was lucky enough to land in some long, soft grass on the riverbank. As she scrabbled to recover from what had happened, she looked around and saw Pete was face down in the water. She managed to crawl over to him and mustered enough strength to roll him over so he wouldn't inhale the water and drown. Within seconds, he was coughing and spluttering.

They were gone for ages – the bike was undamaged apart from some scratches to the petrol tank and a few small dents, so once they managed to get themselves sorted out, they eventually lifted it and got back on it. By this time, back at the cottage we were desperately worried. Pete's brother Ade and I were just about to head off in the camper to look for them, when we heard the rumbling of the bike coming along the lane.

You assumed that that had been how you (if you really were Pete) had died, but the thing is that he didn't die in the accident, so I've always felt some consolation in the fact that what I told you wasn't a lie. Pete and Hannah had, though, definitely come off much worse than the bike. Hannah mainly had bumps and cuts on her right arm and right leg from being catapulted through the air, but she'd had a soft landing. Pete had a bruised shoulder and a cut to his forehead. After a check-up at casualty, they were both discharged from hospital later that evening.

Back at the cottage later that night we all thanked our lucky stars that they'd fallen on the riverside, and not on the other side of the road where there wouldn't have been such a soft landing. There might even have been a vehicle coming around the bend. The accident dampened our enthusiasm for the holiday, and we returned home the following day.

Riding pillion on the battered bike on the way back, I felt as though things had changed, as though my whole world was collapsing around me. The others went on in the van. I was tempted to as well but didn't want Pete to make that journey on his own so soon after the accident.

So, yes, there was someone I loved back then, Nate, and he did have a motorbike. I don't know whether what I've said so far is enough evidence for you. But what really did it for me, what really confirmed everything you were saying to me, and that a person can be reunited with people they have loved before, was the painting. Not the fox one, but this painting, the one with the mute swans. There is no way you could have known about it – few people did. For many years I had this painting on the landing in mine and Jackson's house.

It was 1985 when the accident happened, winter had been on its way, yet the weather had been mild for the time of year, hence our visit to Wales. Pete was in the final year of his art degree. His parents had bought him fresh stocks of everything he needed for the final stretch of his course. In the days that followed the accident, Pete told me he wanted to do some paintings of me. He wanted to paint, he said, the essence of me in shades of nature. He said that mere words would not express the depth of his love and how sorry he was for having scared me when we were in Wales. I laughed at him and told him I knew he loved me, despite the worries I'd had about Hannah and him. I felt his love, you see; I felt it with every breath I took and every beat of my heart.

Anyway, I digress ... in the weeks after the accident he said he wanted to paint me in every season and in each season, I would be sitting on our favourite bench at the entrance to the woods, amid the trees and flowers we both loved so much. It had turned wintry outside, but in his bedroom that day he began his mammoth task.

As I sat for him, he created 'Spring'. The picture, of course, which somehow ended up in your hands. The image was, as he'd planned, in shades of green and representing the renewed life of the time of year, and in the bottom left-hand corner of the painting he painted the small, dark red fox cub. He painted the cub so he looked inquisitive, with his head cocked to one side as though he was carefully watching me. The abnormally large red admiral butterfly was something he added to make the picture not just of a girl and a fox. To make people think about the natural world he loved so much, he wanted to somehow depict a sense of beauty and freedom on a carefree day, with warmth and the promising signs of warmer days.

A few days after finishing 'Spring', Pete spent a few days creating 'Summer', this painting with the swans. You'll find similarities between this and 'Spring'. That had always been his intention. I don't know, I think he had some idea that by creating a series of images through the seasons, it would mean our love would be eternal, that there would be no time when we would ever be apart – he the painter, me the subject of his work, his muse, I suppose. Silly really, but I guess artists have been inspired by many things. I felt flattered, but also that I didn't deserve such admiration.

That day once Pete had finished painting 'Summer', we were in my bedroom, and I lay on my side on my bed admiring the picture, where he'd left it on his easel. Pete was behind me with his body spooned around mine. Together, we admired his work – he with a far more critical eye than mine. I loved it, and yet he could only see fault in his painting. He

*said he wanted to work on it some more to get it
how he wanted it to be. In the picture there are dark
silhouettes of birds in the sky, and clearer, pastel
blue birds sitting amid the deep green leaves on the
branches of the trees. I loved that the swans were
beside me in the pond at the mouth of the wood, and
that he'd painted me turning to the side, looking
over towards them and smiling.*

*Once he'd left for home that night, Hannah came
into my room to admire the painting. She said she
hoped she would find someone who would love her
as much as Pete clearly loved me. I hoped so too. I
don't know whether by then she'd got over her
crush on him. I never challenged her about it.*

*At that point 'Spring' was already adorning his
parents' sitting room wall, and Pete said that once
he was happy with it, he wanted me to have this one
with the swans. I told him I would treasure it
forever. He had intended to paint autumn next. He
said there would be no animals in it. Just trees in all
their autumnal glory. And me, sitting on our special
bench. That night, he left the swan painting at my
house.*

*Pete never managed to paint 'autumn' or 'winter',
because the next day he collapsed in my parents'
kitchen as he was peeling a banana to make a jam
and banana sandwich. It sounds so ridiculous that*

someone could go in such a way, peeling a banana for heaven's sake, but an hour later at the hospital he was declared dead by the doctors in casualty. A blood clot on his brain had shifted and he had suffered an intracranial bleed – a brain haemorrhage. The doctors thought it was as a delayed result of the accident. The clot had been sitting there like a timebomb. Just waiting.

He'd had an intermittent headache after the crash, but no one had thought anything of it as he and Hannah had both been so battered and bruised. Once he was back in classes working on his portfolio, he'd had little time with his busy schedule to do anything about those headaches. Perhaps if he had, then the clot would have been discovered.

Like I said, Pete was at our house when it happened. We'd been for a long walk with the two dogs, and he was back at ours for something to eat. We'd all thought everything was okay – he and I were planning our lives together. Although we'd been with each other for less than a year, we'd been looking at houses. In that moment when I saw him die, my whole world disintegrated around me. Suddenly, in that instant, there was nothing left.

The 'spring' painting that somehow ended up in your collection, Nate? I can only imagine Pete's parents moved on, that when I married Jackson, they wanted to let go of me and of what might have been. They had plenty of other pictures Pete had drawn or painted for them over the years. Maybe they'd downsized their home or something, I don't know, it just seems like such a strange decision for them to have made.

I wish that when they had no longer wanted it that they'd offered it to me. I would have loved to have looked after it. But then if they'd done that, I imagine you and I might not have discovered that link, that tie which somehow had been forged between us.

But time moves on, and we become what the world and our circumstances make us. I kept in touch with Pete's parents for several years. Until Jess died really. I used to go and walk her for them; take my dog Buddy to see her. But the memories were too much, and I think eventually that as time passed Pete's parents found it difficult to be around me. They never said, but I sensed it – I even felt it with his brothers Ade and Julian. I suppose in the end, likewise, they too were a constant reminder to me of what Pete and I had been through together. And what we had lost. But then they all moved away – Pete's brothers opened a photographic business in Cornwall, and as grandchildren came along, their parents followed them down there.

I moved north, and I suppose that in the end all Pete's family and I really had was social media – delicate links which didn't stand the test of time.

The paintings, though they are of me, they are also of a time of innocence and beauty, and the only other person who could have truly known their detail and of the things you said was, indeed, Pete. He knew every stroke of each image.

When you emailed the photograph of the fox cub painting to me, my world felt as though it had collapsed, and all the anguish of those years before came flooding back. I tried to hide the sheer intensity of what I was feeling – that's why it took me a few days to write back to you. I felt I couldn't be objective. It took every cell in my body to write back without becoming emotional. All I wanted was to fly home, meet you, take the picture from you and run – hide from this world and try to recapture the feelings I'd had all those years before. In the end, though, while there were times I hated myself for it, it was easier to deny what was happening.

When I did get back in touch with you and we'd arranged to meet, in the days that followed I thought about cancelling our meeting. The photograph you had sent me had been enough for me to identify the picture, but I wanted to see it one more time. I wanted to feel what I'd felt all those years earlier. I needed to hold that picture in my hands and feel the emotions I'd experienced back then.

When I met you at the cafe, I did feel something. Never before nor since have I felt like I did that day. It's a feeling I can't describe to you, but I imagine it could have mirrored some of what I think happened to you when we shook hands. Somehow (and I don't know how) I managed to control my reaction to our touch.

I regretted not taking the painting from you when you offered it. I even thought I could have offered to have bought it from you. You know, said something like 'It's not me, but I really like it – can I buy it from you?' At least then I would have had it with me, but it was easier to simply deny all knowledge of the painting ... and, indeed, the painter.

I think, Nate, that if there is such a thing as reincarnation, then it's quite possible that in a previous life we were together. That's the explanation I've concealed from you all these years, and I'm sorry I could never bring myself to tell you; to agree with you, I suppose.

What was it that allowed us to be aware of something which others only imagine? Why is it that you and I, of all the people in the world, have had this extraordinary confirmation that there really could be something more?

When I left you that day and had somehow got through the meeting at the zoo, I went back to my hotel room, and cried and cried; the grief I had felt those years before came flooding back to me. I don't blame you for that; I just need you to know the depth of loss from that time had never gone away. Those things had been locked inside me since the day Pete died.

I thought after you and I met that you would find out about his death and make the connection. Over the years I've worried that you might turn up at my door, flash an obituary in front of me, and ask why I hadn't told you that you were right. I don't know why that didn't happen, perhaps it was because he didn't die straight away when the accident happened, and there was no mention of the accident in the newspaper or the obituary.

Anyhow, I imagine you never found the obituary because it was in a local newspaper back in the Midlands where I lived until I was in my mid-twenties. It was where Pete and I had grown up and had been at the same school. You had no way of knowing any of that though. The obituary never mentioned my name either; it just said Pete had left behind his parents, two brothers, grandparents, a girlfriend, and his beloved dog.

For many years I felt I couldn't ever love anyone else. When Mum, Hannah and I followed the ambulance to the hospital and the doctor very quickly confirmed Pete's death, I felt numb. I felt as though there was a way I should be, and that certain actions or facial expressions were acceptable, and others weren't. At his funeral, I thought back to TV programmes I'd watched with my mum when I was in my early teens, and how those characters would have reacted to such events. I looked around me at all the other mourners and held my emotions; feelings of numbness continuing to dominate my body.

But then, once we were outside the crematorium, I collapsed and sobbed until I could sob no more. All the plans we'd made together; the life we'd hoped to spend together – how we were going to save the world, all of that had been lost in that instant. The little power I had had to stop it I had dismissed, all because I'd been angry with him that night.

Perhaps he would have been more careful if he hadn't been perturbed about our quarrel – it was such a silly row, I had been concerned he was taking my younger sister out on the bike with him as it was clear she had a crush on him. I hadn't wanted her to feel encouraged. Perhaps he might have taken the corner more carefully if he hadn't been worrying about me and rushing to get back to me on the wet roads.

There were ordinary things, personal things you knew, Nate, which only Pete would have known. Everything you said matched what happened back then. I should have told you and I am so very sorry.

The man with the old collie dog, Arthur, his wife had been ill when we met him, and she died about the same time as Pete did. I bumped into Arthur shortly afterwards and he still had Eric by his side. He hadn't heard about Pete's death.

It's strange how people's lives do that fleeting thing where for part of your life you have a connection with someone and then they're gone. I stayed in touch with Arthur, and as he got weaker, I used to go and walk Eric for him, often taking Buddy and Jess. I went with him when he made the decision to have old Eric put to sleep. Within weeks, Arthur, too, had died. It was such a sad time.

Having lost Pete and then watching sweet little Eric and Arthur fade away, I threw myself into my work. Eventually I realized that nursing animals wasn't enough for me, and so I went and studied for almost twelve years to fill my head with the knowledge and experiences I needed in order to work with animals across the world.

But there's more you should know, Nate. Every time

I was with Pete, I felt there was nowhere in the world I would rather be than with him. That day he'd finished painting 'Summer' and we were lying on my bed together; I was relaxed and content with everything. I felt myself drifting to sleep, but then he suddenly pushed himself up to lean on his elbow, clearly wanting to talk. I flipped over on my back to look up at him. The side of his face was still bruised yellow, and he had the remnants of a wound on his brow. I gave him a weak smile and reached up to gently touch the wound.

What Pete said next shocked me, and his words have resonated through the years – mainly because of you, Nate. He told me he would love me for eternity and that even if he died, he would find some way of getting back to me. I told him to stop being so ridiculous; that he and I would be together forever – we were meant to be together. We were going to have three children – two boys and a girl (in that order), and four rescue dogs and a couple of cats. We would live in a house near to a forest, grow our own vegetables and plant lots of fruit trees.

Pete gently took hold of my face and looked deep into my eyes. The sea of blue I saw each time I looked at him, the sea that made my heart sing, had clouded over, becoming a tempestuous, stormy, steel grey.

'No … listen to me, Dayna, if there is another life beyond this one, I SHALL find you and I'll give you a sign – you'll know it's me … I'll make sure you know it's me.'

I felt a dark wave of fear pass through my body as his voice tapered off, leaving the statement hanging in the air and open-ended. I'd always felt so safe with him – as though nothing could invade our world and break the happiness we had when we were together. I'd never seen that bleak side of him. Not ever.

To lighten the mood, I sat bolt upright and picked up a pillow and hit him across his shoulder with it. I laughed and told him he was giving me the creeps and we should go for a walk. The two dogs were lying patiently beside the bed, so we said the magic word, 'Walkies,' and headed out into the wintry cold.

Although we chatted as we walked along, and Pete watched as I had races in the park with the dogs, he was distant for the rest of the day. I'll never know for sure whether he'd had some kind of premonition. Had he really seen his death, or was it just a coincidence, in that the only reason he was thinking so despairingly about the world, was because of his accident?

The 1980s was a time when we embraced the 'mix-

tape'. Years ago, I transferred onto a digital drive the contents of a mix-tape Pete recorded for me when we started going out. There's a copy of it here for you – I re-loaded them onto an earpiece some years ago, so I hope it still works. I was often tempted over the years to send it to you electronically, to try to do it anonymously so you wouldn't know it was from me, but I always worried that you would realize I had sent it. And then, well, those old scars would have been opened up.

I hadn't spotted an earpiece in the parcel, so I put the letter to one side and scrabbled to find it amid the letters and photographs. I thought it must have got lost, and then I saw it taped to the edge of the picture frame. She had been determined it wouldn't get lost. I placed it carefully on the dashboard shelf and went back to the letter.

There are a couple of things still to say, Nate, and I don't know whether these are perhaps the pinnacle of what happened – they are certainly odd, and I think they're worth mentioning to you.

The summer before we went to Wales and the accident happened, we spent six weeks in Scotland - Pete, me, my sister Hannah, Pete's brother Ade, and our friends Rachel and Jake – you'll see the pictures from that summer of 1985 in with the painting. I've labeled and dated the backs of some of the photographs showing where we were and who was who in the picture.

It was a mysterious time and things happened which stayed with me. Four of us quite by chance went to see a fortune teller. The things she warned came to pass, for all of us. I don't know how she could have been so accurate in what she predicted, or perhaps because of what she said, then by the power of suggestion we went on to live our lives that way. She told my friend Rachel, for example, that she would go to live far away, which she did, she went to live in New Zealand with a German man she met on holiday in Berlin. Her boyfriend of the time was Jake, and while they stayed together for ten years, they eventually went their separate ways, him moving to France with his broken heart and marrying a girl he met there. These were things the fortune teller suggested would happen. I don't know, I really don't. To me, she said there was a warning to say no, and then strangely she began to sing 'It's raining, it's pouring ...'. As you can probably imagine, I was terrified.

The warning from her though, strangely, that wasn't the starkest warning we received that summer. No, that came when the six of us, on our way home from our Scotland trip, encountered some sort of paranormal occurrence which resulted in us finding a letter. You told me you recalled in your regression about a woman who sent a letter with a warning about something to do with souls. I must say that it almost floored me when you said that.

The letter was from a woman named Annie, who'd died years before. She had previously owned my aunt's house. One day Annie was confronted by a woman who had a warning. The thing about this strange woman which was alarming, was that she was described as having had a scar on her neck, just like mine.

Call it coincidence, I guess we'll call it what we will, but Nate, she warned that if the people to whom the message related didn't act on the warning to, strangely, listen to one who knew, then their souls would separate across time. You'll see that the last part of the message says:

'Our lives are entwined as one. We must reach inside ourselves and prevent our worlds from drifting, for if we drift, we cannot reunite … '.

That part of the message has haunted me, Nate. My aunt had no need for the note, so she gave it to me. It was obvious who the message was intended for, so there was no point in her keeping it at the house anymore, hiding it in the dark cupboard. I've enclosed the letter for you. I imagine you, too, won't be able to fathom what she meant. I went on to assume the 'one who knew' was the fortune teller at the fete, but over time, Nate, I've come to think that maybe it was you.

When you and I met it was like opening a huge can of worms – what would I do? What if somehow you really had been here before as Pete back in the 1980s? What if I'd stopped Pete from leaving that rainy night? Perhaps our worlds wouldn't have drifted, Pete would have been with me all these years and we would have grown old together.

Pete and I separating from one another in that way and not meeting properly in your new lifetime, perhaps that broke the link? Maybe if I had warned you (sorry, I mean Pete) that day, then the joining of our souls (or whatever), would have continued to have been strengthened across time? Perhaps that woman with the scar was actually a previous incarnation of me? This stuff has blown my mind for so many years, Nate.

I picked up the other letter, its paper fragile from the years of storage. As I read the words there was a sensation which I can only describe as being like the passing of time running through my veins. I rested my head back on the headrest of the car and tried to make sense of the thoughts scattered across my mind. I closed my eyes, and in the darkness, faces began to appear. Faces, so many faces.

Chapter 4

I don't know for how long I sat there with my head against the headrest, but when once more I became aware of my surroundings, the day was dimming, and dusk threatened its eerie presence.

I looked down at the pages I still had to read, there were only a few, so I decided to sit it out and finish reading what Dayna had to say:

Do you know that Nate is a north American name meaning moon, and that there was a full moon on the night you were born? Such meaningless information and I don't even know how I came across it, but so often since Pete died, I would look above at the moon and the stars and feel that somehow he was watching over me. But then when you came along it confused me ... how could he still be up there watching over me, if he'd been reincarnated as you? When I found out the thing about your name and the moon it made me feel that maybe he was still watching over me, in a strange kind of way.

After he died, for several years I didn't date, but then Jackson came along, and I gave my heart to him. I've heard it said that there is more than one person in this life who could be right for us, you just need to be in the right place at the right time and fate just lends a hand. Jackson understood as much as he could about what had happened with Pete – to the extent that when our first daughter was born, it was his suggestion to call her Pieter. That made me love Jackson more than I ever thought I could love anyone who wasn't Pete.

But perhaps, Nate, there are more than two souls tied together in the complex network of time. Perhaps it's not just you and me, but your dear Ellie and Jenna and my Jackson and the girls. I hope, too, the animals we have loved. If Pete hadn't died then you wouldn't have been in this world, and you wouldn't have had the experiences of your life with Ellie, nor I with Jackson. He has been a wonderful husband, and while I continued to love Pete, Jackson stole a huge piece of my heart. For the world, I wouldn't have wanted to have missed out on that love.

Perhaps we are all linked and it's conceivable that in time and space we will all be connected once more, however fragile that connection. This is far too big a thing for any of us to fathom; in the end, I suppose, all we can do is speculate.

I have so, so many unanswered questions. I don't know, Nate, whether you and Pete are truly connected, and whether, by default, because of the love I've held all these years for Pete, you and I are somehow tied together; inextricably linked.

Our modern technology has not been able to answer the question of what happens to us once we pass. Through much more meticulous, detailed brain imaging, we now know more about the initial stages of death, and that there appears to be some sort of stream of consciousness which extends beyond the point at which we no longer have a functioning body or mind.

We've for a long time had reports of people describing near-death experiences, and there are many stories of people being regressed like you were, but some were hoping that by now we'd know something more; something which could be evidenced, rather than be simply hearsay. I suppose we're really no further forward in understanding death than we were when I was born back in the 1960s.

And so, here we are, and it's likely that because you're reading this letter I have now passed away. A couple of years after our last meeting in the café, I realized my mind had been unfairly distracted by you and that it was interfering in my everyday world with Jackson and the girls – my work even! I decided then to remove the swan picture from the wall. I placed it and photographs of Pete and the rest of us from those days in this package, so that one day you might know as much as I know. I couldn't face you with it, and I apologize with all my heart for being so cowardly. I knew, though, that for my sanity I had to parcel all evidence of you up, package you away, along with all that had been to do with the time I shared with Pete.

I told Jackson and the girls what I'd done, and I think they understood. I told them that if ever anything happened to me, they might come across you. I just felt that you were still watching over me, Nate, I'm not sure whether that is true, but I felt it. If it helps, even though I had stored you away, I admit there were times when I spoke at animal protection or environmental conferences, I would scan the audience looking for you. I wanted you to be there, because if there was a chance that you were right, then I wanted that remnant of Pete to be proud of me. Likewise, whenever I heard you had a big exhibition I would try to visit – sometimes with Jackson, and I hope he understood. And how strange that Pete had been an artist too – I've thought about that a lot, and whether in new lives there are things we can't let go of. If, indeed, that is what happened.

You have done some amazing work for wildlife and the environment, Nate. I have felt great moments of admiration for you – and the timing of those huge anonymous donations coming whenever your art

343

books were published, I guessed it was you and Ellie – so thank you both!

So, farewell Nate, and if we are meant to be together in some far-flung place in the universe, or even somewhere not of this world, I'll see you there ... or perhaps I will find you another time here on Earth.

Yours (eternally?)

Dayna

Chapter 5

I fought back my tears. Time had not resolved anything. Even with the sense of confirmation that had come with her letter and the painting, there was still doubt and I, too, had so many more questions to ask.

What was it that had allowed me to apparently traverse lifetimes? If that really was what it had all been about? What was it that had created the sense that she and I had some sort of ethereal connection? Had it been something that would have been better left unsaid? Would it have been better if I'd fought back the urges to follow the notions I had?

Perhaps everyone has those impulses of recognition, those flickers of familiarity? Is that what we feel as part of our sixth sense, that feeling of déjà vu, a connection with someone we've never met before? Strangers passing in the street, unknowing, unaware, because something closes when we are reborn, sealing that portal to the other world, completely redacting any link to what may have been before. But then, one day someone does remember that someone else, and reconnections are made. Perhaps that is how we end up being with the ones we end up being with.

Perhaps there is something in it, or maybe there is

only coincidence. But coincidence does not explain the depth to which I felt I knew Dayna and, it would seem, the degree of accuracy in what I told her.

I shuffled the photographs to find one of Pete on his own. It was a head and shoulders shot which had him looking directly into the camera. He had a wide smile and clear blue eyes. Across the barriers of time and consciousness, I tried hard to make a connection with him – attempted to fill my mind with memories of who he was and what he was like. But just as before when I had looked at the picture of them all together, there was nothing.

I felt an overbearing urge to go back to see Dayna's daughters, to tell them what the letter had said. To find out how much more they had known about Pete. It seemed strange thinking that all along Dayna, Jackson, and their daughters had kept what they knew a secret. I understood why. Just as Dayna said to me when we last met, we had separate lives, separate loves, and we couldn't have travelled down an avenue of such emotional magnitude.

I felt sad that I hadn't got to know her better, that all I had was a bunch of fleeting meetings with her, and what I knew of her from her great work in preserving our dwindling wild species. There were also the vague recollections from a life only known to me through some feelings, random dreams, and emotional sessions in a hypnotherapist's surgery.

I looked through my rear-view mirror at the road outside of the memorial garden car park as it curved behind me; the road that would lead back to Jackson, and the wealth of information he may have. I bundled the photographs and pieces of paper on top of the picture on the seat beside me and told the car to start. The electric engine started with a soft purr, and to my right ear I connected the music drive Dayna had left for me.

Once on my way, I left Jackson and his daughters to live the rest of their lives behind me and kept to the sycamore-lined road in front of me. I told the car to take me home. Back to Ellie, Jenna, and Jenna and her husband Eddie's two-year old twin boys. I asked the car to adjust the volume of the music, which would accompany me on my three-hour journey. I smiled to myself as the first few bars of a very old Jon and Vangelis song drifted into my ear … '*I'll find my way home.*' It appeared as though that, too, had been right.

On the ride home and as I listened to the music from a long time ago, gosh, sixty years or more, something was eating away at me. I had missed something! I searched the photos and pieces of paper in front of me. What was it that Dayna said in her letter?

No, no, of course, it wasn't Dayna! It was the woman with the scar who visited Annie, the lady at Dayna's aunt's house.

With a heavy heart, I realized this wasn't over. I needed to see Mick again. We hadn't gone far enough back in time – we needed to go back to the 1950s. I could let it go, but it could be that the woman with the scar and I were linked. What if this note that was almost a hundred years old held the key to everything that had happened with Dayna and me?

I told the earpiece to switch to phone. Within seconds, Mick responded. 'Mick, hello. It's Nate Campbell here. I need to come and see you.'

A Dog Like Ralph

… A Book for Anyone Who has Ever Loved a Rescue Dog

The true story of Ralph—a rescue dog with a difficult past—who loves other dogs, is frightened of people and cars, and mesmerized by cats, rabbits and 'Santa Please Stop Here' signs. Clare, his new human, tells with equal amounts of humour and sadness about the joys and challenges of having him as a companion.

His story is partly told through his eyes and describes how what he may have experienced before has affected how he interacts with those in his new 'forever' home. When Ralph's compatriots, Peggy, and Luella (Lucy to her friends), enter his life, it becomes clear that they have their own 'version of events' to add to the story!

Clare also writes about the pitfalls of a society that has resulted in Ralph being the way he is, and of how small changes could transform the plight of abandoned dogs. This book is a tribute to the rescue dog.

A Dog Like Ralph gives some of the back story to The Diary of a Human and a Dog and A Dog Like Peggy, but it's not necessary to read it first.

The Diary of a Human and a Dog (or Three)

The story of a human and a dog sharing their unanticipated grief

When a dog loses their human companion, it results in the upheaval of everything they've ever loved. When a human loses their parent, it is the most heart-rending thing to have to deal with.

Lucy had been rescued just two years earlier and thought she had found her forever home. She was living as the sole dog in charge of an old woman. When the old woman passed away, Lucy found herself thrust into a life in which she would have to share her new humans with two other dogs. She had encountered Ralph and Peggy before and, quite frankly and in her stroppy terrier way, was not that keen on them.

This is the diary of Clare and Lucy. It is a story of how dogs can help humans heal, and how humans can help dogs to overcome their own very special sort of grief.

This book is Clare's most personal book as it focuses on the way in which grief can affect us, but how dogs and people can help one another along the road to recovery. She wrote it in the time following her mother's unexpected death.

A Dog Like Peggy ... the life and times of a rescued greyhound

The book is narrated by Peggy the rescued greyhound, as she tells of her life on the tracks, and of the horrors she's witnessed. She also tells of the canine and human attachments she has made along the way.

She gives her (very frank) greyhound opinion of what she thinks about racing, the lot of a racing greyhound, and then eventually about the dogs she finally meets in her home that's forever – with Ralph and Lucy.

It is a heartwarming story because, after all, Peggy has been one of the luckier of these noble, gentle dogs.

Clare wrote this book (with Peggy, of course), in honour of all the racing greyhounds who are born into this cruel sport. She has a love of all dogs, and the plight of greyhounds touches her heart.

A Soldier Like Jack

Like millions of other young men, Jack was plunged into a war which was to change his life, and the lives of his loved ones, forever. Jack's war would take him to Salonika (Thessaloniki), in Greece.

Jack's wife, Grace, tells the harrowing story of what happened to the men and the families they left behind. It traces their lives from the time of Jack and Grace's marriage in 1912, until Grace's death in 1957.

This is a true story based on the lives of the author's great grandparents, Jack and Grace Cogbill.

Clare wrote this book after feeling touched by a story she came across when embarking on the genealogy of her family. This story is the reason Clare chose the name Cogbill as her pen name—in tribute to the three Cogbill men in her family who lost their lives because of The Great War.

Lilac Haze

You don't remember your childhood in detail, so your memories thirty or forty years on have become hazy; times you had back then are painted in colours that have become distorted.

This is a love story. In the end, anyway, that's what it will be. A love story gives you hope, whatever you have lost; whatever you have to gain. For me, as someone on daily kidney dialysis, when an offer of a kidney came along which I couldn't possibly refuse, there was everything to gain.

But the past has a way of interfering with what seems to be the right path. And how do you ever in this life repay such an immeasurable debt?

Clare wrote this book because of her own experience of losing her father to kidney failure in 1970, and then receiving her husband's kidney in 2002 when her own kidneys failed.

Vegan Cookbook

Delicious soups, tempting starters, wholesome main courses, naughty and nice, sweet treats. More than 100 tried and tested recipes for you and your friends to enjoy, vegans and non-vegans alike. These recipes are nutritious, fun, easy, and naturally free from dairy and eggs ... and all other animal products. Clare became vegetarian in 1977 and has been vegan since 2002. Her whole family is vegan, and these are some of their favourite dishes.

The Indie Gluten Free Vegan

Following her husband's coeliac diagnosis, Clare has revisited many of the recipes in her vegan cookbook and created more, all for this 100% vegan gluten free cookbook. 120 recipes – soups, suppers, and sweets.
No frills, just useful recipes for those beginning a vegan, gluten free diet.

If you've enjoyed any of my books, do please get in touch through Facebook or Goodreads.
Reviews on Amazon and/or Goodreads are very gratefully received.
Thank you so much for reading my book.

ABOUT THE AUTHOR

Clare Cogbill was born in the mid-1960s, and like many youngsters from an early age she developed a deep passion for animals and their welfare. She had fifteen years' experience of working with domesticated animals in rescue shelters, and as a qualified veterinary nurse in both welfare and private practice environments before, in 1991, becoming a lecturer in animal care and veterinary nursing.

In 2020, she took early retirement from lecturing and has since been concentrating on writing books, something she began doing in 2012 while still teaching. While much of her writing to date has been about dogs or autobiographical, she has now ventured into fiction – Picture Me Now is her first novel of this kind. Naturally, because of her love of animals, the occasional dog or cat character finds their way into the pages of her fiction.

While animals have always been her greatest interest, she also loves to read, and where those books contain some reference to the human-animal bond, all the better. She also enjoys reading books which have been made into films but can't quite work out whether it's better to read the book or to see the film first!

Clare lives in Scotland with her husband, son, and two rescue dogs. When she's not writing, she can be found pottering around the garden with the dogs following her around, or watching films – cinema being her other great love.

Printed in Great Britain
by Amazon

65084977R00215